T0304805

Alexandra Wilson is a junior barrister in England and Wales, and an attorney in New York State. She grew up on the border of East London and Essex and is the eldest of four children. Her mother is white British, her father is Black British and her paternal grandparents were born in Jamaica and came to England as part of the Windrush generation.

Alexandra studied at the University of Oxford and was awarded two prestigious scholarships, enabling her to research the impact of police shootings in the US on young people's attitudes to the police. She went on to study for a Graduate Diploma in Law (GDL), a Master of Laws at BPP University in London, and a Master of Laws at Columbia University in New York. Alexandra was awarded the first Queen's scholarship by the Honourable Society of the Middle Temple, a scholarship awarded to students showing exceptional promise in a career at the Bar. She has since also been awarded the Morris Fellowship by Columbia University.

Alongside her paid legal work, Alexandra helps to facilitate access to justice by providing legal representation for disenfranchised minorities and others on a pro-bono basis.

X @EssexBarrister
essexbarrister

THE
WITNESS

ALEXANDRA WILSON

SPHERE

SPHERE

First published in Great Britain in 2024 by Sphere

1 3 5 7 9 10 8 6 4 2

A CIP catalogue record for this book
is available from the British Library.

Hardback ISBN 978-0-7515-8340-3
Trade paperback ISBN 978-0-7515-8339-7

Typeset in Garamond by M Rules
Printed and bound in Great Britain by
Clays Ltd, Elcograf S.p.A.

Papers used by Sphere are from well-managed forests
and other responsible sources.

Sphere
An imprint of
Little, Brown Book Group
Carmelite House
50 Victoria Embankment
London EC4Y 0DZ

An Hachette UK Company
www.hachette.co.uk

www.littlebrown.co.uk

To my partner, my best friend,
my greatest supporter, Aisosa.

To Mum, Dad, Lew, Soph and Dee
who never stopped believing in me.

And, to my Nanny Jan, who now lives
in the stars. May this tale reach you.

CHAPTER 1

The men bounced off one another rhythmically, as though in a synchronised dance. There were grunts and groans as fists and elbows were swung in different directions. The shorter of the two darker-skinned Black men, Tyrone, stumbled backwards. He cursed out loud and stepped back towards the others, hands raised in front of his face like a boxer in a ring. Emmett, the lighter-skinned Black boy, tugged his shirt to pull him back but Tyrone slapped him away. He glared at him and Emmett knew what this look meant: if he wasn't willing to support his friends at a time like this, he wasn't 'a real one'.

Emmett took a deep breath and raised his own hands. He stepped back in. One of the two white men growled and clutched his calf. He wobbled back, stretched his leg out and combed the sweat on his forehead through his reddish hair, pausing for a brief second before returning to the commotion. A ray of light bounced off something metallic and then disappeared. The other white man, with darker hair, let out a loud, pained cry.

A knife dropped to the floor.

The other bodies dispersed like pigeons as the dark-haired white man fell to his knees with a thud. He clutched his chest. His hands slowly changed from peach to red as the blood seeped through his clothes and stained his skin. His knees held him for just a few seconds before he rocked back and collapsed onto the earth. Splashes of scarlet scattered across the green blades of grass before a river of deeper red oozed through and tinted it all.

Emmett looked back at the man on the ground and exhaled heavily. He scanned the park around him. The red-haired man was limping away. Tyrone and Jayden had already reached the entrance to the park and were calling out and beckoning him to follow. He could barely make out their faces, but could see their deep brown skin against their brightly coloured tracksuits. He imagined the desperation and fear on their faces before looking back at the man bleeding out on the grass.

Emmett stepped towards the man on the ground. He'd never seen so much blood and wasn't sure what to do; he could see people walking towards him and heard a woman scream – perhaps the one with the baby. Instinctively, he tugged his jumper off and scrunched it into a ball, pushing it against the man's body, against where the blood appeared to be leaking from, and applied pressure, as he had seen people do on television.

He leaned closer to the man and lifted his heavy head, cradling it in his left palm like a newborn baby. With his right hand he gripped the man's shoulder and shook him firmly as if waking him from a deep sleep. The man's expression had slipped away, and his jaw hung slightly ajar.

'Come on, bro,' he whispered. 'I've got you. Come on.' His voice was quivering but he continued to plead.

'Stay awake, pl-pl-please, man.' The words left Emmett's lips but drifted away in the air.

He felt a tear trickle down his cheek and wiped it with the back of his hand. Something was warm and sticky – his hands were coated in blood.

People had swarmed around them. A couple were crying, others on their phones – some of them pointed at him. Emmett glanced back down and saw that his once white jumper was a saturated crimson.

A stocky woman in a bright fluorescent jacket asked him to stand to the side as she and her colleague approached the now limp body. Emmett froze, paralysed by the shock. Someone tugged on his shoulders and pulled him behind the crowd that was slowly being cleared. The face bent towards his and asked his name, a male voice. He answered. Slowly, emphasising the hard 'T' sound at the end.

The man paused and gripped Emmett's shoulder more tightly.

'Emmett, you do not have to say anything ...'

Emmett looked up at the person speaking, and slowly let his eyes scan down the body. Now he noticed the police uniform, the body-cam, all the way down to the hard, black boots. His gaze settled on his own stained fingers, which he rubbed desperately against his trouser leg.

'But, it may harm your defence if you do not mention when questioned something which you later rely on in court. Anything you do say may be given in evidence.'

CHAPTER 2

Rosa scrubbed her naked body with a discoloured pink loofah. She pulled it closer to her face and saw small hairs embedded in the netting but knew she didn't have time to clean it. She discarded it on the shower shelf and rubbed the shower gel in her palms, spreading it methodically all over her body. Her wide-toothed comb had knots of hair trapped at the base and congealed shampoo in the corners. She ripped the hairs off with her nails and ran the comb under the water for a few seconds. Placing the comb at her roots, she attempted to tug it through to clear the knots, but the ripping sound of the clumps of tangled hair made her discard the comb with a huff. The hot water began to scorch her skin. She twisted the tap off and stepped out onto the fluffy white bathmat.

A matching snow-white towel hung from the radiator, and she pulled it towards her, draping it around her body. She tapped the mirror that hung evenly above the sink, and it lit up. Her fingerprints remained on the glass, and she noticed other smears that hadn't been properly cleaned.

Her own bathroom mirror at Nana's flat was dated and lopsided, but the glass was always perfectly polished. Nana was immaculate.

A white T-shirt bra hung from the bathroom door handle and Rosa leaned to grab it, wrapping it around her chest. It felt slightly too tight, and she adjusted it to the loosest hook. She trotted into Tristan's room with the towel still wrapped around her waist.

They swapped places as Tristan departed for a shower. Rosa stared at herself in the full-length mirror and was horrified by her reflection. Her skin still looked scarred and uneven. Dark, tired circles were stretching around her eyes like a panda's and her lips looked cracked and dry.

She'd been working ridiculously late recently, being instructed as a junior on an 'advice on appeal' in a fraud case being led by Gillian Folkestone KC. Gillian merely performed the advocacy that Rosa worked late into the night scripting, and the appeal was no different. She'd admired Gillian for a long time and was delighted to be working alongside her role model, but so far she had been sorely disappointed. Gillian had no time to speak to her as she spent a large amount of her day pretending to be busier than she actually was. She brunched with solicitors she had known for years and met others for drinks after court. But worse than her constant intoxication was the fact that Gillian was impatient and shouted ferociously when she was unhappy, like a spoilt child. She expected things to be done at least a week before the deadline she'd set. When Rosa had delivered the work, it was already late.

She squirted a heavy dollop of moisturiser into the palm of her hands and rubbed it into her skin. She placed the bottle on the side but quickly picked it back up and put it into her bag, conscious that she might need it throughout the day. Whenever she was stressed, her eczema would flare up and there was nothing worse than the urge to scratch her flaking skin while trying to concentrate in court. Next was hair oil. She drizzled a generous amount into her already greasy hands and massaged it into her scalp.

Rosa didn't take as much pride in her appearance as Nana did. It was something that irritated her grandmother. Rosa remembered that when she was younger, she would try to rush her showers, barely washing and forgetting to put cream on her body so that an ashy white layer of dead cells would show on her brown skin. Nana would mutter to herself, 'Wa de goat do, di kid falla.' As a child she hadn't understood the saying. She remembered foolishly questioning how not moisturising or not plaiting her hair had any bearing on goats or their offspring. As an adult she now understood what Nana was insinuating. Rosa didn't want to be anything like her mother.

With nimble fingers, Rosa divided her hair into two sections and plaited it backwards away from her face. It was still knotty, but it looked neat to the naked eye. She massaged her concealer under her eyes to hide the growing dark circles and dabbed it across the various spots across her cheeks. Brushed some chestnut-coloured powder over her cheeks. Better. It almost masked her acne-scarred complexion.

She picked up the television remote from the floor beside

the bed and switched on the breakfast news. The presenter appeared solemn at the desk while the news jingle played, and the cameras slowly focused in. Rosa reached into her handbag, retrieved a pair of tights, and stretched them over her feet, pulling them up towards her knees.

'The Metropolitan Police say that they are investigating a serious incident that took place yesterday, in a park in Walthamstow, where a man has been stabbed.' The presenter spoke with conviction, his tone measured and his pace slow. Each word was enunciated carefully.

Walthamstow? She glared up at the television and waited, still clutching her tights with both hands.

'There are reports that a man, said to be white and in his twenties, is seriously injured.'

Rosa hoisted up the tights, flexing her foot and adjusting the dark fabric around her toes. Tristan had already turned off the shower in the bathroom leaving a suffocating silence to fill the room each time the news presenter paused.

'The police have arrested a man named Emmett Hamilton in connection with the stabbing.'

A young Black man's photo flashed across the screen. His hair was styled in a short, untidy afro and he wore a grey sweater, which had an uncanny resemblance to prison attire. The jumper swamped him, like a child forced to wear clothes they would 'grow in to'. The photograph had clearly been cropped but it was impossible to identify its context. Aside from another Black hand on Emmett's shoulder, the background was dark. Perhaps it captured a moment with friends and family, or maybe not. It didn't really matter. There must have been a better photo available; he was squinting as though the flash was too bright and although she presumed his skin colour was similar to her own, the photograph showed it as an ashy brown. The person behind the camera had clearly paid no attention to the lighting. Worse still, his index and middle fingers were up by the side of his face, palm facing the camera. While this hand gesture was a widely recognised 'peace' sign, performed by the hands of a young Black man, it would likely be misunderstood.

Her phone rang loudly. It was her chambers.

'Hello, hello,' she answered, slightly flustered. 'Oh, hello, Steve, yes, I'm well, thank you.'

Steve spoke quickly. He told Rosa that a solicitor, Craig Rowling, had called and asked her to cover a case for him, today.

'Craig Rowling?' she said, with slight astonishment. She knew who Craig Rowling was, and had even met him a few times, but she had never been instructed by him before. Coincidentally, Nana used to clean his home when she was still working, and he had been the last of Nana's clients to go.

Steve confirmed the name and emphasised that he had specifically asked that she covered it. He said that he'd be happy to ask someone else, but Steve said he'd like to give Craig his first choice. Apparently, the solicitor sent a lot of work to chambers and always rewarded people who helped him out.

'Erm, I'd be happy to, but I have a PTPH in Snares—'

He interrupted her to tell her that he'd already found

someone to cover that case. He needed an answer now. The case was in Harlesden Crown Court, starting at 10 a.m.

'Yes, erm, yes, of course. Can you send the papers?' She'd have to read them on the way to court.

He thanked her and ended the call.

Tristan walked back into the bedroom and glanced at the television. He still had his toothbrush in his mouth and droplets of minty spittle sprayed outwards as he spoke.

'Isn't that where you grew up, Rose?'

She hated that he called her Rose, but just nodded silently, her eyes remaining fixed on the screen. He patted her shoulder sympathetically and walked towards his chest of drawers.

'Do you know him?' he called out. 'It's awful, isn't it? So much Black-on-Black crime nowadays. It's so sad,' his voice trailing slightly as he bent down to thread his feet through the legs of his boxer shorts.

Rosa shook her head slowly before realising that Tristan wasn't looking in her direction. She didn't know either man, not the *white* victim nor the Black suspect. To be fair to him, Tristan had missed the beginning of the report but why had he assumed both men were Black? For someone who purported to be intelligent he sometimes irritated her with his ignorance.

'No, I don't know them. And, Tristan –' she inhaled deeply, simultaneously filling her diaphragm and rejuvenating her confidence – 'the victim was white. You can't assume that it's "Black-on-Black crime" just because it's a stabbing.' She spat the words out.

'Babe. Rose. I didn't say anything about his skin colour. Please, listen. It's your area, I just thought you might have known him.' He shifted his weight between each foot, standing awkwardly and obediently like a dog awaiting instruction.

It had been a slip of the tongue. He hadn't meant to be malicious. Rosa looked at his wide eyes and for some unknown reason a wave of empathy swept over her. After all, there was a constant stream of media articles criminalising young Black men. If she hadn't seen the whole report, perhaps she too would have assumed they were both Black. Tristan wasn't a bad guy, not really. In the past, in her twenties during law school and her training years, Rosa had dated 'bad' guys. Without even being her official partner, Tristan already treated her much better than many of her exes. He was just a product of his upbringing. That wasn't his fault any more than it was her fault that her grandmother had been left to raise her and Toby. At least she was aware of this; sometimes Tristan just showed such little insight into how privileged he was.

As if reading her thoughts, Tristan seemed to detect the sea of frustration churning between them and reached out his arms. Rosa stepped towards him, grateful for his embrace. She rested her head on his bare chest, letting the small, soft hairs tickle her cheeks. They held each other for a moment. Tristan released his hold and gently lifted Rosa's head, placing a soft kiss on top. She smiled.

'Look at us!' he chortled. 'Are we OK now, Rose? You know I hate arguments. We don't want all of that, we just want to have fun, right?'

She felt a slight pain when he mocked them and another when he used the word 'fun', but she reminded herself that this was what *she* had wanted. No strings attached. She didn't have time for a serious partner, she barely had time for her friends.

'Of course,' she eventually responded. 'But seriously, Tristan, please stop shortening my name. It's Rose-ah, there are two syllables.' How would he like it if she called him 'Trist' or just 'T'? She realised before he answered that he would be unlikely to care. His friends all called him Hughes, his surname. It seemed that there was a pattern in his friendship circle of them only being able to manage one syllable, never using a person's actual first name.

'Sorry, Rose-ah!' He smiled and planted a kiss on her forehead. 'I didn't realise you hated it so much. I promise I'll stop. It's just, you're so beautiful, like a rose, my little rose.'

His compliment was a little trite but made her chuckle.

'I've brought croissants for breakfast, if that helps you to forgive me,' he said, his blue eyes glistening in the sunlight as it crept through his blinds. 'They're not just any croissants either, they're Marks and Spencer's ones. I know they're your favourite!'

She tried to hide her grin.

The contents of her overnight bag were sprawled out across the sofa in the living room. Scrunching her dirty knickers into a ball, she stuffed them alongside yesterday's clothing in the side of her bag. Hopefully the security staff at court wouldn't require her to empty her belongings into a tray.

Wouldn't that be excruciating? She imagined pulling each item out, unravelling her worn underwear to demonstrate that there was nothing concealed inside.

Delicately, she slipped each foot into her high-heeled leather shoes and headed towards the front door, almost forgetting to say goodbye before turning back.

'Trist, Tee, Tristy ...' she hesitated, having run out of shortened versions of his name. 'I've got to go.'

'Ha. Ha. Very funny,' he called out in response. 'See you soon, my sweet rose.'

A smile crept across her face, and she felt a little warm. She was far too old to be feeling like this.

CHAPTER 3

Rosa tapped her foot impatiently. It was 9.30 a.m. and the line for security checks stretched out of the doors to Harlesden Crown Court, and slithered down the steps and on to the street.

Her rhythmic foot taps had no effect on the pace of those in front of her. Feeling hopeless, she continued trying to read the papers for her last-minute case on her phone – defending a Mr Adebayo – just as two messages arrived, both from Orissa. The first was a small picture of Michelle Obama with white calligraphy writing over the top. Rosa pressed on the image to enlarge it.

> Here's to strong women. May we know them.
> May we be them. May we raise them.

For a successful and extremely busy thirty-one-year-old businesswoman, Orissa could be exceptionally cringeworthy. It was supposed to be sweet, but Rosa was not in the mood for exchanging quotes like teenagers. She took two large steps forwards, mirroring the person in front of her, and double clicked on the picture to revert back to her messages.

> This made me think of you. You deserve the
> world. Miss you.

Rosa felt a pang of guilt. Orissa was only trying to be kind. She typed in reply.

> Miss you too. Let's catch up this weekend.

She knew that was a false promise, but it felt appropriate. This weekend she had far too much work to do to fit in a gossip-filled catch-up. Maybe next week? Surely it didn't really matter, it was the thought that counted. Rosa stepped forward in unison with the people in front of her.

> Yes, definitely. Let's! I have loads to fill you in on.
> Have you been on any dates since breaking up
> with Tee-who-we-shall-not-name?

Her message forced a small snort. She'd forgotten that she hadn't updated Orissa on the latest. There was no rush. Yes, of course Orissa was her best friend, but they were adults. They both had private lives and didn't need to share every bit with each other.

> Not yet! Give me a chance! At work but speak to
> you at the weekend. X

The kiss was to emphasise the end of the conversation. The queue ahead of her shuffled forward and she opened her bag to put her phone away. It buzzed again.

It's been WEEKS Rosa! This isn't like you. Let's
get cocktails at the weekend! XXX

The queue continued to move, picking up speed, and she climbed the concrete steps up to the huge arched doors. There she waited. The man in front of her sported a black rubber bracelet around his ankle, adorned with greyish plastic on the outside of his leg. He made no effort to hide his electronic tag, wearing tracksuit trousers cropped just above his ankle. She couldn't see his face but as he scratched his head small flakes of dandruff floated to the ground like snowflakes.

Once through security, she charged to the advocate's robing room and tipped her blue bag out onto the table. Another female barrister turned to look at her and smiled kindly. The woman had glossy straight blonde hair, combed back into a perfect bun. Her eyebrows were tamed into tidy arches and her eyes framed with dark mascara and a soft honey eyeshadow. Her face was unmarked by either wrinkles or blemishes, and she was clearly a lot younger than Rosa. Perhaps she was newly qualified, yet to suffer the stress of this job, or maybe she was even a pupil barrister. There was no doubt that she looked a lot more put-together than Rosa and it made Rosa's cheeks feel hot. She returned a friendly smile and rushed to wrap her bib collarette around her neck.

The bib stuck to the droplets of sweat forming on her chest as she desperately tried to tuck it neatly into her dress. Her attempt to straighten it out was futile. She tugged, but her dress was slightly too tight, and she regretted the previous weeks of comfort eating. It was impossible to pull the bib down and flat without taking off her entire dress.

'For fuck's sake!' Rosa muttered under her breath.

She reached for her gown – at least this would go some way towards disguising the bulge of her gut – and the ornate tin encasing her wig, on which gold lettering spelled out her name. She tipped the lid open and retrieved the ringleted, horse-hair prop. Placing it gently on her head, she strode towards the mirror. Another barrister, who she recognised but could not recall the name of, was significantly closer and stood up at the same time. It was a race towards the mirror. Rosa didn't have time for this today. She used her phone camera as a make-shift mirror and tried to even out her wig via the small screen. Tiredness crept through her. It crawled through her weak feet, where her shoes pinched swollen toes. It clambered up her legs and spread through her whole torso, making her crave the breakfast she'd missed, and trickled into her head, forcing her to blink and shake her head from side to side as though it could be shed through her ears.

She sat for a moment to catch her breath and found herself scrolling through news websites on her phone. Her polished fingernails scratched at the plastic screen protector, thumb gliding from the bottom to the top of the screen and then repeating the motion again as she exhausted the stream of articles. The headlines were repetitive, as though the journalists were competing to reword the same sentence in as many ways as they could.

Man stabbed in a park in Walthamstow.

Walthamstow stabbing: Police arrest 18-year-old man.

Paramedics rush to the scene of a stabbing in East London.

The stories had been published over the past few hours. She refreshed the page and the stack of headlines disappeared into a blank ocean of white, a small circle of dots dancing in the middle of the screen. Rosa rubbed her thumb smoothly around the black silicone casing of her phone as the bold, black-lettered words slowly re-emerged. A new article popped up. Her finger hovered over it and in a small grey font besides the headline she read the words 'one minute ago'.

Breaking news: Man confirmed as dead after
being brutally stabbed in East London park.

Her eyes darted back and forth over the words, each time tripping on four letters in the middle of the sentence. D-e-a-d. This was now a murder. The news story had a small square image of a reporter embedded within the text, with a grey triangle hovering over the top showing that the video was ready to be played. Turning her volume down to zero, she pressed it.

The image jolted and began playing, showing the

sealed-off park, emptier than Rosa had ever seen it. Crowds of enquiring people surrounded the secured greenery, seemingly trying to find out what had happened. The image froze and Rosa tapped her screen repeatedly to nudge the video back into action, but her attempt was futile. She paused, giving the signal a chance to catch up, but it stayed still. At the top of her screen a revolving arrow offered her a chance to refresh the page, which she did obligingly. She waited again and the page reloaded. She dragged the slider to where the video had previously stopped and clicked play. The image jerked again and Nana's block of flats now appeared, an unsightly dull grey concrete high-rise building sticking out sorely among the neighbouring properties. The roof of the building stabbed through the sky. Identical rectangular balconies and blue doors adorned the front in a utilitarian design. Nobody had tried to make this building look attractive, yet Rosa felt a slight warmth in her chest looking at it, even in these dreadful circumstances. Nana's flat was her home, and she was more like a mother to Rosa than her real mother.

Closing the news app abruptly, Rosa opened her text messages and typed n-a-n— then stopped, remembering how much Nana hated texting.

'Mi always prefa fi yuh tuh ring me,' Nana would say in her strong patois. Nana could speak perfect English but chose not to, preferring the creole language of the country she'd been raised in. It gave her another language, a way to communicate with her family and friends privately.

She tapped in Nana's landline number, which had

remained the same for as long as she could remember, tucked the phone in between her ear and her shoulder and left the robing room, pacing down the long dark corridor to try to find a signal. A petite woman sporting a suit not dissimilar to Rosa's awkwardly hobbled in uncomfortable heels. Her wig was slightly lopsided, making the curled ringlets look asymmetrical. The flowing black woollen gown, which should have offered her some gracefulness, had slipped off her shoulders and hung too loosely like a fancy-dress cape. She looked Rosa in the eye and smiled warmly and Rosa noticed that her flamingo pink lipstick had transferred to her teeth.

This building had clearly been designed to rob people of sunlight, a cruel design that made it difficult to distinguish between day and night. The windows were sparse and so high up the walls that you could not peer outwards. A lanky security officer, who Rosa estimated to be at least six foot five, nodded at her as she passed him; even on his tiptoes he wouldn't have been able to reach the window's handles to let some fresh oxygen into these stuffy halls.

Her phone finally showed two bars of signal, and her call to Nana began to connect. She stopped and leaned her back against the wall, her dark suit contrasting with the faded lemon wallpaper. The dado rail prodded her spine. She adjusted herself, grating her heels against the carpet to stabilise herself. Nana answered the phone almost instantly.

'Mercedes, mi dear, mi pickney, yuh OK?'

Rosa hated her legal first name, and her grandmother was the only person she allowed to use it. But she was glad to hear Nana's soft voice. She was her 'pickney', her child. Even now, at thirty, she was closer to Nana than anyone else.

'Yes, Nana. I'm OK.'

Nana lowered her tone and Rosa sensed her discomfort.

'Mi need yuh tuh send me sum funds please. Mi haffi buy Toby's new school uniform. Him only haff one pair ah trousers dat fit.' Her voice shook a little as she spoke.

Rosa's throat suddenly felt dry, as if filled with sand. 'Of course, Nana. Sorry. You shouldn't have to ask.' Embarrassment swept over her.

'Yuh si di news?' Nana changed the topic abruptly. Pride drowned out any glimmer of gratitude in Nana, which made Rosa roll her eyes but then smile, just as she felt a strong finger poking at her shoulder, and she turned sharply to face Albert, another barrister from her chambers. Her smile quickly faded.

'Fancy seeing you here, Rosa! Long time, no see! Good to see you still have a Crown Court practice, a few of us were worried you'd joined the dark side.'

Calling solicitors' firms 'the dark side' was pathetic and Rosa knew that the assumption had only arisen because she was of child-bearing age. The 'we' club of men in her chambers assumed she would give up self-employment to reap the benefits of maternity pay. She signalled with her index finger at her mobile phone and offered a pretend expression of awkwardness, as if to suggest that had she not been on this call she would have loved to have conversed.

'Oops, I hadn't realised you were on the phone. Last-minute instructions?' This was clearly a rhetorical question as he didn't pause. 'I'll let you get on.' The tone of superiority had dampened in his voice, and he turned away, strode towards the door of the advocates room, and clicked in a code.

Rosa felt a moment of relief. She was mortified that she had no idea how long he had been standing beside her before digging his finger into her shoulder without invitation as she talked about sending Nana money. She watched as he stabbed an assortment of numbers on the small metal keypad and tried to twist the knob, before pushing the door with some force. It didn't budge and he pushed again, more forcefully this time. A piece of white A4 paper had been affixed to the door, which from Rosa's memory had reminded advocates to ensure that the door closed behind them. The paper had flown from the door with Albert's shove, and now lay in the middle of the dusty brown-tiled floor face down, with a small blob of Blu-tack sitting on top. He shoved the flimsy wooden door for a third time, and it looked like it would soon burst open without unlocking, leaving the keypad and doorknob behind in his hand.

'Rosa. Did yuh si di news?' Nana's voice chimed through her handset. Rosa lowered her voice so that Albert couldn't hear.

'Yes. It's so sad. Are you OK, Nana?' Rosa meant the question genuinely but regretted it instantly. She knew that she had invited a lecture.

'Nuh worry bout mi! Worry bout yuh likkle brudda. Yuh likkle brudda easily led.' Nana interrupted herself with an involuntary cough. She tried to start again but was held back by her splutter. Albert had finally opened the door and slammed it in frustration behind him. Rosa pulled the phone from her ear and glanced at the time in the top corner of her screen. She had to go.

'Nana . . . ' Rosa tried to take advantage of the coughing fit but was quickly silenced.

'Wah mi did say? Yuh likkle brudda easily led.'

'Yes, Nana.'

'Yuh know dat dem likkle stupid boys wi try fi get him involved inna dis big gangsta life.'

'Yes, Nana, I'm sorry to cut you . . . ' Rosa's voice sliced through Nana's, 'I'm really sorry to have to go.' Knowing this wouldn't go down well, she quickly continued, 'I'm about to go into court. I'll have to speak to you this evening. Please take care and don't believe everything you see on the news.' She hadn't meant to patronise Nana, but her words were rushed and clumsy. 'Love you loads.'

Nana scoffed and paused. The apparent condescension had not gone unnoticed.

'Mercedes Rosa Higgins, mi kno betta dan most people ow dangerous dis area. Don't tell me wah tuh believe.' Rosa waited a beat, knowing that she couldn't hang up yet. Nana continued, not bothered about whether she was invited to do so or not.

'Si yuh dis evening if yuh bodda coming home.' The sarcasm didn't signal the end, not yet.

'I am di one dat needs fi guh, mi need fi guh a drop yuh likkle brudda's inhaler tuh school.' There it was – Nana had to have the final word. 'Even when mi haf bigga tings on mi mind.'

Instinctively, Rosa wanted to protest but Nana ended the call abruptly. For a brief second, she wondered about the 'other things' but quickly pushed the thought to the back of her mind.

CHAPTER 4

Rosa pressed the doorbell of the court cells, stared straight into the camera, and waited for the buzz. The door released and she leaned her weight onto it to force it open. The officer, a round woman who wore high-waisted trousers that stretched across her stomach, greeted her in the walkway. She had short grey hair with a light streak of purple and a number of studded earrings in her left ear. Her right ear looked maimed. Rosa diverted her gaze and smiled politely. The officer, wasting no time on niceties, focused on unlocking the hanging small black box with a code. She retrieved a single key and forced it into the lock of the next door, which was tall with no windows or peepholes. Rosa stepped through cautiously, which seemed to irritate the officer. The officer locked the box and then locked the door behind them both.

As the female officer stepped in closer to Rosa, she could smell the strong aroma of coffee on her breath. Her badge was now visible and in small square letters read *Kelly Bolan*. It had a small photo of a much slimmer woman with longer hair. There was so little resemblance between this small photograph and the woman stood next to Rosa that she considered it likely this woman had picked up the wrong badge.

The woman purporting to be Kelly abandoned Rosa in this walkway and plodded back to her desk, plonking herself back into her chair with a huge sigh. The desk was untidy, with piles of confidential white paper spread out like spilt milk. The office was small. A woman shared Kelly's desk, cramped in the corner, hunched over her phone watching videos. None of the officers seemed to acknowledge Rosa's existence.

'Ahem. Hi,' she said mildly.

The officer sharing a desk with Kelly tapped on the clipboard next to her without looking up from her phone. Rosa tiptoed over and picked up the pen.

Name. She scribbled 'Rosa Higgins' in the box.

Chambers. 3 Straw Court.

'Who are you here to see, miss?' The woman closest to her finally looked up.

Rosa, slightly startled, looked back at her.

'Mr Oluwafemi Adebayo. Is he here?' she replied.

'Yep. Give us a second. Leave that. We'll fill the rest in.'

The officer leaned over the clipboard and ticked the box to say Rosa had shown ID, which she certainly hadn't. The wig and gown were evidently enough for them to take her at her word.

Rosa was led through yet another heavy, locked door into a corridor. This door was bright blue, with brown marks where the paint had chipped off. Again, she paused, waiting for it to be locked behind her. The walls were once white but were now discoloured and the floor was a similar shade, covered in tacky linoleum. There was a line of doors on the right, each leading to a small conference room. She was directed into the second door, and as she passed the first, she could see the bobbing wig of another barrister talking to their client.

The room was small, and the walls unevenly painted. The ceiling, walls and floor blended into one. An alarmed dado rail was the only decoration. The furniture was sparse. There was a rectangular table, which had been bolted to the floor, and two wooden stools, that had been similarly secured, one on each side. Rosa sat on one stool and stretched out her legs under the table. She tapped her fingertips on the table and then, upon reflection, wiped them down the side of her gown as a feeble attempt to clean them. Someone had engraved the name 'Mazza' into the edge of the table closest to her, which reminded her of her graffitied school desks.

Mr Adebayo was brought into the room without hand-cuffs and offered the vacant seat closest to the door. The officer muttered to Rosa that she should knock on the small plastic window when she was ready to leave. She left without waiting for a response and the door was locked from the outside.

Rosa was frequently reminded how dangerous her job was; if she needed help, it may take some time to even get someone's attention.

Reassuringly, her client today was not an alleged violent offender. He was sitting in these dimly lit, poorly decorated cells because he had been accused of dealing drugs. Like many other young Black boys that Rosa represented, he had been remanded in custody in the interim. Rosa's job today was to make a bail application. She wouldn't ordinarily do cases like this, but Craig might yield more work if she got a result, and she needed the money – though she was barely going to make any today. This is how she understood things worked at the Bar: solicitors expected barristers to do the low-paid, unsexy cases to help them out and in return they would repay them by sending them better cases. She was yet to receive any big cases through this exchange, but she had received some good cases and the occasional 'great' one; her clerks, the people in her chambers responsible for liaising with the solicitors to secure her work, promised her that it was all to come.

Mr Adebayo sat in front of her, wide-eyed and ready to absorb Rosa's legal advice. She introduced herself by her first name.

'I'm Femi. Good to meet you, Ms Rosa,' he replied. There was a childish softness to his voice. She smiled warmly. 'Ms Rosa' would do.

There was little time to speak to Femi. The cells only opened at 9.30 a.m. and there was always a long queue.

'I'm afraid we don't have long,' she said apologetically. Femi sat still and listened.

She wanted to describe the bail application hearing in detail, but the clock was ticking. Instead, Rosa confirmed the information that the solicitor had given her about where he would be able to stay, and what conditions he was willing to abide by.

'And so, whatever happens today, like I've said, I will come back down here to the cells, and we can talk about next steps. Either you'll be going home, or we'll be rethinking our options.' Rosa paused for breath.

'So, Miss Rosa, what you're saying is that basically I have a 50:50 chance of getting bail?'

'Well, no, not quite.' She tried to offer him a reassuring smile but her face betrayed her. 'I'm afraid it is not quite as straightforward as that.'

His face scrunched up a little, and he looked confused.

'As I say, it's not quite 50:50, it depends a lot on what the judge is like.'

'What is the judge like?'

'Unfortunately, I don't know HHJ Robinson.' Rosa knew it didn't really matter who the judge was. This was a hopeless application; he didn't stand a chance.

Femi looked even more perplexed, as though he hadn't really understood anything that she'd said.

'Look, I think that your application for bail, well, the one we are making on your behalf, is quite difficult. I think lots of judges might be worried about granting you bail. I think the court are going to be most concerned that you will be a flight risk, that you'll abscond. They are going to look at your previous convictions, and it seems like there are a few "failure to surrender" convictions on your PNC – your record. I think that's the main thing I'm concerned about, isn't it?' Her question was rhetorical, but she looked at him and waited for him to shake his head to ensure that he was following. 'You don't pose a danger to yourself or others.' She realised that listing the objections to bail was doing little to reassure him and he opened his mouth to speak.

'So, am I going to be able to go home today?' His voice was more vulnerable than before – he was barely an adult.

Rosa looked at the previous convictions for failing to surrender –

2018

2019

2019 again.

They were fairly old, but for some judges even one previous conviction for failing to surrender was enough to refuse to grant bail.

'Er . . .' she looked up to answer his question. 'I hope so. I really do, but I can't promise anything. I hope that the judge sees that you don't need to be kept in prison until your trial. I am going to try my very best to persuade him or her of that, OK?'

'But what about my aunt? She's said I can stay at her house. Did Craig tell you that?'

Rosa nodded. 'Yes, Susan Adebayo?'

'Yeah – has he spoken to her?'

'I'm not entirely sure, from his note it isn't clear.'

'Have you called her?' he interrupted.

'I haven't, no, but I do have your solicitor's assurance that she has offered her property as a place you can stay. It wouldn't be ordinary for me to call her, as your barrister.'

Femi lowered his head and fiddled with his hands on the table.

'So, what you're saying is, you've given up already? You

don't think I have a chance?' he muttered. She felt like there suddenly wasn't enough oxygen in the room, like someone was squeezing her throat. Nana's voice echoed through her head, *Neva give up on nobody. Mi neva did.*

Time was up. She stood up to leave, also leaving his question unanswered. Femi remained seated, staring through her and at the blank wall. She turned her back to him and tapped on the plastic panel of the door, and when she looked again she saw him still staring blankly.

'I'll see you upstairs,' she whispered and exited the cell.

CHAPTER 5

Rosa walked into the courtroom, sneaking into the back, bowing her head to the judge as she entered – a sign of respect and deference. Being careful not to make too much noise, her fingers crept over the edge of the folding seat at the end of the back row, lowering it slowly. It softly creaked under the weight of her hand. Rosa held the seat firmly, placing her weight on her left palm to prevent it springing upwards and loudly notifying everyone in the courtroom of her entrance. She slowly sat down and dropped her handbag to the floor.

She listened carefully to the judge, trying to get a feel for her style. With some, she would rush her submissions, conscious that an extra unnecessary point could sway them against her. With others, she took her time. Rosa was careful to prioritise her best points but never neglected the weaker ones, hopeful that the cumulation of relevant points would persuade the judge.

'Yes, Mr Davenport. What is the Crown's explanation for continually failing to disclose the phone records? Why have they not been provided yet?' The judge's shrill voice commanded the attention of the courtroom.

A man a few rows in front of her stood up and adjusted his black gown, dragging it up onto his shoulders. The back of his neck changed from a pale white to a clammy red as he answered the judge's question. His face was out of sight and from this angle he could easily be mistaken for most other barristers in this court building. His once white-haired wig was discoloured, the yellow-tinged curls clinging desperately to each other.

Rosa watched and listened. This judge seemed irritable and short-tempered. In the short five minutes Rosa observed her, she didn't allow the advocate to finish a sentence before interrupting. She had a sharp nose, which contrasted with her gentle eyes, covered partly by a feathery brown fringe peeping out from under her silvery wig. Her ornate robes were freshly pressed and her collarette snugly fitted her slightly chubby neck.

Rosa pulled her phone from her bag to make sure that it was on silent. Out of habit, she quickly flicked through social media, hiding her device behind the seat in front of her. People were sharing yesterday's murder across her social media channels.

Sarah Lawrence, from school, now a social media influencer, had shared a photo of the victim with *RIP* and a small love heart. The photo already had over 10,000 likes. Rosa scanned the comments. He'd been named as Thomas, and she learned that he was a nurse. One person commented that he'd helped deliver her baby just a few months ago.

Peter Mann had shared the same picture of the victim but with the words *A fallen brother, a fallen soldier. RIP bro.* Joe Collins, who she had strongly disliked since he had bragged in their French class that his parents supported the British National Party, had posted a status.

It's time we take our country back from these thugs. Black on Black crime is ruining Britain. Like if you agree.

She clicked on his profile. His picture was of him with an England shirt on and a tall glass of beer, with a cheesy grin. Swiping up, she exited his profile photo and clicked on the blue button beneath his photo. *Unfriend.* Was she sure? She tapped again to confirm that she was.

Rosa wasn't surprised that the accused's race had become a feature in this offence so quickly. In almost all of her cases where the client was Black, race was mentioned in some capacity. It began with police statements subtly dehumanising Black defendants. Many officers described 'an IC3 male' or 'a group of IC3s'; a short-hand code for Black people. This contrasted with reports for most white clients, whose race was rarely stated other than in the ethnicity box. Being white was the norm, anything else made you 'other'. In court, Rosa often corrected judges or prosecution barristers who used the term 'gang' too lightly, referring to any group of Black males as such, again without the same treatment of white groups of friends. Even outside of the criminal justice system, in the news and on social media, being Black clearly seemed to affect whether a murder was a tragedy worthy of public sympathy, or whether it was fuel for the government to announce their intention to be 'tougher on crime'.

The barristers in front of her got up to leave and Rosa stuffed her phone into her bag. She stood and stepped forwards to take her place in the front row, ready to address the judge. She placed her laptop carefully on the desk next to her and propped her blue paper notebook on the acrylic lectern. She lined her two pens and highlighter like soldiers next to her notebook and took a seat. The prosecutor remained seated and didn't look up at her. Her wig was wonky, and Rosa could see that she had kicked her shoes off underneath the desk. The courtroom remained quiet, and the judge embraced this moment, taking her time to finish her handwritten notes of the previous case. The dock was empty as the jailor had departed to retrieve Oluwafemi Adebayo from the cells.

Rosa breathed slowly and lapped up the silence. She focused on the intricate artistic work on the royal arms that hung above the judge's head. A mystical white unicorn mirrored a gold-painted regal lion on his hind legs. The imagery gave a false impression of the criminal justice system. There was nothing magical about it. The chair she had chosen wobbled even though someone had attempted to jam a paper wedge underneath to stabilise it. There was yellow tape across the desk behind her as it had partially collapsed some months ago and there were clearly not yet funds to replace or repair it.

The keys of the jailor jingled into a crescendo as she unbolted the door at the back of the courtroom and brought Femi in. He took his seat behind the sealed glass of the dock.

'May it please Your Honour, I appear on behalf of the Crown and my learned friend ... uh ...' the prosecutor scrambled around, realising she hadn't asked for Rosa's name.

'It's Ms Higgins,' Rosa whispered.

'Uh ... Ms Higgins. And, yes, my learned friend Ms Higgins appears for the defence.' Rosa partially stood up and nodded respectfully to the judge.

The prosecutor, whose name Rosa later discovered was Ms Gayle, opened the case by attempting to set out the facts. She explained, as Rosa had predicted, that Mr Adebayo was linked to local gangs and then claimed that there had been a rise in violence in the area. Rosa wondered whether she had any real clue about this, or whether she'd just taken this fact as face value from the Crown Prosecution Service.

'Your Honour, the court may also wish to take into consideration the fact that Mr Adebayo has a history of failing to surrender,' Ms Gayle stated.

Femi had failed to attend court hearings when he was thirteen and fourteen years old, Rosa had calculated. It was frustrating that the prosecution relied on this in asserting that there was a high risk of him not attending his trial in this present case.

She stood up, straightened her collarette and addressed the court.

'Your Honour, there are a number of conditions that we have proposed, which we hope may alleviate any concerns the court might have.'

35

The judge lifted her pen from the paper, pausing her note writing, and nodded for Rosa to continue. This was not reassuring.

'Mr Adebayo's aunt has agreed for him to stay at her house and for an electronic tag to be put at her address if needed. I understand that she is a police officer, Your Honour,' Rosa said.

'Do we have any evidence of this, Ms Higgins?'

'Erm, well Mr Adebayo's solicitor has instructed me that ...' She stumbled slightly as she looked at the note she'd prepared.

'Ms Gayle! I'm not asking you about your instructions, I'm asking about hard evidence. Do you have any evidence that Mr Adebayo's aunt is a police officer and has offered him a place to stay?'

Rosa tried to ignore the judge's indifference to using her correct name. The prosecutor seemed unable to do the same.

'I'm Ms Gayle,' the prosecutor said, standing up to address the court.

'What?' the judge asked curtly. Rosa sat down, abiding by the rule that only one advocate stands up at a time.

The prosecutor sat back down. 'Nothing, Your Honour.'

'Your Honour, can I say something?' Femi called out from the back of court.

'No, you cannot. You have instructed lawyers and it is their job to do the talking on your behalf. Please stay quiet.'

Rosa felt her face flush red. She stood back up, slowly.

'Your Honour, could I please check and return to that point?' She didn't wait for confirmation and continued. 'The boy who didn't attend court at fourteen years old is not the same man you see before you today. He is nineteen and has matured considerably over the past five years.' Rosa asked that the court did not weigh this against him being granted bail today.

'That may well be the case, but I don't have any real choice if I cannot be sure, do I, that he will be somewhere the court deems satisfactory. This is a case where I am concerned that he may revert to his old ways,' the judge retorted.

Out of the corner of her eye, Rosa saw the once shy prosecutor smile to herself. Rosa felt desperate. Nana's voice again intruded her thoughts. *Neva give up on nobody. Mi neva did.*

'Your Honour, may I please just be excused from court for just a few minutes. It really is important.'

'For what, Ms Higgins?'

'I am not at liberty to say, Your Honour, but I would be very grateful for this small courtesy.'

'Very well. I shall allow you five minutes only. We shall resume at 2.35.'

The jailors stood up and took Femi back through the dock door. Rosa scribbled a number on her notebook, from her laptop.

'Court rise,' the usher called out. The judge rose, bowed her head, and then left through the judicial door.

Rosa dashed to the back of the courtroom with her notebook under her arm. She stood in the corridor and tapped the number into her phone. The ringtone sounded. Once. Twice. Three times. She really needed an answer. Four times.

'Hello?' a voice answered.

'Hello, hello. Thank God. Is this Susan Adebayo?'

'It is. Who is calling?'

'Brilliant, OK. I don't have long. Your nephew, Femi, I understand that you are happy for him to stay at your house.'

'Sorry, who is this?' the voice asked again.

'Oh, I'm sorry. I'm Rosa Higgins, Mr Adebayo's barrister.'

Rosa rushed through the conversation, barely pausing for breath.

It was already 2.36 p.m. She darted back into the court-room. The judge was in place inside, and Femi was in the dock behind her.

'Your Honour, I am so sorry for keeping the court waiting.'

'Ms Higgins, no need to apologise, just please get on with it. Is there anything else you wish to say?'

'Yes, erm, Your Honour.' Rosa tried to catch her breath, she inhaled deeply and exhaled softly. 'Your Honour, this is perhaps unconventional ...'

The judge looked up and raised her eyebrows in anticipation.

'I've just had the opportunity to speak to Mr Adebayo's aunt. She's confirmed that she is indeed a police officer.'

'Ms Higgins, are you giving evidence?'

'No, Your Honour, what I am proposing is that Mrs Susan Adebayo, his aunt, gives evidence, to satisfy the court that she is in fact a police officer.'

'Well, is she here?'

'No, but she is available by video call. I have her telephone number, which I can provide to your clerk.'

The prosecutor stood up.

'Your Honour, the Crown cannot be sure who this person is. This is highly inappropriate.'

Rosa remained on her feet, not allowing Ms Gayle to finish.

'Well, Your Honour. Mrs Adebayo has just sent me an email from her Met—, sorry, erm, Metropolitan Police email account, and has attached a photograph of her police badge, ID documents and has provided her police number. I am content to provide this to the court.'

The judge paused for a moment.

'Send it to my clerk and to the prosecutor, please.'

The prosecutor stood up again. 'This person could be impersonating an officer!'

'Nah, she's *actually* a police officer!' Femi called out.

'Quiet! Please. This is a courtroom not a playground. Mr Adebayo, I've told you before, you have a lawyer. Ms Gayle, I've heard your objection. Let's see what is in this email. Ms Higgins, this might, quite rightly, be considered an ambush.'

Rosa nodded. 'Yes, I can appreciate that, Your Honour, but no disrespect is intended to the court. I am obliged to act in my client's best interests, even if unconventional.'

'Well, I'm not so sure about that,' the judge muttered.

The courtroom fell silent as the judge read the email and looked at the pictures. The clerk tapped at his keyboard and the prosecutor bounced irritatingly in her seat.

'I suppose I'd better hear from her, then,' the judge said at last.

CHAPTER 6

Rosa turned to Femi and was met with a huge smile. He was going home. She waved him goodbye, knowing it would take some time for him to get his belongings downstairs, and headed out of the courtroom.

She paced down the corridor and dialled the number Steve had given her for Craig, her instructing solicitor. A phone trilled behind her. There he was. He was sporting more facial hair than when she had last seen him. She tried to calculate how long ago that was and figured that it must have been about four years ago when she'd bumped into him with Nana. He was also a lot shorter than she remembered – maybe she'd worn flat shoes then? From her aerial view of his head, she could see the pink tint of his scalp in the circle of baldness.

'Well done!' he exclaimed.

'Oh, hello, Craig. Long time, no see. Well, yes. He is on bail. Lots of conditions, including a tag, but he's on bail!'

'I had to pop by to cover a hearing myself. The bloody barrister dropped out last minute.'

'Oh, I'm sorry to hear that.'

'Not at all. It's worked out well, I was able to sneak into the public gallery and see you in action.'

Rosa felt slightly mortified.

'You really are good. Creative and thorough. I'm sorry I didn't get a chance to call his aunt, but well done for just getting on with it. It takes a lot to impress me, and I am impressed. I can't believe I haven't ever instructed you before. I remember your gran saying you were a barrister.'

Rosa smiled internally but kept a poker face. 'I'll send you my attendance note as soon as I'm home. As I said, there are quite a few conditions, and he needs to give the police his number and PIN code within twenty-four hours so you'll have to help him with that,' she began to ramble. 'Of course, you know that, don't you?'

'Yes, but send me the note anyway. My memory is like a sieve. I'll call Mrs Adebayo and thank her. I reckon he's a referrer, we'll get a chunk of cases off the back of that win. Great stuff.'

'Yes, I'm so pleased.' She spoke a little too enthusiastically and had to remind herself that this was, after all, just a bail application.

'Steve said you were the right person for the job. Look, Rosa, I'm about to start on a big case and need to dash.'

'Oh gosh, yeah, so sorry. Of course. Sorry! Here I am chatting away about a bail application.'

'No need to apologise. You know, Rosa, I look after *my* people. Your grandmother looked after me, in a way – did she ever tell you about the time she had to call an ambulance because my wife collapsed? She was so much more than just our cleaner.'

Rosa felt embarrassed and wished she didn't.

'What a result that you're actually a decent barrister too. We just need to find the right big case for you – you've got potential. Speak soon!'

Craig turned his back without waiting for a reply and paced down the corridor.

Rosa headed for the advocates' robing room and stripped off her gown, ripped open the Velcro fastening of her collarette, and dismounted the wig from her head. Hurriedly, she stuffed the pile of costume into her blue bag and flung it into her suitcase. The zip of the suitcase jammed, just as her phone started ringing. She leaned her knee onto the bag, slowly shifting her body weight over it, and continued to tug, ignoring her phone for a few seconds. It gave and she toppled backwards with the zip. Rosa flushed pink and clambered to her feet. She picked up her phone, now silent.

Nana.

CHAPTER 7

The walls of the police station cell were a shiny yellow, with a thick blue strip dividing the top half of the room from the bottom. Emmett sat on the hard plastic-coated mattress, which reminded him of safety mats he'd once used in PE at school. This bedding, if it could be called that, was a different shade of blue, more intense and deeper, compared to the strip along the wall. If he stretched out his legs, perpendicular to the mattress, his toes grazed the metal toilet basin. There was no toilet seat, and he couldn't see any toilet paper. The police station had deprived the room of any comfort, and even basic necessities.

Emmett pulled his fingers into a fist and pressed his fingernails firmly into his palms. He squeezed his hands more tightly until the skin broke and bled lightly. The pain gave him a small rush. He opened his palms and looked at the small crescent-shaped cuts. The window behind had an opaque plastic border, with five small panels of lighter translucent plastic that allowed a small amount of light to struggle through to the room. That light now bounced off his hands, revealing the remnants of the blood stains, not just his newly formed cuts, but the blood of the man in the park. He seemed unable to scrub them clean.

A jangle of keys grew in volume and ended abruptly with a thump on the door. The rattle of a key and the cell door burst open.

'Your solicitor is here, kid,' the officer said, with an expressionless face.

'My solicitor?' Emmett asked, bewildered.

'Yes, his name is Craig something?'

Emmett nodded as though he remembered but was overcome with confusion.

He followed the officer out of the cell, treading lightly on the linoleum flooring. They passed numerous windowless doors until the officer stopped and reached for a handle. He led Emmett inside and then said he'd return in fifteen minutes.

'Hey, Emmett, I'm Craig, it's good to meet you, although, of course, I wish it was in better circumstances.' Craig smiled out of the corner of his mouth and stood up, extending his arm out to greet Emmett.

Emmett peered at him cautiously. Craig's lips were thin and when he smiled, they almost disappeared. He had clearly tried to shave, but his dark facial hair defiantly poked through his pale skin. The stubble contrasted with the thinning hair on top of his head, which was pale and wispy. He had the confidence of a much taller man. Emmett let his eyes fall to Craig's extended arm. His suit jacket sleeve had risen up his forearm revealing a plain white shirt with personalised cufflinks; an expensive-looking watch and a gold wedding band on his finger. Emmett extended his own hand, conscious of his bitten fingernails and the 'grandma' tattoo in gothic handwriting across the underside of his forearm. Slowly, he clasped Craig's hand in a firm handshake.

'Who are you? How are you my solicitor?' he asked suspiciously, looking at the watch adorning Craig's wrist.

Craig caught his eye and followed it to the watch. He grinned.

'Oh, don't be fooled by that. It's a fake. I wouldn't risk wearing a real Rolex around here. A pretty good one, though, huh?'

Emmett didn't laugh with him.

'Sorry, more important things to talk about. Well, you have me because your dad called me. I've come to know him well over the years. He's a long-standing client.'

'My dad?' Emmett gasped.

'He said you might react like this. Yes, your dad. I assume he saw you on the news – along with the rest of the country. Look, we don't have much time, so we probably need to get to the meat of it.'

Emmett paused, thinking about his father. He could barely remember the last time he saw him; he knew it had been years.

'Emmett?'

'Nah, thank you, but I'm OK. I don't have anything to do with my dad and this feels weird. He saw me on the news? Nah, I don't need his help. Definitely not now.'

'Look, son, I understand things might feel a bit rushed

and confused, but you are going to need all the help you can get. Your dad said something about your grandmother calling him too.'

'Granny called him?' Emmett whispered.

'Yes.'

'You're sure about that?' Emmett said slightly louder.

'That's what he told me. Look, so sorry son, but we really don't have a huge amount of time. They want to start interviewing you within the hour; that gives us only about five more minutes to see where we're going with this.'

Emmett paused and thought carefully for a moment.

'Honestly, I don't want to owe him anything. I'm OK. I'll get a duty.'

'A duty solicitor?' Craig laughed and then stopped abruptly. 'Son, this isn't a joke. You haven't been charged with possession of Cannabis – someone has been killed. You need to sharpen up. I'll be representing you today, OK. You can have a think about whether I stay on the case afterwards, but we need to get going.'

Emmett remained silent.

'Is that OK, Emmett?' Craig's voice softened. Emmett nodded.

'Right, OK. So, do you want to start by telling me just yes or no, whether you stabbed that man, we can start from there.'

'No. I didn't.'

'Right, OK. Do you know who did?'

'I'm not going to say anything else. I didn't stab him. I didn't kill anyone.' Emmett's voice started to grow higher in pitch.

'OK, deep breaths, son. We don't have much time today anyway, and it won't help anything by you giving a comment interview in this state. My advice is that you answer no comment to every question, is that clear? No matter what they ask, you say "no comment". Have you got that?'

Emmett bobbed his head up and down.

A now-familiar jangle of keys approached the door and the door swung open.

'We ready?' the officer asked. Craig nodded and stood up.

Emmett was led by the officer to another room and Craig followed closely behind. The officer placed a key into the lock and twisted it firmly, but the door didn't budge. He flicked to another key and tried again. It opened. He clapped his hands together at his minor achievement and led them inside. As Emmett and Craig took their seats next to each other on black plastic chairs, another male officer joined them.

The desk was too small for the number of people in the room, and the air conditioning unit whirred loudly. A sweaty aroma filled every corner.

A recording system was set up on the desk, which the new officer fiddled with. The machine bleeped. There was a short pause once the bleeping stopped.

'This interview is being recorded. I am Detective Sergeant Matthew Willis and I'm based at Walthamstow Police Station, and I am joined by my colleague . . . ' he paused and nodded to the other police officer who introduced himself. He then turned to Emmett.

'Could you please tell us your full name for the recording?'

'Emmett Hamilton.'

'Could you also please confirm your date of birth for us?'

Emmett looked at Craig, wondering when he should begin answering 'no comment'. Craig nodded approvingly and Emmett answered with his date of birth, before Detective Willis continued.

'The date is 5 September 2023 and the time, by my watch, is 16.07. This interview is being conducted in Walthamstow Police Station ... '

Emmett began to let the officer's voice drown under the whirring of the air-conditioning unit. He noticed that the room's colours were almost the inverse of the cell. The walls were a duck-egg blue, neatly divided into top and bottom by a beige wooden strip, lined with an alarm belt. He realised the voice had stopped and looked at the officer.

'Is that OK, Emmett?'

'Sorry, what?'

'I'm just going to read the caution to you, OK?'

Emmett shrugged.

'You do not have to say anything ... ' The officer hesitated and then coughed into his elbow. 'Sorry.' He returned his elbow to his side. 'But it may harm your defence if you do not mention when questioned something you later rely on in court, and anything you do say may be given in evidence.' Again, he coughed into his elbow and thumped his fist on his chest. His colleague shifted his chair slightly further away.

'What this all means Em-art, is that how I say your name?'

'It's Emmett. Eh-met.'

'Yes, sorry, OK, well Eh-meet, what this all means is that

you don't have to answer my questions if you don't want to, but if you don't answer a question today and later answer it at court, they may ask you why you didn't answer it now, here, today.'

Craig turned to Emmett to reassure him, but Emmett stared at the officer and nodded.

'So, we're here to talk about ...' The officer started setting out the parameters of the conversation, but Emmett had tuned out again. He watched the officer's lips move quickly over the next hour, overusing his tongue, sending small droplets of spittle out onto the table in front of him. There was something about a knife and wanting to test it for fingerprints. Each time the officer's mouth stopped, he answered 'no comment'. They were taking his blood-soiled clothes too. He could feel the other officer's eyes burning a hole into his cheeks and saw Craig's pen move fluidly recording the most important pieces of information. A witness, at the scene, pointed to him.

Finally, the interview came to an end. The officers informed Emmett that he was going to be charged. The tape stopped and the officers stood up. Emmett waited in his chair. Craig stood up expecting Emmett to follow but he remained seated. Craig beckoned him towards the door. He remained still while his eyes flickered like the flame of a candle, and eventually he stood up.

In the corridor, the four men stood alongside each other awkwardly. One of the officers walked away while the other slowly led Craig and Emmett to the custody sergeant's desk. Again, Emmett could barely focus. In the low hum of voices he detected the words 'Emmett Hamilton, you are being charged with the murder of Thomas Dove'.

The custody sergeant discharged them and after a few steps back towards the cells, the accompanying officer stood back against the wall, giving Craig and Emmett a few seconds of privacy.

'You'll be at the magistrates' court in the morning. We'll speak properly then. Keep your head up,' Craig said confidently.

'I might still use duty – you said I could change my mind.' Emmett avoided making eye-contact with Craig but there was no malice in his voice.

'Sure, no rush but I'll be there tomorrow.'

CHAPTER 8

Rosa tipped the last few droplets of her red wine into the back of her throat and reached across the table to grab some peanuts from the small dish they all shared. There were hardly enough peanuts for each person to have a couple, but Rosa grabbed a small handful, leaving only a few with some crumbs behind.

'John, you will never guess who I was in front of today ... the witch herself!' Sally shouted over the buzz of conversation in the pub. Her voice pierced Rosa's ears, which were less than a ruler-length from Sally's mouth.

'HHJ Robinson?' he answered, equally as loudly. 'God only knows why she's become so shit on the bench, I heard she was a decent advocate. The power must have gone to her head!'

'Oh my god, seriously I had a PTPH before her today and my client was a young ...' Sally yelled. Rosa excused herself from the table in a desperate attempt to protect her eardrums. She stepped towards to the bar and ordered another glass of wine.

'Did you hear about what happened in HHJ Robinson's

court today? Supposedly it was utter mayhem,' Chloe shouted across the table.

The response was inaudible from where Rosa was standing, but as she looked over her shoulder, she could see her colleagues' faces lighting up like lamps in anticipation of more gossip.

'I heard that a barrister just pulled out their phone and started FaceTiming a witness in the middle of a bail hearing! Imagine that!' Sam said.

Was that supposed to have been *her*?

'Controversial opinion but maybe it saved a hell of a lot of time, we all know how shit the court technology is,' a voice shouted from the group; Rosa couldn't match it to any of the faces.

'No, it's not creative, it just shows a complete lack of respect for our traditions and courtesy. The system will fall apart if barristers start acting like smart-arse teenagers in court,' another voice chimed in. This time it appeared to come from Peter, an older colleague in chambers who had never had much time for her.

'That'll be £9 please, miss,' the bartender stated, holding out a card machine. Rosa paid with her phone, took three large sips and looked back at the group. Everyone was laughing, which she assumed was at her expense – whether knowingly or unknowingly. She lifted the glass and glugged down the remainder of the drink. Time to go.

A hand grabbed her arm as she went to leave.

'Rosa! You're leaving already?' It was John. He and Rosa had completed their pupillage together, and he'd initially introduced her to Tristan. His eyes were slightly bloodshot and his words beginning to slur. He'd clearly been here most of the afternoon.

'I have quite a lot of work to do this evening. Have fun,' she said curtly, shaking her arm free.

'Always working, never having fun. How are things with you and Trist?' he said with a wry grin.

'Fine,' she said, with a straight face.

'Such a good lad. I still wouldn't have put you together but hey, love wins, eh!'

Rosa smiled politely and turned her back to leave.

On the train home, Rosa's phone buzzed. She was tempted to ignore it; she'd soon face Nana. It rang again and she took it from her pocket. Craig.

'Rosa, your clerks have said that you are free tomorrow?'

'Erm, yes, I think so, do you need something covered?' She tried to slow down, realising she'd spoken in one breath. She inhaled deeply before continuing. 'I can imagine you've got your hands full.'

'That's what I'm calling about, Rosa. I'm instructing you in a murder case, the one in Walthamstow Park, you'll have seen it on the news. I think you'll be perfect.'

'Sorry, what?' She pulled the phone away from her ear to check that she really was speaking to Craig. 'I don't think I heard that right.'

'You did, I'm instructing you in the murder case. His name is Emmett Hamilton. I'll email your clerks now and join you at the magistrates' court tomorrow.'

'You're instructing me?' she gasped, finally registering that she wasn't mistaken in what she'd heard. She hadn't intended to sound quite so shocked, but it came before she had a chance to stop it.

'Yes, you've done a murder case before, haven't you?' Craig asked in a playfully sarcastic tone, with a hint of genuine enquiry.

'Erm, yes. Well, yes, of course,' she replied, trying desperately to disguise her panic.

'Great. I looked you up properly today too. An Oxbridge graduate! I know the sort of family you come from, so I'm doubly impressed. I look forward to our first murder together – this should be fun. I'll see you tomorrow.' He ended the call before Rosa had a chance to respond. She pulled the phone away from her ear and looked at it again. She shook her head. *No way.*

A woman on the train, who had previously been tapping at her smartphone, was glaring at Rosa. Her long fingernails were perched over the edge of her phone case, and her chin pointed upwards as if in contempt. Rosa whispered an apology and picked her suitcase up from the floor. She shuffled down the carriage and sat at the other end, out of sight.

Rosa was, unusually, a little lost for words. Craig was instructing her on the murder case. She'd been led on murder cases before, but she'd never defended one on her own. She'd not told Craig that; although she hadn't lied, she had let him believe she was more experienced than she was.

She thought back to her ethics exam at Bar School, it must have been at least ten years ago now. It was an easy question on any professional ethics paper: *a barrister does not have sufficient experience to do a complex case, but an important instructing solicitor instructs them unknowingly. Should they:*

Do the case anyway, to impress the solicitor, or . . .

Return the case, and explain to the solicitor that they are not suitably qualified

Option *B* was obviously the correct one, but it rarely happened in reality. People were constantly doing cases out of their depth, that was the nature of the Criminal Bar. This was different. This was a murder case. Rosa would have to return it; this was not the time to be treading water in the deep end. There must be someone in chambers who could do a better job than her.

Rosa scrolled through her contacts and found Steve, her clerk. She dialled and he answered after a couple of rings.

'Rosa? You all right? Great news that Craig has instructed you on that case.'

'Yes, erm, yes, great news. Hi, yes, Steve. I need to tell you something.'

'He seems pretty keen to have you,' he said, ignoring Rosa. 'Not sure why, no offence – I don't mean it like that. You have the best qualifications of any of our lot. But you know, you haven't done many like this, have you?' Steve spoke quickly and, evidently, without thinking. 'Anyway, what did you want to tell me? Fire away.'

'Well, I was going to say.' She paused, considering what Steve had just said. 'I think, I'm maybe too junior to be doing a case like this *on my own.*'

'Well, as I say, Craig doesn't think so, does he? Mind you,

if you aren't keen, I can send John down there tomorrow. He loves a murder case. Especially the high-profile ones. Up to you.'

John had apparently always known he was going to be a high-flying criminal barrister because his dad was a judge in the Court of Appeal and had practically coached him to the Bar since he was a young teenager. She'd spent most of her professional career feeling that she lived in John's shadow.

'Is there anyone else?' Rosa blurted out.

'What? Not John? Why, is there something wrong with John?'

John this, John that. It appeared that Steve was challenging himself as to how many times he could say his name during this single phone call. Rosa had always got on well with Steve; he was old school in his clerking style. He was a sweet-talker and loved to say nice things to the female barristers but didn't hide the fact that he thought crime was a boys' game. It was one of the reasons Rosa had been so impressed with Gillian Folkestone: she was the only female KC in their chambers, and she'd made it to the top despite these attitudes.

'No, nothing wrong. It's just . . . well, it's just that John is the same call as me.'

'Yes . . . ' Steve seemed oblivious to Rosa's sentiment. This wasn't the first time Rosa had drawn his attention to the disparities in hers and John's practice, despite them having been in chambers for exactly the same length of time.

'Well, surely if John can do it, I can do it,' she mumbled.

'Er, yeah, I guess so. Well, he has a lot more experience

in murders, doesn't he?' Steve had a way of making Rosa feel as though it was her fault that she wasn't getting a fair distribution of the exciting cases. 'But look, yeah. Craig has chosen you. What do you want me to do? You at least gonna go to the Mags tomorrow?'

'Oh yes, yes, sorry. I'll be there tomorrow. I just need to think about whether I'm up to doing this case.'

'Right, sure, OK. Well, it's in your diary and I've just sent you the papers. Go to the Mags tomorrow and let me know about keeping the case. Speak soon.'

'Thank you. Bye.'

Rosa had felt an ache growing in her stomach.

CHAPTER 9

'Mercedes, laas night yuh seh yuh wudda send me di funds. Mi emailed yuh telling yuh ow much it did an yuh nuh send it. Yuh know mi wi nuh aks again.' Nana's voice echoed around Rosa's bedroom as she tugged at the duvet to get Rosa's full attention.

Rosa stretched her arms, hitting her headboard and squealing quietly, exaggerating the pain. This was the first day in weeks that she didn't have to wake up at 6 a.m., and she was desperate for a few more minutes of sleep. Nana flicked the switch by the door. Rosa narrowed her brows and raised her palms over her eyes to shield herself from the bright light that now bounced around her room.

'Yes, Nana, I said I'd send it. I'm so sorry.' She heaved herself up, embarrassed that Nana was having to wake her up. She glanced at her phone screen. Six a.m.

Nana walked around the bed. Her legs were thick and her large bottom jiggled as she walked. Nana was barely five feet tall, but her short grey afro made her a few inches taller. Besides the colour of her hair, Nana didn't look old enough to be anyone's grandmother. Her dark brown face was soft and plump, with no wrinkles at all.

'Sorry nuh pay di bills, Mercedes. Yuh get di email?'

'Nana. It's not an email, it's a text message but, yes, I saw it. I'm so sorry,' she said realising that she'd repeated the apology that Nana had scorned her for. She swivelled her legs to the side of the bed and hopped out. 'I promise I'll sort it before lunchtime.' Rosa wasn't entirely sure she could keep that promise: she had a pile of 'aged debt' – work that she had done but that the Legal Aid Agency had not yet paid her for. The legal aid rates were so poor that even when she *was* paid it was hardly enough, but she didn't withdraw her promise. She was *needed*.

Nana sighed and mumbled something in patois that Rosa couldn't hear and left the room. Rosa could feel a headache creeping through her skull.

A few minutes of silence passed before her phone started ringing. Reluctantly she tapped the green answer button and lifted the phone to her ear.

'Hello, Rosa, you all right?' Steve greeted her chirpily. He was oblivious to how much he'd frustrated her yesterday. She answered affirmatively but kept her answer short, hoping that this interruption wouldn't further prevent her falling back to sleep.

'Sorry to call you at this time but Craig has been on the phone. Are you ready for today?'

She remembered their conversation yesterday and John's face popped into her head.

'Rosa?'

She began to pace back and forth across her bedroom.

'Rosa? Can you hear me?'

Rosa realised she hadn't said anything yet. Her heart was racing. She took a deep breath and announced: 'Yes, Steve. I heard you. I'm ready.'

Those words felt so powerful, but the opposite was true. She was petrified and prayed that Craig's faith in her ability was not misplaced. She had done plenty of serious cases on her own: GBH, rape, firearms and even attempted murder. But murder felt different.

'Excellent. Excellent, OK, well, I'll wrap things up on our end.' Steve sounded genuinely enthusiastic, despite having put such effort into replacing her on the case with John.

Rosa nodded furiously before realising that Steve couldn't see her.

'Yes, thank you. I'll get ready now.'

Rosa had always been academically gifted, and many of her instructing solicitors knew what a talented barrister she was, but she didn't have connections in the same way that others did. Sometimes she was envious of people like John who grew up going to school with the same solicitors who instructed him now. Rosa needed a chance to prove herself. She'd been in this job for over ten years, yet still so many solicitors didn't know her name. The publicity around this case could be career changing.

She pulled her phone away from her ear and typed frantically, messaging Orissa as she walked into the hallway.

You will never guess who is doing her own
murder trial?!?! xxx

This was terrifying. She copied the same text message to Tristan and pressed send.

'Sady!' Toby called out, pulling her attention away from her phone. As a young child he hadn't been able to manage 'Mercedes' and had shortened it himself. He'd now kept it as a nickname for her. Rosa smiled at him, crouched, and pulled him in for a quick cuddle.

'You OK, Toby?' she whispered into his ear. His grin spread across his face as he nodded into her chest. She pulled him back to look at his face. Eyes dark and warm like little puddles of chocolate.

'Shall we go out this weekend? Maybe the park?'

'Nuh mek promises yuh cyan kip, Mercedes.' Nana's voice appeared, followed by the stout figure of the woman herself, packing Toby's reading book into his bag.

'Yes, yes, or can we go swimming, Sady?' His beautiful round eyes lit up as he spoke.

'Maybe. I'll see what I can do.' She offered a less definite answer this time. 'Go on, Toby, I need to get ready, and you need to get ready for school!'

Without giving him a chance to respond, Rosa stood up and scurried back into her bedroom, attempting to close the door behind her. It didn't quite close properly, but the clock was ticking. Rosa grabbed some wet wipes and attempted to wipe her body clean. Pulled some big knickers out of her drawer and held them up against her groin before returning them to the drawer. Hopefully she'd be spending tonight with Tristan and these knickers had the potential to ruin that. Her hands reached to the back of the drawer and pulled out a strappy thong, which clearly used to be black but was now a faded grey. Rosa looked disappointedly at her huge dirty washing pile and realised she had little choice. Without showering, she stepped in between the strings of the thong and pulled it up around her thighs. Her underwear didn't match, but at least this thong was a little bit sexy.

Lying on the top of the dirty washing pile was the dress Rosa had worn in yesterday's hearing. She picked it up, brushed it off and examined it for stains. She pulled it over her head and smoothed out the creases, picked a pair of black tights and pushed her foot into them, tearing a small hole in her inner thigh. She didn't have time to change so stuffed a spare pair into her handbag.

Maybe she was more like her mother than she realised.

The carpets in Nana's flat were a tattered grey but she knew better than to wear shoes in the house. She carried her shoes to the front door and dropped them, before tiptoeing to the kitchen and peering around the doorframe.

'Nana, I'm off. It's urgent. I've been called to work.'

Nana looked up, kissed her teeth, and went back to chopping strawberries into neat little hearts. Rosa had expected a worse response and smiled back.

'Love you, Nana,' she called out.

Nana remained silent and a reply from Orissa popped up on her phone.

Not the one in Walthamstow Park? The grandma of the man they've arrested, Joyce, she goes to my church!

CHAPTER 10

Leytonstone Magistrates' Court was far more pleasant than most others. It was brightly lit, and the security staff were friendly. Rosa unlocked her phone and accessed her digital wallet, ready to show the staff the electronic pass that she had finally bothered to download.

'Morning, miss. You've got a pass, right?'

'Yes, right here.'

'OK, great. Could you head over to my colleague, and he'll just scan it for you?'

Rosa followed his instructions and walked over to the other security officer who scanned the QR code on her screen.

'All done, love. You have a good day.'

Rosa thanked him, walked to the back wall, and pressed the lift button.

A voice sounded behind her. 'Rosa, good morning!' She turned to see Craig grinning.

'Craig! How are you?' Rosa smiled back.

'I had an absolute nightmare getting in and hardly any

sleep last night. My wife, Sarah, couldn't get the baby to sleep – you know what newborns are like – and I honestly must have only managed a few hours.' His face had aged, lines spreading across his forehead as he spoke.

'You have a newborn baby? Congratulations to you both!'

'Yeah, yeah. It's our fourth. Didn't your gran ever tell you about our eldest, Daphne? She was so fond of her. Anyway, don't have kids. Stay being a brilliant barrister. Trust me on that.' He laughed at himself. Rosa didn't laugh but maintained her smile, less warm now.

Oblivious to Rosa's reaction, Craig switched the conversation to their client.

'I thought it made sense for us both to attend. You know how much of a nightmare booking prison conferences can be.' She did have a vague idea, having heard similar complaints from other solicitors. 'If you don't mind, I'll head down to him now. Meet me down there?' Rosa nodded and secretly felt glad he was there to assist.

Emmett was an unusual name, but it rang a bell. She tried to remember where she had heard it before but struggled to put a face to the name. Nana came to the forefront of her mind, and she distantly recalled a story her grandmother had told her many years ago. *White men killed a young bowy inna America fi being Black.* She could now remember exactly how Nana had begun the account of what happened. It was alleged that the boy had flirted with a white woman, and he was tortured and lynched. A small wave of terror trickled through her veins.

Rosa found an empty room and shut herself in. It was

small and windowless, and far too warm. There was only one chair and no table, and Rosa wondered what this room had ever been designed for. She perched on the lone chair, pulled out her laptop, placed it onto her knees and opened the screen. Emmett's case files were already open but she'd not had the chance to properly read them. She turned to the first page of the MG5 – the case summary prepared by the police.

Defendant 1: *Hamilton*

Defendant 2: ...

The second box was blank. Emmett was the only identified defendant.

Rosa continued to make her way through the document.

Anticipated plea: *GAP – NSST*

GAP. Guilty Anticipated Plea. *NSST.* Not Suitable for Summary Trial. Despite it being obvious that this case, a murder case, was not suitable to be decided in the magistrates' court, the form had spelled it out in neat black typed font. More importantly, she observed, the police thought that he was going to plead guilty.

The next box on the page set out a summary, divided into two parts: key evidence and key witnesses.

Key evidence. On 4 September 2023, police were called to Walthamstow Park, East London. They'd received a call about a fight. On police attendance at the park, at approximately 10.05 a.m. officers saw the following.

Rosa's eyes quickly absorbed the blunt description of the scene. *There was blood on the grass. The victim, Thomas Dove, appeared to have been stabbed multiple times.*

The stabbing was said to have taken place at around 10 a.m. The officers arrived just minutes later.

Dove was taken to Whipps Cross hospital. That was the hospital she was born in.

This was a sparsely filled-out document. The officer had clearly been in a rush to complete it. The police summary stated that there had been a group of Black boys and Rosa checked the top of the form again to confirm that there was only one identified defendant in this case.

Hamilton was identified by members of the public in the park. He was cautioned and detained.

The court speaker system called a defendant into the courtroom. Rosa would have to speed up her reading given that their case would soon be heard. She flicked to the last page and read the disclosure officer's name. *PC 20201 Hadley.* She turned back to the summary of the evidence.

PC Hadley had recorded that there were two key witnesses, besides the arresting officers. The first was Claire Smith, a mother with her baby in the park. The second was Mark McEvoy, a man who claimed that he momentarily intervened in the fight to try and break it up, and who appeared to have been stabbed in the leg in the process. According to this summary, both witnesses agreed that there was a group of Black men, at least three, and that they were all dark-skinned, except for one. Both also agreed that the lighter-skinned male was the person carrying the knife. And, they said, they saw him stab the victim multiple times.

She let out a long exhale, realising that she had been holding her breath while reading. Rosa felt deflated. There was more than one witness, and they'd clearly identified Emmett as the person who was carrying the knife and who'd stabbed the victim. There appeared to be no reason why two random members of the public would make that up, and there was no obvious explanation for them being mistaken. The murder had taken place in broad daylight in an open park.

This was her first murder case, on her own. It was all over the news. And she was going to lose.

CHAPTER 11

A musty smell wafted through Rosa's nose as she entered the confined court cell space at the magistrates' court, a combination of stale body odour and clinical hand sanitiser. Resisting the urge to take a deep breath, she pursed her lips tightly and arched them into a smile in the direction of both Craig and Emmett. Craig didn't acknowledge her and continued tapping at his laptop keys. She greeted Emmett with a nod and her forced grin became more natural. Emmett did not smile back, acknowledging her presence merely by moving his gaze in her direction, his stare passing blankly through her.

Emmett had a light complexion, as described in the witness statements, much paler than her; his skin resembled a milky latte. His hair was short and had been neatly shaped to frame his small rectangular forehead. The lack of facial hair made him look boyish, which was emphasised by the small dimples in his cheeks as he flexed by pouting and then relaxing his mouth.

Rosa perched on the edge of the bench, beside Craig. The

seats were bolted down on either side of the room and there was a rectangular table affixed to the floor in between. She spoke softly and extended her hand out to Emmett.

'Hi, I'm Rosa. I'm going to be your barrist—'

'Let's skip the introductions, we don't have much time,' Craig interrupted. 'He knows who you are and, look, he is nervous. He wants to know what's going to happen today.' Craig's curtness surprised Rosa and forced her to sit a little more upright. His eyes remained fixed on his laptop screen as he spoke. Craig spoke about Emmett like he wasn't sitting directly in front of him.

Before Rosa had the chance to respond, Craig spoke again, this time more quietly so that only she could hear.

'Please, let's just get cracking with what's going to happen today because I need to be out of here by lunchtime.'

He stretched upwards and lifted his head above his screen, offering Emmett a friendly wink. Emmett's face was motionless aside from a slight flare of his nostrils as he inhaled and exhaled.

Rosa mirrored his breathing, letting out a soft exhale with his. She slightly raised her eyebrows, making sure that Emmett saw but knowing Craig wouldn't care to look. Her duty was to Emmett, not Craig.

'As I said, I'm Rosa, your barrister,' she said purposefully.

Craig shuffled irritably. She felt her neck growing hotter. She regretted being so forthright, remembering that Craig was doing her a favour in giving her this case. She tried to relax and forced a smile again.

Emmett remained still and expressionless. He continued

to stare into nothingness. She noticed that the left side of his face was swollen, making one eye more almond shaped than the other, encased in a perfect circular purple patch. On both cheeks there were small cuts, but the cut on the left cheek looked deeper. Rosa imagined that with the lightest touch of the cut, fresh blood would ooze from the wound. Her eyes slowly travelled down his face and rested on his lips, which looked remarkably untouched.

'Are you OK?'

He seemed to acknowledge her concern and bobbed his head slowly without saying a word. She stared a little longer at the cuts on his cheeks and the bruising, noticing now his big, coffee-coloured eyes, kind and childlike – like Toby's.

'Emmett, you've been charged with murder. That means the prosecution has said that you have unlawfully killed another person. That person being . . .'

Rosa paused and adjusted her language; she wasn't in court now.

'The person they have said you've killed is called Thomas Dove. The prosecution will try to prove that you stabbed him and that's how he died.'

Her words were delivered without any embellishment. Droplets of tears began to trickle from Emmett's eyes. He said something so softly that neither Rosa nor Craig noticed that he had spoken.

'They'll also be trying to prove that you had the intention to kill him, or to cause him grievous bodily harm – in other words, really serious bodily harm.'

Emmett muttered something again.

'Sorry, Emmett, I didn't catch that. What did you say?'

His fingers were trembling, and he sat on them to calm his nerves.

'I didn't do it,' he repeated.

He lifted one of his hands from underneath him, wiped his eyes and then his nose, smearing a small trail of snot towards his ear, before his hand disappeared again under the table.

Craig sighed impatiently as if he had seen this scene before.

'I didn't do it,' Emmett whispered, slightly louder this time. 'I didn't kill anyone.'

Craig clapped his hands together. 'Of course you didn't. You've said this. That's why we're here to help.' Rosa was again surprised by the lack of empathy in his tone. 'Now it doesn't really matter to me whether you did or didn't – my job, as your solicitor, is to make sure that the Crown can't prove that you did.' He stood up and edged towards the door.

Rosa looked at Craig, astonished. She'd just heard Emmett say he didn't do it and Craig was telling him that it didn't matter either way. Their client's liberty was on the line. Emmett could face life in prison and Craig was sitting there talking about it as though he was talking tactics in a gameshow.

'What you tell us is extremely important.' Rosa's voice sliced through the quiet. 'We act for *you*, Emmett. I've heard what you've said, you didn't do it . . . '

Emmett's hands were now on the table. He looked down at his fingers and pulled each one in turn.

'But, Emmett, I have a responsibility to make sure that

71

you understand that if you *did* do it, by owning up to that right now and pleading guilty, you could benefit from up to one-third off a sentence you would otherwise get if you were found guilty at trial.'

Emmett started sobbing. Not just slowly crying but howling hysterically.

'I didn't do it!' he cried.

Craig glared at her. She felt a flood of panic rush over her. She wondered if she, Rosa Higgins – Craig's ex-cleaner's granddaughter – had gone too far. She was struggling to balance her gratitude to Craig against her obligations to Emmett. There was no doubt that Craig was far more experienced than her and she contemplated whether she should be following his lead. But Emmett . . . he was her client. His freedom was on the line.

'No, no, I know. I wasn't trying to suggest you did. I just need to make sure that I advise you properly.' Her words were scrambled. She paused for breath. Craig leaned back against the wall, with his hands in his pockets. She watched Emmett helplessly. He wiped his face again, this time with the underside of his fingers, and sniffed repeatedly until he had calmed himself down.

'Why were you in the park that day, Emmett?'

'I can't remember, I probably just wanted some fresh air with my friends.'

'Was there any particular reason that you went to *that* park on that day?'

'I've already told you, no. No, not that I can remember.'

'And your friends, did they travel to the park with you, or did you meet them there?'

'I'm not talking about my friends, they're no part of this.'

'Could I talk to them?'

'No,' he said flatly. He looked from Craig to Rosa and back to Craig again. 'Surely there is CCTV. Can't you get that to prove my innocence?'

Craig scoffed. 'How many times have you seen CCTV in a park, son?'

Emmett lowered his head, and tears rolled down his face and off his chin again.

'We will look into whether there was any nearby CCTV,' Rosa said, gently this time. 'Craig will make some enquiries.' She looked hopefully at Craig who nodded and addressed Emmett.

'Keep your head low in prison, son. I'll be in contact soon.'

Rosa stood up awkwardly and offered Emmett an apologetic expression. Emmett avoided eye contact and glanced back down at his hands, repeating the motion of pulling each finger. Craig tapped on the glass and a cell officer came to unlock the door. They told Rosa and Craig to wait while they cuffed Emmett and led him back to his cell.

Rosa followed Craig back upstairs. She knew that it shouldn't matter whether or not she believed Emmett. Over the years she had represented many defendants who she didn't believe for a second, but had managed to successfully persuade a jury they were not guilty. Right now, however, she believed him. Her gut told her that he didn't do it. And, in that moment, she told herself that she would do everything in her power to help him.

CHAPTER 12

'Can we have *just* counsel in the case of Mr Hamilton come into the courtroom, please,' the usher shouted from the doorway. Her hair was covered in a caramel-coloured headscarf, which complemented both her light honey eyes and toffee-coloured lipstick. She glared at the group of people in the waiting area who had crowded around the door. Rosa pushed through the crowd and emerged at the front.

'I represent Mr Hamilton,' she said. 'This is his solicitor.' She turned to look for Craig among the crowd. His head bobbed up and then disappeared. The usher's eyes searched with Rosa's.

'Hello. I'm Mr Hamilton's solicitor,' Craig said, slightly out of breath.

The usher looked sceptically at them both but allowed them to pass her into the courtroom. Rosa pressed her hand against the modern silver push plate on the second door and bowed to the judge as she entered. She was appearing in the magistrates' court before District Judge Whitman, who she didn't recognise. Craig followed her into the room and copied her bow.

Rosa sat on the left, closest to the public gallery, Craig directly behind her, and the prosecutor took his place on her right. Rosa plugged in her laptop and typed the date into a blank Word document. She glanced at the prosecutor, Jeremy Pankhurst. She didn't know much about him other than that he was a fairly experienced barrister at a rival set to hers – 10 Green Park. A few wispy grey hairs protruded from underneath his horsehair wig and Rosa estimated that he was in his sixties. He had clearly missed any opportunity he might have had to be King's Counsel (or Queen's Counsel as it would have been at the time he'd have been appointed). Today, he looked rushed off his feet. A pile of papers spread untidily across the desk next to him and his suit jacket collar stuck up awkwardly at the back. Rosa wanted to tell him but strongly suspected that he would not welcome the feedback.

DJ Whitman pushed his glasses up higher on the bridge of his nose. He had dark hair that was combed neatly to the right-hand side.

'Counsel, are we ready? Are we all set to go?'

Mr Pankhurst remained seated and nodded. Rosa stood up.

'Yes, sir, we are.' She sat back down.

'Good. This will be straightforward but I'm sure you both have gathered how much public interest there is. This is not a show or a circus. There will be order in my courtroom.'

Rosa stood up again like a jack-in-the-box.

'Yes, of course, sir.' She sat again.

'Good. Now, Rameen, could you please let members of the public in. Please make sure that only members of the media sit in the press seats. I cannot be dealing with those complaints again.' DJ Whitman again pushed his glasses back along his nose.

'Sure, sir. Will do,' the usher replied.

This courtroom was unusually modern but whoever had designed it had tried to emulate the traditional décor of the typically older courts. The back wall, behind the judge, was panelled with cheap laminated wood, and the royal crest looked out of place hanging on it. All the desks were constructed out of the same cheap wood, with the surfaces of the advocates' covered in a grey plastic material. It rather undermined the attempted elegance of the space, as did their rigid black office chairs, which only coordinated with the tall giraffe-like microphones that poked out of each desk and the single black computer monitor on the clerk's desk.

Rosa followed the usher's steps with her eyes as she passed the press seats and the red-carpeted public gallery. The chairs there were also red; uncomfortable, hard, plastic things, fixed firmly to the floor. They slowly filled as the usher beckoned people in. A plump-faced woman wearing an excessive amount of blusher squeezed herself through the row of chairs to the end and collapsed into her seat with relief. She opened her notepad and pulled a pen from her handbag. The man next to her, who seemed squashed in his seat so as not to be touching her, pulled a small tablet on to his lap. A few elderly people lined the back chairs, while some younger people who looked like a mixture of students and court reporters, remained standing, all the way to the doorway.

'Can everyone please make sure that their phones are switched off?' the usher said as she walked briskly to her seat at the front of the courtroom.

The familiar jingle of the dock officer's keys grew louder as Emmett was brought into the dock. The dock was entirely glass-fronted, like an animal display at a zoo.

'Sir, this is the case of Mr Emmett Hamilton. Number six on your list,' the usher said.

'Please stand. Are you Emmett Hamilton?' A different voice spoke from just beneath the elevated desk where DJ Whitman was seated – the court clerk. She stared at Emmett awaiting his confirmation.

'Yes.'

'What is your date of birth?'

'Erm. My birthday is 23 November 2004.'

'What's your address?'

'Flat 240, Seabridge Estate, Sade Hill, Walthamstow, E17 8QA.'

The court continued with a few formalities before declaring that this case could not be heard at the magistrates' court. Rosa felt grateful that this judge was not wasting any time; this court did not have the power to deal with a case of this magnitude and the hearing there today was merely part of the process.

'This case, of course, will be sent to the Crown Court. My clerk will find the date,' DJ Whitman announced.

The clerk tapped at her keyboard and lifted the small landline phone beside her. She whispered ferociously into it.

'Ms Higgins,' DJ Whitman said and then paused, waiting for her to stand. Rosa did and straightened her jacket. 'Has legal aid been granted yet?'

'No, not yet, sir, but it's been applied for.' Rosa could feel a slight tremble in her hand. She gripped the lectern in front of her in a desperate attempt to calm her nerves. This was the magistrates' court, she'd been here hundreds, perhaps even a thousand times before. She didn't know why she felt so nervous.

DJ Whitman nodded.

'Thank you. As you know, I can't consider bail today. Is there anything else?'

Rosa knew that this court couldn't make decisions about bail in murder cases. Did the judge think she needed that reminder? Was it obvious that she was out of her depth?

'Ms Higgins? Is there anything else?'

She shook her head. 'No, sorry, sir, there is nothing else.' Rosa avoided looking back at Craig or the boggling eyes at the side of the courtroom and sat back down. It had been a simple question, if she couldn't handle the magistrates' court how on earth was she going to do an entire murder trial?

'Mr Hamilton, please stand,' DJ Whitman commanded.

There was a shuffle at the back of the courtroom as Emmett rose to his feet.

'Mr Hamilton, I am sending your case to the Crown Court sitting at the Central Criminal Court. You may know this as the Old Bailey.'

Rosa made a note on her laptop. *Sent to the Old Bailey.*

'You will appear there in just a few days, on ...' DJ

Whitman paused briefly to read the note the clerk handed him. 'On the fourth of October.'

Rosa added the date to her note and opened her calendar. She had a conference with a client in the afternoon but should be able to fit this hearing into the morning.

'I don't have the power to consider the question of bail today, as you may have heard me say to your counsel.' Rosa felt too warm and slightly embarrassed – would Emmett think she didn't know what she was doing? Would Craig?

'Bail can be considered, if you wish to make an application, on the fourth of October. The judge at Old Bailey will be able to make that decision.'

It was difficult for Rosa to see Emmett, who was behind glass at the very back of the courtroom. She was worried about him. He was still standing, clad in a grey tracksuit.

'Mr Hamilton, you are remanded in custody until the fourth of October of this year, and your case has been sent to the Crown Court. That's it for now.' DJ Whitman paused and looked at both legal representatives. 'Thank you, both.'

The hearing had been swift, and Emmett was taken back to the cells as quickly as he had been brought up.

DJ Whitman folded his laptop closed and stood up.

'All rise,' the usher called.

Everyone stood up. DJ Whitman bowed his head and left the room. As the door shut behind him, everyone sat back down in unison. There was something remarkably synchronised about the courtroom.

Rosa reached into her bag to check her messages. She texted Tristan.

> We still on for tonight? Need some rest and
> relaxation with this heavy case. X

He replied instantly, which was unlike him.

> Sure, I'm busy until about 11 p.m. but you're
> welcome to stay over. Let me know.

She replied rapidly too.

> I'll see you then.

She stuffed her phone back into her handbag and collected her belongings from the desk. The crowd at the doorway had begun to clear but she waited a few moments for the last few people to leave before exiting herself.

Someone stepped out in front of her outside the courtroom, blocking her path. She recognised him as the man who looked squashed in his seat during the hearing.

'Ms Higgins, I'm Matthew Weisberg, I'm a journalist with the *Daily Mail*. Could I ask you a few questions?'

'No, I'm afraid I'm in a rush,' Rosa said, avoiding eye contact and sidestepping past him.

'Excuse me, are you Emmett's barrister?' a woman's voice called out.

Without looking back, Rosa walked onwards down the corridor away from the courtroom. She didn't want to talk to any journalists. 'I am, but I'm afraid I can't speak to the press.'

'I'm not the press,' the voice said, and now Rosa noticed it had the shake of someone much older.

Rosa stopped, turned her head and let the woman fill the silence.

'I'm his grandmother, Joyce,' the woman said. 'I'm the only family he has.'

Rosa felt embarrassed and walked back towards the elderly woman. Her face was barely visible as she wore a silk scarf that she pulled up over her chin, and her fluffy black hair covered most of the top of her head. Rosa guided her into one of the small conference rooms.

'I'm so sorry, we've been meaning to reach out to you,' Rosa babbled.

Joyce's small beady eyes were glossy with tears, and her frail fingers were crooked with what looked to Rosa like arthritis. She sat down on the chair and let out a little breath of relief.

'Can I please go to see him in the cells?' she asked.

'I'm afraid not,' Rosa replied. 'They don't allow friends or family to go into the cells, it's lawyers only.'

Joyce reached up with a bent knuckle and rubbed a tear away.

'I can pass a message to him if you'd like?' Rosa suggested. She knew the offer was inadequate, but it was the best she could think of in the circumstances.

'Just tell him that I love him. I haven't told him enough. And . . . ' she stopped, and her bottom lip quivered. 'Please tell him that I believe him.'

Rosa listened and made a note of the message.

'Miss, his life is in your hands. I know he didn't commit this horrendous crime. I know my grandson and I saw his face.' Her voice croaked as more tears tumbled. When silence fell between them, she gave Joyce room. The grandmother gathered herself. 'My sweet boy wouldn't do that. I've raised him as my own. My daughter . . . died in childbirth. Nobody prepares you for that kind of thing.'

There was something about Joyce that reminded Rosa of Nana. It wasn't the way she spoke; Joyce enunciated every word and had no trace of anything but a London accent. It wasn't the way she looked; Joyce was thin and her body hunched, showing her age. Her face appeared gaunt and drained of energy. Nana, on the other hand, was plumper than her doctor wished but her cheeks were full of life, and she looked at least ten years younger than she was. Perhaps, Rosa thought, it was the love they both felt for their grandchildren.

'And his father, let me not even start on his father. He has contributed very little to Emmett's life other than trouble. He's probably been to places like this more times than you!' she exclaimed pointing at the floor of the conference room. 'I know you're thinking I'm just saying that he's a good boy because he is my grandson. I am not. He is a very clever young man.'

Joyce reached into her bag and pulled out a small square of folded paper. She handed it to Rosa.

Rosa unfolded it and skimmed the page. It appeared to be a printout of Emmett's school report, showing almost exclusively A grades. She glanced back to the top of the headed paper, which read Green Tree High School – that wasn't far from Nana's. Rosa carefully pressed the report in half, and then quarters, and smoothed out the creases. She handed it back to Joyce.

'I'm telling you now, this system was set up to keep people like us down – don't you forget that you're one of us too,' Joyce said, taking the report back from Rosa. 'I have a good feeling about you. I trust you. Please save my gran—'

'There you are!' Craig burst in, interrupting Joyce. She didn't turn to look at him.

'Craig, this is Emmett's grandmother.'

Craig extended his hand to shake hers, but Joyce merely looked down at the piece of paper in her hand and put it into her handbag. Slowly, she lifted herself out of the seat and looked Rosa squarely in the eyes.

'It's you I trust,' she whispered, and hobbled out of the room.

CHAPTER 13

Rosa knocked at Tristan's front door at 11 p.m. on the dot, having waited outside for at least fifteen minutes in the hope of not appearing too enthusiastic for yet another late evening. He opened the huge, weighted door and greeted Rosa with a smothering kiss, which caught her slightly off guard. He had answered in the blue underpants that hugged his groin, which she couldn't help but stare at. She playfully pushed him away.

'Too much, baby?' Tristan smirked. 'Wait and see what I've got for you.' His words were slurred. Slow R&B music was playing in the background. He winked and Rosa forced a laugh. He was clearly drunk, or tipsy at best. She followed him into the kitchen as he pulled a half-empty bottle of wine from the fridge.

'I'm OK, thanks. I don't think I'm going to drink tonight,' Rosa said.

Ignoring her, he pulled two glasses from the cupboard and emptied the bottle between them. She went to retrieve a glass of water but was grateful for the glass of wine, as she figured that she probably did need something to help her relax.

Tristan crept up behind her and pinched her bottom. She abandoned the stem of the glass and turned to face him, and pulled him closer towards her, sandwiching herself between him and the kitchen countertop. She slid her right hand from his hip to his groin and caressed the bulge of his penis in his boxer shorts. He let out a soft moan and stepped back to allow Rosa more room. Instead, she pulled away and beckoned him to follow her as she walked through the kitchen, into the hallway and up the stairs to his bedroom.

'Whoa, you want to get straight to it.' Tristan chuckled and followed her obligingly.

'I've had a stressful day,' Rosa said, pausing on the staircase and bending towards him. She planted a soft kiss on his lips. 'But I'm glad to be here.'

'Tell me all about it,' he said, dragging each word.

Rosa winked. 'Not yet, I want to enjoy you first.' He followed Rosa into the bedroom where she had already begun to take off her clothes.

They both climbed onto his bed, kissing passionately. Tristan began to kiss down her neck, and then across her chest until he reached her left nipple. She placed her hand gently on his head and guided his lips down her body, until they reached between her thighs. She moaned softly. As minutes passed her moans grew louder and she clenched his head with her legs. Her body grew tense as she let out a loud gasp and then relaxed into an orgasm. Tristan smiled at her pleasure and lifted his whole body up, so that he could place himself inside of her. He thrust for a few minutes, and she wiggled her hips rhythmically. He, too, let out a loud moan and collapsed onto her, resting his head on her chest for just a few seconds before rolling to the side.

A moment of thoughtful silence passed between them.

'I was a bumbling mess in court today. I've been anxious since the hearing – it's for the Walthamstow murder case I'm doing. I keep thinking about it and worrying that my client thinks I'm an idiot. He really needs me to be excellent and honestly, I don't know if I am.' Rosa was giving herself a pep talk more than she was conversing with Tristan. 'I genuinely believe that he didn't do it.'

'I thought – well, in fact, you told me – that it doesn't matter whether you thought the person committed the crime.' His tone was clumsy but not unkind.

She reached for a bottle of water beside his bed and took several gulps.

'I know it *shouldn't* matter. Of course, it shouldn't. Everyone deserves a fair trial, and I believe that.' The shaking in her voice made it unclear whether she was trying to convince herself or Tristan. 'Maybe it's because this happened so close to home, or maybe it's something more. It's a gut instinct: I think he is innocent.'

'You and your bloody gut instinct,' he said jokingly.

Silence filled the room as Tristan picked up the same bottle of water and tipped most of its contents into his mouth, and Rosa decided to interrupt it. She continued to talk about Emmett and how scared he looked when she spoke to him, how terrifying it must be for someone so young to be transported to a police station, then straight to a court cell, and now to a prison.

'It's just not really something to joke about, Tristan. He had never been in trouble before. It really could be anyone caught up in his position. It could have been you!' she blurted.

'Hmmm, yeah I guess so.' Tristan tilted his head against the pillow. His eyes slowly closed.

'Trist, I'm telling you about someone being arrested and charged with murder . . . who clearly didn't do it.' Rosa could hear her the frustration growing in her voice.

'Oh, Rosa,' Tristan said calmly. 'The trial hasn't happened yet. He's not been acquitted – nor has he been convicted. You need to calm down.'

'C-c-calm down?' Her voice was louder now but she stumbled slightly over her words.

'Yes! Calm down. You criticise everyone else for speaking about cases as though they've been decided but you're doing the exact same thing.'

The conceit was overwhelming and was making Rosa's blood boil. 'I think I'm just going to go home. I can't be bothered with this.'

Tristan shrugged his shoulders. 'Leave if you want, Rose. You don't need to. You're being really sensitive. Can we just have an evening where you don't talk about work?'

Rosa reached for her clothes, which were sprawled out on the floor, and quickly dressed. She pulled her bag up from the floor and flung it over her shoulder. Tristan paid her no attention and fiddled with the remote as she dramatically rearranged her bag across her body and loudly clanged her keys on the side. Without saying goodbye, she stormed out of the front door. The stones crunched under her feet as she walked down the front path. She pulled out her phone to order a taxi.

The car took a few minutes to arrive and when it did the driver barely acknowledged her existence. He turned up the radio and it was the football again.

'Excuse me, could you please turn off the radio?' Rosa asked.

'Sorry love, what?' They caught eyes in the rear-view mirror and Rosa felt a pang of embarrassment. 'What did you say love, I didn't catch it?'

She took a deep breath.

'Nothing, nothing. Just having a bad day,' she muttered.

He offered her a sympathetic smile.

'Sorry to hear that, love. Man issues? We can be right idiots – us men. Can't believe anyone would be mean to a pretty lady like you.'

Rosa returned a half-smile and remained silent, not wanting to encourage any further conversation.

'Fancy a bit of music, love? To cheer you up? How about some Magic FM? Oh wait, do you like that stuff? I know. I've got it. What about Magic Soul? Oh, I do love a bit of soul, I do.' The cab driver didn't wait for a response and tapped at his radio. Marvin Gaye began to play, and he tapped his fingers on the steering wheel and mouthed along to the lyrics. Rosa let her lids close and drifted into a nap.

'Sorry to wake you, love, but we're here. This is your house, right?' Rosa opened her eyes, startled. She thanked the driver and waved him off as she approached the door to her block of flats.

Freddy was asleep in the downstairs lobby by the lift. He was tucked into his sleeping bag surrounded by knotted plastic bags of his possessions. He had been homeless for as long as Rosa could remember, and occasionally slept on the cold, damp concrete at the bottom of the stairwell when it was raining outside. She tiptoed past him and pressed the button to call the lift.

Rosa reached the tenth floor and turned the keys slowly in the front door, trying not to wake Nana or Toby. She crept inside and closed the door gently behind her.

'Mercedes, dat yuh?' Nana's voice was quiet but cross.

'Yes, Nana. It's me.' Rosa carried on into her bedroom, unbuttoning her blouse as she walked.

'Mercedes, yuh mada call.' Rosa kept walking, pretending she hadn't heard. The silence was interrupted by heavy, chesty coughing. It sounded like she coughed up phlegm. Rosa poked her head around her door.

'Are you OK, Nana? Do you need anything?'

Her grandmother cleared her throat and sipped some water.

'Actually, yea, Mercedes, could you pick Toby up pan Monday? Him finish at 3.30 p.m. Mi haffi duh sumting,' she asked while breathing heavily.

Rosa agreed and asked if Nana needed anything else, as Nana struggled to slow her breaths.

'Mi need yuh to call yuh mada,' she replied.

CHAPTER 14

Monday morning had flown by as Rosa had covered a remote hearing for a colleague. She'd just finished eating her lunch and sat back at her desk. It was 2 p.m. already. She looked at her electronic diary: the only thing today was a meeting at 2.30 p.m. with Gillian Folkestone to debrief following the fraud trial she had been led in. The last time they'd spoken, Gillian had seemed surprisingly delighted that their instructing solicitor, Paul Fox, had said that the client no longer wanted to be represented by him in an appeal, and by extension that meant that Gillian and Rosa were also no longer required on that case. Rosa was also secretly pleased, given that she'd been the one doing most of the work and she simply didn't have that much time while also doing Emmett's case.

She opened her inbox and scanned her emails for the link to the online meeting. A new email appeared in her inbox, from Gillian.

Rosa, sorry to cancel. I don't think we're going to need this meeting given the circumstances but in any event

something urgent has come up this morning that I need to
attend to. Feel free to call me if there's anything you want
to discuss about the case.

G

Her afternoon was now free. Rosa closed her laptop. She
knew exactly what she needed to do today.

By 4 p.m., Rosa had reached the tall olive-coloured gates of
Green Tree High School. The gates protected the staff car
park, and behind the car park stood the three-storey red-
brick schoolbuilding. A tall, slender man, wearing a checked
shirt and suit trousers but no jacket, packed a crate of exercise
books into the boot of his car slowly. She pressed the intercom, gave her full name and explained that she was a visitor.

'Who are you here to see?' a female voice asked.

'Emmett Hamilton's teacher. I'm his barrister,' Rosa
replied. There was no response on the intercom but after a
few seconds passed, the magnet on the gates clinked as it
released. She pushed one side open and squeezed through
the gap. Once on the other side, and in the concrete car park,
she followed signs to the main office.

There was another set of locked doors to enter the building, but this time she was buzzed straight through. A
woman with a sharp bobbed haircut and long fingernails
greeted her with a wonky smile. Rosa typed her name on a
tablet and showed her driving licence to confirm her iden-
tity. The woman with the bob squinted at the little plastic
card before returning it to Rosa.

'If you just take a seat over there,' she said extending a finger and pointing to a short row of plastic chairs, 'she'll be with you shortly.'

In less time than Rosa had expected, a petite woman pushed open the door opposite the one through which Rosa had entered. She looked a little older than Rosa, but her eyes seemed much more tired and wrinkled. Neatly above them, her eyebrows were pencilled on thinly.

'Rosa Higgins?' she said warmly. 'I hope you don't mind me using your first name. Sheila told me you're here to see me? I'm Tanya. How can I help?'

'Is there somewhere a little more private that we could talk?'

'Yes, of course,' Tanya replied, turning back towards the door. 'Follow me.'

The floors of the corridors were carpeted in grey, which softened the sound of their footsteps. On one side of the wall there were blue lockers, which looked remarkably new and unused. On the other were photographs of the school sports teams by year. They reached the end of the corridor and Tanya turned to the door on the right and unlocked it with a code, before inviting Rosa inside. She glanced at the sign outside, which read HEADTEACHER'S OFFICE.

'Oh,' Tanya followed Rosa's eyes, 'this isn't my office, but we can use it for now. She's on long-term sick leave, so we actually use it as a meeting room. Come in.'

The small room was exactly as Rosa imagined a head-teacher's office to be. There was a desk at the far end, with a big leather chair tucked underneath it. Behind the chair were large windows, which flooded the office with light. Where Tanya stood was a small table with a number of chairs.

'Please, take a seat,' she said. She reached into the cupboard on the wall and retrieved a small tin of biscuits, which she opened and put on the table. Rosa sat down on the chair closest to the door. Tanya walked over to her desk and flicked on the switch of a kettle that Rosa hadn't noticed before. She turned over two mugs and placed a teabag in each one.

'They're clean, I promise!' Tanya said with a slightly nervous laugh.

They waited in silence as the kettle water boiled loudly. Eventually the switch clicked as steam erupted from the top. Tanya lifted the kettle and poured the water evenly into the two mugs.

'Milk? Sugar?' she asked.

'No, thank you,' Rosa said. 'I prefer it black.'

Tanya ripped open a small packet of artificial sweetener and tipped it into her own cup and stirred. She then brought Rosa's tea over to her.

'Thank you,' Rosa said softly. 'I'm so sorry to interrupt your day, I know you must be incredibly busy.'

'I can always make time for something important. I'm actually just planning for tomorrow, so you've caught me at a good time,' Tanya replied, pouring a small amount of milk into her tea.

Rosa began to ask her questions about Emmett. Tanya explained that she had been his form tutor since he'd joined the school in year seven, at just eleven years of age. As she spoke, tears gathered in the corners of her eyes. She'd known him for seven years and she'd been devastated by the news. As Joyce had said, he did well at school. Tanya added that he'd said that he wasn't applying for university this year because he wanted to take a gap year and earn some money, but she'd had no doubt that he would go on to higher education.

'He really was a straight-A student,' Tanya said with her mouth full of chocolate biscuit, steadying herself. 'But . . . erm. Sorry.' She chewed faster and swallowed. 'But what I would say is that he, unfortunately, always seemed to be making friends with people in the wrong crowd.'

'What do you mean?' Rosa asked.

'I mean, he seemed to befriend the "naughty children". I know we shouldn't call children naughty but that's really what they were.'

'Would he misbehave too?' Rosa pressed her for more information.

'Not at all,' Tanya said quickly. 'I really just can't believe that he murdered this man.'

'Do you think it's possible that he would have been friends with someone who did?'

'Oh yes,' Tanya replied firmly. 'Definitely. In fact, I was saying just the other day to a friend, who knows someone who actually saw the attack, I just can't believe he would do it. I believe he was there, but not *that*.'

'A friend of your friend's saw the incident?'

'I think the police have been speaking to him. No doubt you will too. His name is Mark. I can't remember his surname, I'm afraid. I don't know him terribly well but he's a teacher at another school, and a good mate of a friend of mine.'

Rosa nodded, taking it all in.

'He seemed certain it was Emmett, or at least, his description sounded like it was him.' Tanya looked down, as though disappointed in herself.

Something seemed off to Rosa. If what Tanya had said was right, it seemed clear to her that Emmett was in the wrong place at the wrong time. She just needed to prove it.

The table vibrated and Rosa realised it was her phone. She looked at the screen and a message from Nana popped up.

Mercedes. The school called. You didn't pick up Toby. I'm going to pick him up myself. I'll miss my appointment. Thanks for nothing.

She'd completely forgotten.

CHAPTER 15

Dear my darling Emmett,
  First, let me say, I love you. I always have and always will, my precious grandson.

Emmett read the first two lines and stopped. He scrunched the letter in the palm of his hand and shoved it into the waistband of his underpants, the only place he truly considered private. He held back tears and bit his lip to control his emotions. A salty taste made him realise he'd bitten too hard. He dabbed his lip with the back of his hand and sucked gently to stop the blood from dripping.

He sat down on the edge of the lower bunk and stretched his legs out in front of him. His weight was too heavy for the thin mattress, and he could feel the metal ridges of the bed pressing into his thighs. It was a rare moment of privacy – Alf, Emmett's cellmate, was out of the cell. He outstretched his fingers into the discoloured dark green bedding, trying to ground himself in the room. It had been days now and he still woke up every day petrified.

On the small desk in the room sat four packets of instant noodles, which Emmett dare not touch. He knew how valuable they were to Alf, often used as a form of currency. The walls were an off-white, a colour he'd grown used to seeing. They were made more yellow by the single beam of light that emitted a harsh glow in the centre of the cell.

Emmett, on second thoughts, retrieved the letter. If he didn't read it now, he didn't know when he'd next be able to without Alf, or someone else on the wing, peering over his shoulder. He smoothed the crisp paper out, noticing apparent shadows behind the words – the letter was clearly a copy of the original. He cast his eyes over the first two lines and continued reading.

I am writing this letter because I know you must be feeling very alone. My friend from church, Deborah, tells me that her friend's nephew went to prison last year and these letters are not private.

Emmett could hear the warning of his grandmother's voice in his head. Even now, she was looking out for him. Even with all the embarrassment. He knew she would feel ashamed. The letter wasn't dated but he had no doubt she'd written it as soon as she'd found out he'd been arrested. It had only been eight days and he was surprised that the letter had reached him so quickly.

I am disappointed that you are caught up in this situation. I raised you as my own, and I brought you up better than this. Why were you even in the park that day, Emmett? You told me that you were studying.

Emmett had forgotten he'd told Granny he'd be studying with Nathan, a boy he hadn't actually seen in almost a year. Granny was so keen for him to go to university – and he really did want to – but she expected him to study day and night. He'd begun lying about where he was going, but usually only for trivial things. This was different.

He wondered how Granny had found out that he had been arrested. Had she watched the news herself? That was unlikely given that Granny refused to have the news on in her house, and rarely read newspapers. Perhaps it was from someone at church; that would have been mortifying for her. He could imagine her ordinarily stone-hard expression melting into hysteria. He continued to read.

I am worried about you, Emmett. I have prayed to God every single day since the devastating day that you were arrested. I pray that you will come home. My heart is heavy. I believe that you would never harm someone. God tells me to trust that feeling. I hope he is right. I pray that you are not guilty.
I love you.
Granny x

Emmett read the last few lines again, his breathing hastened, and frustration spread through his veins. Most of the words blurred but one line stood out as if written in neon. *I pray that you are not guilty.* His leg started to tremor, and his hands tightened into a fist. He dashed the letter onto the floor and stood up unsteadily.

'Yo, bro, you alright?' Alf looked into the cell cautiously. He was a short man, or boy, depending on whether you deemed his tender age of eighteen to be a marker of adulthood. He had mousy brown hair, which he cut sharply at the front, giving his small face a rectangular frame. His facial hair was sparse but where it did grow, on the end of his pointed chin, it sprouted in a reddish colour that brought out his many freckles. He wasn't attractive in any conventional sense, but his green eyes had a glint of charm that made him seem both friendly and cheeky.

Alf stood close to the doorway, resting his slight weight on the handle of the door. He lifted his other bony arm and reached his nail-bitten fingers to scratch, or rather rub, his head.

'ARGHHHHH!' Emmett let out a roaring shout that was unfamiliar to himself, and evidently also to Alf, who took two steps back out of the cell.

Emmett's hands began to shake, out of time with his leg. He tried to pace the small cell, but his anger was boiling over. He punched the wall and pulled his fist back, yelping in pain. His knuckles started to bleed but he barely noticed. He grabbed the metal frame of the bed and started to rattle it.

'Bro, you need to calm the fuck down! I'm serious!' Alf shouted into the cell.

Emmett's movements slowed and he collapsed onto the floor, lying star shaped, his limbs pointing to each corner of the room.

Alf stepped back into the room and perched on the bottom bunk, as Emmett had done moments earlier.

'Wanna talk?'

Emmett just pointed to the letter on the floor. Alf stepped over him and picked it up.

'This? What on earth about this could make you lose it like that?'

Emmett closed his eyes and mouth and breathed through his nose. He opened his mouth again to talk.

'Read it.'

'Erm, nah, bro, I can't really read all these long words like that . . . but just tell me what it says.'

Emmett opened his eyes and sat up. He took the letter from Alf's hands and folded it into his palm, his breathing shaky.

'Sorry, bro. Just my Granny. She was the only person I had, and she's praying that I'm not guilty. I think she thinks I might be.'

'Yeah? So, what? Why are you so angry?' he replied calmly.

'What do you mean why?' said Emmett sharply.

'Watch it bro, I'm not the enemy here. I'm saying . . . look, we all think you're guilty, most of the country does, but what difference does that make to you? The only people that matter are those twelve jurors when you get to trial. Right?'

Emmett glared at him. 'If only it were that simple.'

'Well, it is, ain't it?'

'Well, surely you want your family, at the very least, to believe you.'

There was a long pause as Alf approached the desk, opened the kettle, and emptied a pack of instant noodles into it. He added water and then put the kettle on.

'I don't have no one, so nah, doesn't really matter to me. Mum left when I was young, and my dad was killed.' He spoke so matter-of-factly that Emmett had to pause to take in what he'd just said.

'I'm so sorry to hear that, bro.'

'Don't be sorry, it ain't your fault, is it? Just life. Just stop being ungrateful for the family you do have.'

The men sat in silence in the small cell. The only sound was the kettle steaming and shaking slightly as it heated. It clicked off.

Alf sighed as though he'd exhausted himself, and emptied the now-cooked noodles into a bowl. He clambered onto the top bunk and began to slurp food noisily, putting on his headphones, which sent a strong message to Emmett that their conversation was done.

Emmett left the cell and approached the payphones. His phone credit was finally working, and for once there wasn't much of a queue. He dialled his Granny's number, typing each digit to the tune of a nursery rhyme, as he had once memorised. The phone rang. One ring. Two rings. Three rings. Four rings. Granny was clearly not going to answer. Five rings.

'Hello.'

'It's me, Granny. I just wanted to say, I got your letter.'

'Emmett. Are you OK?' she asked with sincerity but without warmth.

'Granny, I didn't do it,' he replied, his voice slowly breaking.

'I hope not but I can't trust you at the moment, Emmett. You lied about where you—'

'Granny, I think they record these phone calls too,' Emmett interrupted.

'OK. Well, Emmett, I am praying, I am praying every day,' Granny said softly.

'Granny, I didn't do it. I'll be telling the court as soon as they let me speak. I promise, I didn't do it,' he pleaded.

She hesitated before speaking.

'I know. I've got to go now, Emmett.' He could hear the quaver in her voice. 'I love you and let's keep praying.' She hung up without waiting for Emmett's goodbye.

Emmett dragged himself back to his cell. Alf didn't pay him attention, and he assumed he was still immersed in his music. He'd never met anyone who knew every single lyric of every single rap song. He'd quickly learned that it wasn't even worth testing whether that was true because Alf really did know them all.

He crept into the lower bunk and pulled the itchy, dark blanket up towards his neck. His toes protruded out of the end, and he reshuffled and bent his legs to allow the blanket to engulf his whole body. Granny's contempt hurt, and he pinched his thigh hard trying to distract from the emotional pain.

Alf clearly wasn't asleep. Emmett lay awake listening to

the hissing of Alf's whispers. Despite being less than a metre away, in the bunk below, he couldn't make out exactly what Alf was saying, or even if he was speaking in English. The only thing he could be sure of was that he was speaking to someone. He climbed out of his bunk and stood next to the bed, staring at Alf's bunk. He could see the small glow of a mobile phone screen shining on the side of Alf's head.

'Alf, is that a phone?' he whispered. Alf didn't respond. 'Alf, bro, is that a phone?' He poked Alf's shoulder, temporarily forgetting where he was.

Alf stopped talking and turned to face Emmett. 'Are you crazy, bruv?'

Emmett looked back at him.

'Hey, I was just asking, is that a phone?'

'Can you not see I'm busy? It's a "mind-your-own-fucking-business" situation. Just go to sleep, fam.'

Emmett wasn't in the mood for quarrelling and climbed back into his bunk. Alf didn't scare him at all but the prospect of the guards finding a mobile phone in their cell terrified him. His bail application hearing was in just a few days, and he couldn't get into any trouble. It really wasn't worth the risk. He climbed back out of his bunk.

'Hey, Alf, look I don't know where you hide that, but can you keep it out of our cell? I want to get bail and I won't get it if I get into any trouble. You know what the guards are like.'

'Bruv, did I not just tell you to go to sleep?' Alf laughed. 'Do you think I give a shit about your bail application? You don't make demands around here, fam.'

Emmett crawled back into bed and tried to fall asleep.

CHAPTER 16

The pale grey linoleum floor shone under the harsh bright lighting. Rosa looked up at the square-tiled ceiling and counted each panel. 1, 2, 3, then a light. 1, 2, then a light. 1, 2, 3, 4, then a light. There was no pattern to the large square bulbs that intercepted every few panels, and the randomness was unsettling.

Nana sat on the plastic chair next to Rosa. Her large, voluptuous thighs flopped over the sides of the chair and brushed against Rosa's. Despite her curves, Nana was physically small, perhaps once five feet, but now her slumped back stole inches from her.

Little black wheels rolled past them, carrying the weight of folded white sheets on rattling metal shelves. An intermittent beep travelled through the corridor. Nana's eyes were closed, and her head rocked forwards and backwards as though lullabying herself to sleep.

'Janice Higgins, could you please come this way?' A petite blonde nurse beckoned Nana to follow her through swinging double doors. Rosa loved that she shared a surname with her grandmother – Nana was the only real parent she had.

Rosa offered her arm for support as Nana heaved herself out of the seat.

'Stay here, Rosa.'

'But I—' Rosa began to argue. She'd booked the day off to come with Nana to her hospital appointment after causing her to miss her appointment on Monday, and she wanted to be there for her now.

'Please. Stay here.' Nana's voice had an unfamiliar wobble. Rosa guided her to the nurse.

'I'm going to stay here, I think,' Rosa told the nurse, sounding uncertain. Rosa had figured out that it must be something serious for them to have rescheduled her appointment just two days later.

'OK, well, we'll come and get you if we need you.'

Rosa turned to Nana, expecting a glare, but instead seeing a fearful softness to her face. The nurse led her down the corridor and they disappeared beyond the swinging doors.

She stood up and walked up and down the corridor, hoping that the physical activity would keep her mind busy.

A photo caught her eye on the nurses' station desk. She recognised the man in the photo. There was a small collection pot that had writing in a permanent marker pen, which she couldn't make out. She leaned in closer.

For Thomas's family.

A nurse behind the desk stared at Rosa and coughed to make her aware of her presence.

'Can I help you?' she asked bluntly.

'Erm, no, sorry.' Rosa stumbled, still looking at the photograph.

The nurse stayed quiet but kept her eye on the collection pot, as though worried Rosa might make be attempting to steal from it.

'Actually,' Rosa said, now turning to face the nurse, 'you might be able to help me, did you know Thomas?'

'Yes, of course,' the nurse said, still watching Rosa suspiciously, who noticed the cold stare and tried harder to build some rapport.

'My grandmother is in hospital today. She's just been called in for an appointment. Her name is Janice Higgins.'

The nurse glanced at the computer screen and appeared slightly more reassured that Rosa was not an imposter, but didn't say anything in response.

'I've seen on the news what happened. It must be so difficult for all of you who knew him. Did he work here?'

'Yes, he did. It *is* really sad. Some of the nurses are upset, and the doctors,' the coldness still in her voice.

'*Some* of the nurses?' Rosa questioned her deliberate use of the word.

'That's what I said, yes,' the nurse replied.

Rosa locked eyes with her and waited for her to expand. She did so, obligingly, and suddenly it was as if a dam had burst.

'Well, obviously it's so sad that he has been murdered, but he wasn't super popular here. People had mixed feelings about him. I didn't know him that well, to be honest, he was new to Outpatients. I know he used to work in Maternity because my friend was there. Some people say he was difficult to work with in the lead-up to his death . . . well, his *murder*. He seemed distracted and stressed. I only worked with him once and I have to say, I got that impression too. There was definitely something on his mind.'

'I wonder what,' Rosa said.

'I don't know why I'm telling you this. It's obviously so sad. Some people really did love him. I think people are still laying flowers outside his flat, you can't really miss it when you walk down Calpol Road. I feel a bit sorry for his flatmates, they must get harassed constantly.'

The telephone on the desk rang and the nurse indicated that she had to answer it. Rosa walked back to where she had been sitting.

Twenty minutes passed and the blonde nurse returned, walking closely beside Nana. The nurse's face bore an entirely different expression to earlier. Her eyes were sombre and her lips thin. She approached Rosa and apologised but said nothing else. Nana shooed her away.

Nana and Rosa stepped into a taxi like strangers. Not a single word was uttered between them for the entire twenty-minute taxi journey home.

'Nana. You need to talk to me,' Rosa said back at their flat, dropping her handbag in the hallway and following Nana into the kitchen.

'Mi nuh *need* fi duh nuhting,' she responded flatly.

'Nana. You are unwell. I want to help you.'

'Mi fine.' She turned her back to Rosa and walked towards the kettle, switching it on. She reached for a mug and placed a single teabag in it. The room was still as the kettle glowed fluorescent purple and slowly started to shake as steam escaped from the lid. It clicked and Nana grabbed it. She slowly poured the boiling water into the mug, her hand shaking.

'I know you're unwell.'

'Yuh nah kno nuhting.' Nana's voice sounded more tired than angry.

'I do, I know it's serious. Stop pretending that everything is OK!' Rosa felt her eyes welling up and clenched her fists to control her energy.

'Wah yuh chatting about? Did dat nurse speak tuh yuh? Dem chatterboxes! It a fi mi business!'

'No. No one told me anything. Please, let me help.'

'Mi fine.' Nana's voice was soft now. She placed a small silver spoon in her mug and stirred. The spoon was discarded into the sink and Nana made her way to her bedroom.

'Mi need some sleep.'

The bright daylight had quickly disappeared into darkness like white sugar dissolving in black tea. Rosa desperately thought about texting Tristan. She missed him.

Hey, are you up to much? I was thinking of
popping over . . . x

She sent the text before she had the chance to change her mind, and jumped into the shower.

The shower curtain looked like a wilting flower and needed replacing. The wall tiles, brown and cream, had chipped over the years. This place was home, she thought, but she questioned how long she would be here. It felt as though something was coming towards her faster than she would like. Change.

She pulled back the soggy curtain and stepped out onto the worn bathmat, which partially covered the scratched and dented wooden floors, dried her body, moisturised and got dressed. Her phone showed that almost an hour had passed, with no response from Tristan.

She texted him again.

> I'm assuming you haven't seen this yet and it's getting late, so I'll just head over and see if you're free. I'm on my way. I'll bring wine. x

The visible front of Tristan's home, the first and second floor, was bare brick. The white paintwork of the exterior ground floor was mostly masked with a perfectly cut hedge, which she knew his gardener, Tim, maintained. She felt every crunch of the stones under her feet as she approached the stone steps leading up to the glossy black front door. Each step felt narrower than usual, unwelcoming to her. Rosa ignored her gut feeling and pressed on the video doorbell. A circle around the camera lit up and flashed as the doorbell sounded.

She waited as the ring repeated three times. The velvety black sky masked the stars and the moon stood alone, like a single cactus in a desert.

The light of the doorbell disappeared, and she remained still in the darkness.

She pressed it again, slightly irritated that she'd made the effort to travel here and Tristan wasn't answering. She glanced to her right, confirming that she'd noticed his huge, shiny Range Rover sitting on the drive – she had. He rarely ever took public transport anywhere; he must be home.

She rang the doorbell again and the ring light around the camera lit up again. The doorbell sound repeated. Once. Twice.

'Rosa, erm, what are you doing here?' a nervous voice asked out from the all-in-one doorbell. She recognised it to be Tristan's, although something sounded wrong.

'Hey, Tristan, everything OK?' Rosa didn't wait for the doorbell speaker to respond. 'I just thought I'd … I just wanted to see what you were up to, really,' she replied, surprised by the nervousness in her own voice.

'Oh, could you not have texted me?' he said, again in a way that made Rosa feel uncomfortable.

'I did!' she protested, a little too quickly. 'I said I was coming over. Check your phone.' She realised that she sounded like she was telling him off.

There was a pause on the intercom and a low buzz, which was the only thing letting Rosa know that she hadn't been disconnected.

'Sorry, Rose, now isn't a great time.'

Rosa, ignoring the signs, brandished the bottle of wine in front of the camera.

'I bought wine!' she exclaimed, in a final desperate attempt to be let inside. 'Come on, let me in, it's pretty dark and cold out here.' She imitated chattering in the cold, trying to lighten the stiffness in her voice.

'It's really not a great—'

A distant female voice interrupted him. 'Trist, who is it? Is it the pizz—'

The intercom was disconnected.

Rosa stood there in shock. She wanted to burst open the door but knew that she had no right to do so. Tristan wasn't her partner. They were just meant to be having a good time. She felt stupid. On social media she was constantly bombarded with photos of school friends getting married or having their first (or even fourth in one woman's case) child. She, Mercedes Rosa Higgins, had no partner, no children and barely any friends. Her job was her life.

A cat tiptoed across the wall next to her and leapt down behind the car. She hated cats; she had a slight allergy and had grown up with Nana telling her that they were evil and brought bad spirits wherever they went. She'd believed that as a child and liked to think of herself as beyond myths now, but she couldn't shake her dislike for them. Her mind continued to wander, comparing herself to the animal, walking the streets at night. She looked down to where the cat had pounced, but it was gone.

Slowly she crunched her way back down Tristan's driveway and perched on the wall at the end. He wouldn't be able to see her; a large tree blocked the view of this wall from his bedroom window – no doubt that's where he was. She sat for a moment, with no real thoughts, just watching nothingness.

The whoosh of a speeding motorbike sailed past her and then repeated as it turned and came back towards her. It ground to a halt outside the property. A spotty man, who looked far too young to be riding a motorbike, pulled off his helmet and swivelled round to the back of his bike, opening the heat-proof box. He retrieved what looked like two pizzas and a big bottle of a fizzy drink. He looked at Rosa and smiled with what looked like sympathy, and she diverted her gaze. He walked past her and up the drive.

'Ahhhhh shit!' she heard yelled behind her as the pizza delivery driver jumped backwards. He shone his phone's torchlight and two cats scattered.

Rosa's phone pinged. It was Tristan.

I'm sorry. I can explain.

Embarrassment flooded over her. She deleted the message. Rosa composed a new one. She needed to get out of here.

Orissa. Are you up? Can I come over? I have wine. Long story but could do with some company.

Her phone remained silent. Orissa must be sleeping.

Rosa stuffed the bottle of wine back into her handbag. Her feet felt welded to the pavement as she heaved herself off the brick wall and stomped down the pavement to the main road.

CHAPTER 17

'**M**orning, lads, cell search today. Up, up, up we get. Out of your cells, please.'

Emmett struggled to open his eyes, convinced he was still sleeping.

'OUT, BOYS!' the officer called, shaking the metal framed bed.

Both Emmett and Alf scrambled out of bed in boxer shorts and retrieved their T-shirts from the desk. They stepped outside the cell.

Alf shot Emmett a murderous look. Emmett, unsure of where to rest his gaze, dropped his eyes to the floor. Alf mumbled something but Emmett couldn't make it out.

The guards pulled the blankets from the bed and checked under the mattresses; knocked things off the desk and kicked items around that were on the floor. Alf was seething as one of the officers opened each individual pack of noodles and tipped them out, allegedly checking for illicit substances. At last, apparently satisfied with their destruction, they left the cells.

As soon as they were out of sight, Alf punched Emmett

hard in the stomach, causing him to clutch his middle and keel over in pain.

'What ... the ... fuck ... mate?' Emmett stuttered.

'You're a fucking snitch, I knew it.' Alf looked angry but there was also a certain self-satisfaction there, as though he'd completed an impossible crossword.

'I knew I was right to have my suspicions about you. A FUCKING SNITCH,' he bellowed.

'Bro, look, I do *not* know what you're talking about. I haven't spoken to anyone. I haven't left our cell!'

'Wait till I tell everyone. I fucking knew it.' He disappeared down the corridor.

Emmett returned to his bed and lay on top of the blankets. His mind was preoccupied, he couldn't think about being branded a snitch when there were so many other things to worry about at the moment. His bail application was in a few days, his first opportunity to return home after this nightmare. Surely, they'd think grandma was a safe person for him to live with? He knew that she would do anything to help him.

Hours passed that Thursday morning, and Emmett had only moved for breakfast. His thoughts were again interrupted by the call for lunch.

The canteen reminded Emmett of school. It was a large white hall, with a metallic serving counter with lamps to keep the food warm. He opted for what the sign said was chicken and rice, although the chicken looked anaemic. He carried his plastic tray, walking towards the corner where he usually sat.

A man he'd never seen before stepped out in front of him. He was at least a few inches taller than Emmett, bald, and had both a crooked nose and a greying beard. The unknown man gathered phlegm in his mouth and spat over Emmett's food.

'Dirty snitch,' he declared, before walking in the opposite direction.

Emmett looked around and could see that almost everyone in the room was staring at him. He glanced at Alf, who was smirking and whispering in another man's ear. The man held his hand up and even from a distance Emmett could see a naked blade glistening in his palm.

CHAPTER 18

A fortnight had passed since Rosa had first met Emmett and she was mentally preparing herself to see him again today. This was an unusual feeling, given that her whole job involved regularly meeting people who were remanded in prison, but with Emmett she felt anxious. She worried about how he had been coping and knew that today's bail application at the Old Bailey was more important than most. She had tried to manage her own expectations, reminding herself that the presumption in favour of bail did not apply to murder cases. It felt like the decision had already been made to remand him in custody and she wasn't sure that either she or Craig had properly prepared him for that. Today would be an uphill struggle.

Craig had emailed her a copy of the formal bail application, which set out the strict conditions by which Emmett was willing to abide. She discovered that he too lived with his grandmother, who she'd met the last time she was at court for this case. She felt this was more than coincidental, perhaps a little of Nana's fatalism rubbing off on her.

Rosa's phone pinged and she grabbed it to put it on silent. The message was from Craig.

I'm just outside court having a cigarette. I'll be inside soon!

Another message popped up.

Look up, I'm in front of you!

Rosa lifted her head slowly and saw Craig passing through the security scanners at the end of the corridor. He paced towards her.

'Ready to go straight down to the cells?' he said, still catching his breath.

'Morning! Erm … sure. Let's go,' she said, feeling the complete opposite of ready.

Rosa and Craig headed down to the cells together and were signed in by the cell security staff. As usual, no one asked to see their IDs, assuming that people wouldn't pretend to be legal representatives just to break into the cells – an assumption Rosa thought was dangerous. Craig shoved his briefcase into a secure locker and Rosa followed suit. The security officer led them through to an empty conference room.

After a few minutes sitting in the cold, Emmett was brought in looking more depressed than the last time she had seen him. He had seemingly lost weight and his skin hung a little loosely on his bones, like sheets on a washing line. He had dark circles under his eyes but this time they looked less like bruises and more like he hadn't slept in a while. Neither Rosa nor Craig bothered asking him if he was OK; it was so obvious that he wasn't.

In an attempt to lift his spirits, Rosa outlined the basis of the bail application.

'Your grandmother has agreed for you to live with her if you are granted bail. That should help today. We can tell the court that you have somewhere you can stay, with a responsible adult.'

'How is my grandma?' Emmett asked.

Rosa looked to Craig who nodded enthusiastically. 'Yes, I'm sure your grandmother is well. Well, considering ...' Craig stopped, but Emmett stared, awaiting more information.

'Have you spoken to her?'

'Not since the last hearing. I spoke to her for some time then. Look, our main focus is you, Emmett.'

'I need you to speak to her again. Please. Can you make sure that she's OK?'

'Emmett ...'

But Emmett interrupted Craig. 'I don't have anything to say to either of you until I know my grandma is OK. Can you please just go and find out? I don't have any credit on my call card, I can't check myself. I was the one giving her money, I don't know if she even has enough for food.'

'How were you making money?' Rosa asked. There had never been any mention of Emmett having a job or being employed. She wondered how he had any money to give to his grandmother.

'Just found ways,' he replied.

She paused and thought about her own bank balance. She was still owed money by the legal aid agency. This morning she had just entered her overdraft by finally sending Nana the money for Toby's school uniform.

'Look, I'll get my PA to call your grandmother after today's hearing,' Craig said reluctantly, 'but we really do need to focus.'

Emmett's frown softened and his eyes looked hollower than Rosa remembered. Unlike their previous conference, his eyes were dry, not a tear in sight. He turned away from Craig and stared for a while at Rosa.

'Can you please promise me you'll keep checking in on her? I'm in here and she's on her own. She needs to know I'm OK. Tell her I'm cool. I don't want her stressing. *Please.*'

'I've just said . . . ' Craig started to say.

'I wasn't talking to you,' Emmett retorted.

Rosa nodded, though she didn't know how she would be able to keep that promise.

Emmett looked slightly relieved.

'So, am I gonna get bail? What are the chances?' His voice had a hint of joy that was quickly stolen by the awkward silence that flooded the room. Craig attempted a reassuring smile, but Rosa's plain expression spoke volumes. After a long moment, she spoke.

'It is quite unlikely that you will get bail today, I'm afraid.' She sat on her hands to steady her nerves. 'Emmett, you've been charged with a very serious crime and when people are charged with murder, the courts tend to keep them in custody until the trial.'

Emmett's eyes suddenly became watery, and Rosa tried to console him.

'Look, I promise you, we are doing our best and we will continue to do our best.' She could feel Craig's gaze on the side of her head. They both knew that their best might not be good enough.

Craig slapped his hands on his thighs and stood up.

'I'm going for a cigarette break. Rosa, you coming?' He tapped on the glass to leave. Reluctantly Rosa stood too.

'Bye, Emmett. We'll see you upstairs.'

Outside the front of court, Craig lit his cigarette and blew a thick puff of smoke away from Rosa.

'You want one?' He offered the box of cigarettes.

'No thanks, I don't smoke.'

Craig shoved the packet back into the pocket of his suit jacket. 'He doesn't look great, does he,' he stated, rather than asked.

'No, he looks terrible. And today won't help, he won't get bail,' Rosa said gloomily.

'Well, no. We've warned him of that. Unless you work your bail magic again – you've done it before! Look at Mr Adebayo!' Craig laughed.

The humour was lost on Rosa, who only felt an increasing amount of pressure.

'I really don't think I can get him bail. Not in a case like this.'

'No, Rosa, I know. Look, he's a Black kid that's killed a professional white man. We both know he'll be lucky to be found not guilty, let alone get bail. But look, it's a great case for both of us, and it'll be a nice payer for you if it goes all the way to trial.'

Rosa needed the money she'd be paid for doing this trial more than ever, but that wasn't the only reason she was feeling the pressure.

'Well, no, he wouldn't be *lucky* if he didn't actually do it,' Rosa replied sharply.

'We both know that often doesn't matter,' Craig said, more softly.

Rosa folded her arms. She felt redundant. There was a predetermined outcome in this case.

'And look, his dad is a frequent client of mine,' Craig continued. 'We need to do a decent job, but we need to also be realistic.'

He stumped out his cigarette and held open the door. Time to go into court.

CHAPTER 19

The Central Criminal Court, the Old Bailey, was surprisingly airy. The ceilings were high and there was a huge circular roof light that brought rays of sun into the room. The ceiling connected to the walls with huge decorative arches, one of which had elevated public gallery seating underneath. It looked almost like a theatre stage, with the public having the best seats in the house.

On the floor there were rows of seats with ornate green leather pillowing embossed with a golden crest; these folded down, and in the hands of the unwary, would bounce back up again. There were more on the other side of the large courtroom, this time just twelve, for the jurors. A few extra chairs were fixed around the courtroom, including for the legal clerk and, of course, the elevated seat for the judge. What struck Rosa most was that the wooden dock was in the centre of the courtroom, like a small stage. All eyes were on the defendant, at all times.

The public gallery filled up, and the prosecutor, Mr Pankhurst, took his seat. The jailor brought Emmett into the dock and invited him to sit down. The room fell quiet as the court usher called on the case.

His Honour Judge Douglas KC had a soft voice, which contrasted his stern appearance. His thick eyebrows were overgrown and made him look permanently frustrated, and his lips were thin and pursed. Even his hollow cheeks gave an unfriendly impression.

Mr Pankhurst set out, in great detail, all of the reasons the Crown objected to the court granting Emmett bail. Every few minutes he helpfully reminded the judge that in murder cases there was no presumption of bail.

Rosa stood up next. There were no fancy tricks this time. She made her submissions neatly and succinctly, she expressed that the court could be satisfied that even though the charge was of such a serious nature, the various proposed conditions would mitigate any risks.

HHJ Douglas KC listened and wrote purposefully, apparently taking in every word. He paused for a few minutes while the court waited silently to consider his decision.

'Mr Hamilton, please stand.'

There was shuffling at the back of the courtroom as Emmet stood up. Rosa's palms were sweaty, and she placed them stiffly on her lap, face down. Craig tapped his foot behind her.

'Mr Hamilton, I have listened very carefully to what Ms Higgins has said on your behalf. She has said all that she can say. I am not going to grant you bail today.'

Rosa closed her eyes and took a deep breath. Craig, out of Rosa's sight and sitting behind her, sounded like he was continuing to tap the keys of his laptop.

'As I am sure you have been advised – and have certainly heard during this hearing – bail may not be granted to someone charged with murder unless the court – that is me – is satisfied that there is no significant risk that if I were to release you on bail, you would commit an offence that would be likely to cause physical or mental injury to another person.

'I cannot be satisfied that there is no significant risk, I'm afraid. This is an extremely serious offence, which was committed in broad daylight against a person who it is accepted was a stranger to you. While I appreciate that there is nothing in your antecedents that causes me concern, I cannot be satisfied that there is no significant risk. You will continue to be remanded in custody.'

Emmett howled from the dock, which startled everyone, including the judge who looked up from his papers.

'Officers, please take him down.'

The bawling grew distant as he was taken through what looked like a trap door in the dock and back down to the court cells.

'Ms Higgins and Mr Pankhurst, thank you both. You may leave. I shall not retire yet.'

Both counsels bowed to the judge and departed from the courtroom. Craig followed behind.

'Let's catch up?' Craig barged into the nearest available conference room. 'Oh – I'm sorry, I couldn't see someone sitting in here!' he exclaimed as he stepped backwards out of the doorway, realising someone was inside. He pulled a funny expression at Rosa, but her eyes remained heavy and focused on the ragged carpet beneath them.

'Here we go, let's go in here – it's empty.' Craig propped open another conference room door and Rosa stepped inside and took a seat. Before the door closed, Craig started talking. 'Rosa, don't look so gloomy. It was an ambitious application; we both know there was little chance of him getting bail.'

Rosa glared at him, detesting the arrogance in his voice but she knew he was right.

'We have to get him an acquittal. We have to, Craig. He said he didn't do it.'

Craig laughed unexpectedly. 'Don't they all?' Seeing Rosa's frown, he stopped laughing. 'Why are you taking this so personally?'

'I'm not, but we have a duty to act in his best interests and that means getting him acquitted. We need to have another conference with him as soon as possible.'

'Do we? Look I'm hoping for an acquittal as much as you are – I want to win – but we shouldn't get too carried away in a case as hopeless as this.'

'Hopeless?' Rosa gasped. 'You think this case is hopeless?'

'That's not quite what I mean, Rosa.' Craig loosened his tie and unbuttoned the top of his shirt. 'I am just trying to ensure that you stay focused. I wanted you on board because you are a good barrister, and frankly, I thought your gran was a wonderful woman. Look, I think you can win but let's not lose sight of your role here.'

'What is that supposed to mean?'

'I just mean that you are going to focus on delivering the most fantastic advocacy you can, I will focus on getting instructions from him. I'll organise another conference if you really think we need one, but I don't want you getting too emotionally attached. I can see it in your eyes.'

'I don't know what you are talking about, I am just trying to do the best job I can ... for Emmett.' She felt her voice getting louder. Had Craig only instructed her for her to fail, knowing it was a hopeless case? Would she, a young, female Black barrister, out of her depth, be an easy person to blame?

'I know, I know. I am too. I know you will do an excellent job. Come on, let's get out of here. Fancy a pint? I've parked around the corner and could have one before I head home.'

'I can't tonight. But please, Craig. I need to have another conference with him. If you're busy, I'm happy for you to send along a paralegal,' Rosa pleaded. 'I just need to get some more out of him. I don't think it will be a waste of time.'

Craig shrugged.

'Fine. Suit yourself. I'll speak to the office and see who is available to join you. It probably won't be me.' He paused and looked at his phone. 'I've actually just got a message from the cells saying that he's being taken to Pentonville tonight; you know how they move them around with no rhyme or reason. I'm sure he won't be delighted about that. Please, Rosa, you stay focused.' He paused momentarily. 'Have you told your grandmother that I've given you this case?'

She smiled half-heartedly and lied. She suspected Nana knew what she was working on, but they hadn't spoken about it at all. Rosa had wanted to tell her about how pleased Craig was with her cleaning services, but she knew Nana had hated that work and, as a proud woman, was embarrassed the only work she could do was clean other people's homes. Rosa suspected Nana would be mortified that Craig had given her such an important case out of some feeling of loyalty.

'Yes, of course. She's so pleased.'

'I thought she would be! That's the kind of guy I am, I always try to look after people who look after me.'

Rosa felt her phone ring and excused herself. Without looking at the caller ID she answered.

An automated voice informed her that she was receiving a call from HMP Bronzefield. It gave her the option to hang up if she didn't want to receive the call. She waited on the line.

'Mercedes, is that you?'

She hadn't heard her mother's voice in years but there was no mistaking the hoarse sound that echoed through the phone.

'Mercedes, I been tryin' to call you.'

Both women fell quiet. Rosa could hear her mother's heavy breaths.

'I know you have,' she eventually replied.

'Why've you ignored me?'

'What do you want, Mu—' she stopped herself giving her a title her mother didn't deserve. 'What do you want?'

'I wanna talk to you about Nana.'

'What about her? Unlike you to be interested in anyone but yourself.' The spite erupted out of Rosa.

'What's that s'posed to mean?' Her mother's voice croaked,

and a bystander might have thought she was overcome with emotion. 'You know I've always tried.'

Rosa was not as easily fooled. She'd seen this act many times before.

'Tried what exactly? To be a mother?' She spoke quietly and edged herself towards the exit, conscious that someone might be eavesdropping on her conversation.

'Stop it, Mercedes! I was young when I had you. Much younger than you are.'

Rosa wished she could articulate how inadequate that explanation was in a way her mother would understand, but she couldn't find the words.

'I love you, Mercedes, and I love Toby. 'Member all the fun things we did when I was out before?'

'You've barely stayed out of prison. I can hardly remember what you look like.' Her mind flicked to her mother's strikingly beautiful face. It was perfectly symmetrical, apart from a small diamond piercing on her left nostril. Her mum had long hair, which hung in loose curls down her spine. *Loop it over from the right, and then over from the left. That's it.* She could hear Nana's voice teaching her how to plait her mother's hair. She pinched her fingers together, as if she would somehow feel her mother's soft hair between her fingertips, but felt only her own skin. She looked down at her short, plain fingernails. Mum's nails were always perfectly painted, and when Rosa did well at school, her mum would sometimes take her with her to the nail salon for her own mini manicure.

'I don't remember much,' she said harshly. It was a lie,

but Rosa didn't want her mother to have the satisfaction of knowing that Rosa still had fond memories of the time they had spent together.

Her mother quietened. 'Mercedes, this ain't even 'bout me. Please – for Nana – just listen to me for two minutes.'

'Nana? What is it?'

'She thinks she has cancer.'

Now it was Rosa's turn to fall silent. The air was sucked from her lungs and her throat closed suddenly. She felt herself struggling to breathe.

'What? She told you that?'

'Yes.'

'Why would she tell you and not me?'

''Cos, Mercedes, you're so busy.' Rosa imagined her skin reddening and felt herself getting defensive, but swallowed it as her mother continued, softer now. 'Don't be angry at her. You know she's private. Look, she needs to get treatment and she doesn't want it.'

Rosa nodded slowly as her chest tightened. She clutched the landline phone in her hand. Tears rolled down her cheeks.

'Rosa?'

'Yes, of course,' she replied.

'Look, you can hate me forever if you want but we both care about Nana. I can't be there to help 'cos of my bad decisions but she's always helped us, Rosa. Please, for me.'

'I said yes, of course,' Rosa spluttered.

'Thanks. Thank you, Mercedes.'

'Mum ...' The word felt unfamiliar and sour on Rosa's tongue.

'Yes?'

'I don't hate you.'

Rosa walked slowly into Pine Estate. At the entrance there were three green bushes that were protected by long black horizontal, knee-height poles that ran parallel with the ground. Ahead she could see four concrete bollards that were clearly erected in an attempt to stop people parking on the pavement, but since there was very little distinction between the dull grey pavement and dull grey car park, she struggled to understand why this was so important. The whole area was lifeless besides the three bushes. There was no other greenery; no trees or flowers. The silvery grey lampposts differed only slightly from the dirty grey concrete and the rusting grey of the TV satellite dishes. The yellow-brown brick of the ground floor walls was brighter than the small reddish-brown stones that were plastered onto the exterior walls higher up. She'd spent her whole life living here but had never really taken in how many shades of brown and grey there were in this concentrated living space.

Nana had had a metal bar gate on their front door for as long as she could remember. She unlocked it and heaved it open before slotting a second key into the front door and opening it into their hallway.

'Evening, Nana,' Rosa called.

'Gud evening, baby. Ow yuh duh? Yuh friend Orissa is 'ere.'

Rosa followed the sound of her voice into the kitchen, where Nana stood with Orissa.

'Hey . . . Orissa! You didn't tell me you were coming over?'

Rosa said, slightly surprised to see her. 'You are joining us for dinner?'

She'd sent Orissa a message earlier that day, after the frustrating conversation with Craig, asking her whether she could help her meet with Emmett's grandmother, Joyce, but hadn't expected her friend to just turn up. She was the only guest who ever came to the flat. Nana didn't like having visitors, but she loved Orissa.

Orissa's braided hair was divided in two. She'd pulled the top half into a bun at the back of her head but let the bottom half hang loose, the braids stretching down to the middle of her back. Orissa had always been beautiful; she had dark skin with darker, almost black, almond-shaped eyes. She looked slimmer than when Rosa had last seen her. That must have been a few months ago, Rosa realised, given how busy her own schedule had been. But after twenty years of friendship, it didn't matter how frequently they saw each other, it always felt like they hadn't spent a day apart.

'I think so, if that's OK?' she replied, smiling enthusiastically towards Nana. Her teeth were snow white and looked like perfectly arranged pearls in her mouth.

'Of course, mi pretty girl,' Nana said with a smaller smile. 'Rosa, why di long face?' Nana was all too observant.

'I'm not great. I'm not great, Nana.' Rosa walked up to Nana who was chopping vegetables and embraced her from behind. She rested her chin on Nana's soft grey curls and then tipped her head to plant a kiss on them. Nana was so small that Rosa towered over her.

'Wah happen', darling? Yuh acting strange.' Nana continued to slice the carrot in front of her, dividing it into neat
circular discs. 'Mi hope it nuh dat bwoy. Wah fi him name?
Christian?'

Orissa looked at Rosa, who shot her back a look that indicated that she would explain that situation later.

'No, and his name is Tristan. But, no, it's not really him,'
Rosa replied, trying to keep her facial expression neutral.

'Wah yuh mean it nuh really him? It or it isn't?' Nana
kissed her teeth as she tipped the carrots into the large Dutch
pot. 'Mi nuh undastan yuh or yuh muda.'

'What does my mother have to do with anything?' Rosa's
voice grew hostile.

Orissa figured out that it was probably time for her to
leave the room. 'I'm going to just check on Toby,' she muttered as she tiptoed upstairs.

'Both of yuh luv white men. Dem always causing problems,' Nana said, oblivious to Orissa's retreat.

'Nana, it's not Tristan. It's everything. I look like shi—'
Rosa stopped herself, remembering not to swear in Nana's
presence. 'I look awful.'

Nana kissed her teeth again. 'Vanity blossom but bears
nuh fruit. Yuh di same as yuh muda.'

'You keep saying that. What about my father? Am I
like him?'

Nana fell quiet and the warmth slipped away from her
face. She muttered in heavy patois under her breath, which
Rosa could not understand. Something about her father
leaving. She knew that she and Toby had different fathers,

although she'd never known Toby's father either. Sensing Nana's discomfort at her cheap shot, she changed the topic.

'Nana, how are *you* feeling? I heard you coughing.'

'Mi fine. Mind yuh bizniz an me wi mind fi mi.' Rosa knew there was no further conversation to be had. She drifted to the little Formica table and picked up the creased morning paper.

A smiling man's face was spread across the front page, captioned *'Rest in peace, our darling boy.'* The journalist detailed the grief of Thomas Dove's mother at her beloved son being murdered.

He was so dearly loved. He was so special. He was our everything.

Rosa's eyes drifted down the page to a picture of him in medical scrubs.

Thomas was a nurse with big ambitions. He was on his day off when he was murdered. He loved the park – he loved nature and spending time with other people. His death is a real tragedy.

Thomas looked so happy in the pictures. It truly was devastating that someone had murdered him.

For a brief second the horrific thought that Emmett was his murderer shot through her mind. She imagined him stabbing him repeatedly, in the middle of the afternoon, his friends egging him on.

CHAPTER 20

Emmett stepped off the bus at HMP Pentonville. He'd been given no explanation as to why he was being moved that Friday, other than the fact that his bed at HMP Thameside had been reallocated while he was in court that morning. Maybe God really was looking over him. Maybe this was just pot luck. Maybe it wasn't lucky at all.

He was nervous. If he had returned to Thameside, that would have been the end of his life, and he knew it. Everyone believed he was a snitch, despite him never telling anyone about Alf's phone. He had to be smarter this time, keep himself to himself and not trust anybody. *What if they already knew?*

With no possessions on his person, checking into the new prison was a fairly straightforward process. He was given some clean clothing, some soap and a toothbrush and directed into a room with other new and returning inmates. Emmett avoided eye contact with everyone, staring only at his palms. He didn't want there to be any misunderstandings.

He followed the prison guard to his new cell and entered confidently. He lowered his shoulders and held his head high. His eyes were hard, and he tightened his palms into fists. Another young man sat on the bottom bunk.

'I'm Mohammed,' he said enthusiastically, 'but you can call me Mo. You are?'

'Emmett,' he replied, bluntly. He wasn't here to make friends.

Emmett climbed onto the top, apparently free, bunk. Mohammed waited for the guard to disappear and crept up to Emmett's side.

'Bruv, what are you doing?' Emmett screwed his face up as he spat out each word. Mohammed looked unfazed.

'I don't know what you're on about, bro, but I just wanted to let you know that I'm kind of a big deal in here. I can get people anything they want. Drugs especially. I've been helping out some of the big guys on the wing get drugs; and I always sneak a little bit. You're my roomie, I can share with you.'

'Nah. I'm good. And don't bring shit to the cell.' The menace in his own voice surprised him.

'No trust me, bro, no trouble. Just letting you know. You're good with me, I'm respected and I'm a good person for you to be sharing with.'

'Say no more,' Emmett replied flatly.

Emmett spent as much time as he could in the library that afternoon. He was determined to keep his head down and try to make something of his time inside. He realised that he had no idea whether he would be in prison for weeks, months or years, and decided he needed to make the most out of it. He started reading a novel about Native Americans, which he eventually brought back to his cell.

Mohammed was clearly a chatterbox. Emmett welcomed silence in the cell, but Mohammed was determined to break it. It was getting late, and Emmett closed his eyes, pretending to fall asleep.

The low buzz of Mohammed's monologue was interrupted by the cell door bursting open. Emmett froze, petrified, his eyes only slightly ajar. At least five men pushed through the doorway and into the room, the one at the front brandishing a kettle, steam erupting from it. Emmett had a strong feeling they weren't here for a tea party and closed his eyes tightly, pretending to be asleep.

Emmett heard, as did every other man on that wing, a piercing scream from Mohammed. One of the men called him a thief and shouted that this would teach him not to steal again. The crackle and hiss of boiling water on skin. More screaming, then the sound of the men scrambling.

When all he could hear was the sound of whimpering and dripping, Emmett opened his eyes and looked over the edge of the bunk. Mohammed's face was redder that Emmett had ever seen on anyone, and the floor was soaking wet.

Following the sounds of the screams, two guards came rushing towards the cell, moments too late to catch the perpetrators.

Emmett lay still on his bed.

'New boy, did you do this?' one of the guards yelled over Mohammed's screams.

'No,' Emmett answered.

'Did you see who did?'

'No,' Emmett answered, without hesitation.

CHAPTER 21

As Rosa sat in bed reviewing information sent by the Crown Prosecution Service, Nana's favourite Sunday morning lovers' rock anthems played loudly in the kitchen. The emails provided an update on the evidence, with three attachments. The CPS confirmed that there were two witnesses, and finally, after far too long, had decided to provide their statements. There was also an attached schedule of unused material.

Rosa clicked on the schedule first. There was nothing particularly interesting. Thomas Dove's phone was locked with a passcode and the police couldn't unlock it. They'd found a letter about a loan in his jacket pocket. She thought about the loan repayment letter she'd received herself yesterday morning, reminding her that she needed to repay the £5,000 she'd borrowed to tide her over until she was paid from the big fraud case that she'd been working on with Gillian Folkestone KC.

There was also some cash in his pocket, £100. That struck Rosa as quite a lot, but she rarely carried cash and knew that not everyone felt the same. Housekeys. A driving licence. A number of different debit cards and two credit cards.

She exited the schedule and turned to the attached witness statements.

The first was a man, Mark McEvoy, a secondary school teacher. This must be the friend of a friend that Tanya Williams had told Rosa about. She skim-read the beginning of the statement and jumped to the most important part.

There was a lot going on, but I had an unobstructed view of the man with the knife. He was the lighter skinned of the Black men. There were three of them.

Rosa had already confirmed for herself that Emmett was a light-skinned Black male.

I saw him carrying the knife before the victim was stabbed. He seemed to be hiding it in his jumper. He was wearing a big jumper even though it was a hot day. That's why I was initially looking at him.

Until now, Rosa hadn't seen what Emmett was wearing that day. She knew that the jumper had been sent off for forensic testing and that they had agreed with the prosecution that the blood was the victim's, but they continued to disagree as to how these blood stains occurred. She'd already seen another email where the CPS and police appeared to have confirmed that an expert in blood splatter was unlikely to be helpful as the jumper was almost entirely covered in blood.

I saw him stab the victim at least once. I tried to stop him but then he stabbed me in the leg. I can't remember exactly how many times he stabbed the victim because I became focused on trying to save the victim and get help. I didn't have any time to call the police, I just wanted to make sure everyone was safe.

This wasn't a great start. The witness would come across to the jury as heroic, someone who was willing to risk their own life to save another. This would be dire for Emmett's case.

She turned to the next witness statement, of Ms Claire Smith. Her job status was recorded as unemployed. She said that she was in the park that day walking with her young child in a buggy. If Emmett was convicted, the presence of a child would only increase his sentence.

I was standing nearby by my pram as my baby was in it trying to sleep. There were three Black boys altogether and there was a white man with red hair who ran in to try to help the white man who was stabbed. Two of the Black men had very dark skin – I didn't see them with the knife, but they ran away as soon as the victim was on the floor. They were wearing tracksuits, I can't remember exactly what colour, I think they were grey. The other lighter Black man was the one I saw holding the knife. He had a big jumper on, which looked weird because it was so hot. Not just a tracksuit jumper – it was thick, like a Christmas jumper. He looked in total shock. I think he was the killer. I pointed him out to the police, and I saw them arrest him.

This witness corroborated the Crown's case. Emmett had been with at least two other boys; he'd brought a knife to the park hidden in his jumper and had stabbed a random man. The case appeared to be becoming increasingly hopeless, but it still felt to Rosa like there was a missing piece in the puzzle. She couldn't understand what motive Emmett would have for killing a random, innocent man. She needed to know more about her client.

Rosa purchased two caramel-flavoured iced coffees and two slices of banana bread. She and Orissa had always shared the same taste in food and drink – they both had a sweet tooth. Orissa picked up her iced coffee and took a large sip, before diving into conversation.

'So, it must be pretty intense doing *the* Emmett Hamilton case? It's huge, Rosa!'

Rosa wanted to smile but upon hearing his name she was overcome with immense anxiety and sadness. He was still in prison, and every day it was looking more likely that he might be there for a very long time.

Orissa took Rosa's silence as an invitation for her to continue.

'You wanted me to arrange for you to speak with his grandmother, right? The whole church has been praying for the family. I really feel for her.' Orissa looked Rosa in the eyes. 'Everyone thinks he's guilty, Rosa.'

A chill fell across the women, and in this moment, it was difficult for Rosa to believe that they'd been friends for over twenty years.

'Yes, I need to speak to her,' Rosa declared after the extended pause.

'And you can't just speak to her through your work?'

Rosa's mahogany brown eyes shone like polished marbles, hopeful. She considered whether to explain her plan to Orissa, a woman she'd trusted all her life.

'Please, Orissa. Just trust me on this one. Can you help me meet her?'

'So, you want me to help you but won't tell me why?' She folded her arms and leaned back into her hips, pursing her lips.

'Yes, please,' Rosa said softly.

'Fine,' Orissa said reluctantly. 'This better be good. We're actually going to church this evening; there's a soup kitchen and she always helps out. No doubt she'll be there.'

Rosa allowed her faded smile to return.

'Thank you,' she said.

'I'm going to need some answers at some point,' Orissa replied. 'I wish I could see into that busy brain of yours. It must be like a witch's cauldron: spells, and magic bubbling over the top.'

CHAPTER 22

An orderly but stationary queue of people had started to form outside the church, like cars stuck in traffic. Orissa guided Rosa through the small car park and through a rickety back gate that led to the church garden, which was overgrown and abandoned. The grey concrete of the car park blended into the muddy brown ground, which was coated in pieces of fractured tiles and pots, cigarette butts and jagged broken bits of branch. An isolated patch of grass stood out in the corner, untouched, probably for years. The rich green of the weeds contrasted with the otherwise dark soil.

Rosa copied Orissa's movements, lifting her legs high to step over the small row of bricks that obstructed their path. It looked as though, at some point, there had been an attempt to build a wall in this garden, but that too had been forgotten.

Once inside, Orissa invited Rosa to pass over her light jacket, to hang it in the cloakroom.

'You need to get involved, Rosa. Don't make it so obvious that you're only here for one thing. At least *try* to be subtle!'

Orissa said as she watched Rosa scout the room for Emmett's grandmother.

Rosa compliantly took off her jacket and handed it to Orissa.

The volunteers in the church hall were setting up. There was a wonderful aroma of spices as people lifted the lids off big bucket-like pans of rice and mild curries. The smell reminded her of home, of Nana's cooking.

'Here, Rosa, come and grab the bread with me, please.'

Rosa followed Orissa into the small kitchen where a group of elderly ladies hobbled out with their mugs of tea.

Orissa gripped the handle of the oven and pulled it open. A cloud of steam escaped through the gap and created a fog in the room.

Rosa desperately wanted to speak to Emmett's grandmother but wasn't entirely sure what she was going to say. It was unlike her not to have a plan, but it was also unusual for her to feel this invested in a case.

Orissa fiddled with the oven to switch it off and pulled open the door fully. The sweet smell of baked bread crept up Rosa's nose, and she clutched her stomach, remembering that the only thing she'd eaten all day was the coffee-shop banana bread.

As if reading her mind, Orissa leaned in and picked up one of the rolls to share it but dropped it immediately. 'Ah, that is hot! Bloody hell.' Orissa stood up straight and looked around, searching. Rosa, as if she were the limbs to Orissa's body, handed her the oven gloves she had already picked up. The kind of understanding that only comes over decades.

Orissa pulled the trays of rolls out of the oven and tipped them into a few larger deep foil trays for serving, which the two friends picked up and carried back to the main hall.

Women and men, clad in the church's little green aprons, stood behind a row of tables that had been set up as a counter. Members of the congregation were now trickling into the room, making it harder for Rosa to spot Emmett's grandmother. She followed Orissa to the end of the table and mirrored her in placing the dishes neatly on the surface.

'She's by the tea and biscuits,' Orissa said, aware that Rosa was becoming impatient.

Rosa swivelled her head towards the huge, insulated containers of tea. There she was, sitting behind the table, nibbling a biscuit, and listening intently to another elderly woman who was rabbiting away.

As Rosa approached the tea stand, she noticed that Joyce looked older and more haggard than the last time she'd seen her. She was wearing a short grey wig, but it was positioned too far back on her head as though someone had ruffled her hair too affectionately. Her thick-rimmed glasses were tilted to the left, like they needed to assist one eye more than the other. There was no glow to her complexion, and her lips turned downwards as she chewed on the crumbs of biscuit.

'Good morning, Joyce.' Rosa stopped suddenly, remembering where she was and the respect she ought to show. 'I'm sorry, is it Mrs Hamilton?'

Joyce looked up over her glasses. It seemed that her right eye was in fact stronger than the other as while it widened, her left eye drooped heavily behind. The strong

145

eye narrowed and squinted at Rosa, before Joyce suddenly smashed her polystyrene cup down on the table, spilling the milky tea over her twisted fingers.

'What are you doing at my *church*?' she asked in a loud whisper, turning her neck to see if anyone had stopped to stare.

Rosa felt a rush of embarrassment, knowing she was overstepping. She followed Joyce's eyes and was grateful that nobody appeared to be paying either of them any attention. She tried to gather herself, standing up tall and allowing oxygen to fill her lungs. She squeezed her diaphragm and started again.

'Mrs Hamilton, I wanted to talk to you, please. It's about your grandson.'

'My grandson. You want to come to my *church*? The one safe place I have.' She enunciated each word so carefully, despite her bubbling upset. Her voice was now sharp and proper. She didn't really have an accent at all, each word delivered as neutrally as by a news reader.

'Yes, I'm s-so-sorry.' Rosa temporarily crumbled and had to take another deep breath. 'Mrs Hamilton. It really is important. Please.'

'You could have called me. I could have met you at the solicitor's office, but you stroll into my church, making me feel like I've done something wrong. Why would you do that?'

Rosa stepped back and twisted her neck to catch eyes with Orissa. To her surprise, Orissa was only standing a few steps behind, silently observing. Rosa looked at her pleadingly. Orissa stepped forwards and placed her hand on Joyce's shoulder.

'Mrs H, I'm so sorry. It's my fault. Rosa is my friend. I invited her today.' She squeezed Joyce's shoulder a little more tightly and then crouched so that their eyes were parallel. 'Of course, I understand if you don't want to talk to her, I should have spoken to you first.' There was such softness and warmth in Orissa's voice, it melted some of the tension.

'Why *here*?'

'Mrs H, I'm not entirely sure because I don't know the details, but shall we all go into a smaller room? I know you don't want everyone in the hall to hear this conversation.' Orissa released Joyce's shoulder and extended her elbow out for Joyce to hold, which she did obligingly. Orissa helped to lift her and guided her into the smaller room at the back of the hall.

Three of the four walls were painted white, and the fourth stood out in bright lime green. It was decorated with giant scrabble-like pieces of wood, each with an engraved letter arranged in a backwards L shape. Vertically it read S-E-R-V-E and horizontally the letters spelled L-O-V-E, with the letter E connecting to both words. Perpendicular to the design, on one of the white walls, there were numerous sheets of coloured paper, each one cut out in the shape of a child's handprint and covered in scribbles.

Infant-sized tables were pushed up against the wall, and just one adult-sized chair, which Orissa led Joyce to. The older woman breathed a little sigh of relief and lifted her swollen feet off the ground.

Rosa tugged one of the small chairs out from under the mini tables and perched on the edge, feeling like a naughty child called before the headteacher.

'I'm going to leave you both to talk, I'll be right next door if you need me,' Orissa said, speaking mostly to Joyce.

As she left the room, she gave Rosa a thumbs up and smiled. Rosa returned her expression, careful to make sure that Joyce did not to notice.

'Mrs H,' Rosa started, hoping that she'd heard Orissa correctly, 'I want to help your grandson. I want to do *everything* I can to help him.'

Joyce closed her eyes and remained still. Rosa heard heavy breaths emanating from the back of her throat as her lower jaw hung slightly open.

'I have this feeling. I know this might sound ridiculous but I'm hoping that you, his grandmother, might understand more than I do. Something isn't right. Let's just say, it's a gut feeling.' She suddenly had a flashback of her argument with Tristan. *You and your bloody gut instinct.* His voice echoed in her head, and she tried to blink it away. 'Is there anything that you know that you think might be helpful?'

After a long silence, Joyce said quietly, 'One of my kitchen knives is missing. The sharp one.'

'I see,' Rosa whispered. *So much for a gut instinct. The facts were plain. Emmett was found at the murder scene, with blood on his hands, and a knife is seemingly missing from his home. He might as well have confessed. This trial was going to be a disaster.*

Joyce opened her eyes. 'Could you send your friend back in here to help me, please?'

'Oh yes, of course. I'm sorry. I can help?'

'No, thank you. Please send in Orissa. You be on your way.' Rosa tried to hide her embarrassment.

'Look, I wouldn't read too much into the knife at this stage,' she said, trying to sound gentle. Rosa was trying to reassure herself as much as Joyce. She looked at her tired, dark eyes. 'Your grandson needs your support right now.'

Joyce closed her eyes and tilted her head back. Their conversation was over.

'Sady, look at my new shoes!' Toby called out as soon as Rosa returned to the flat. Rosa opened her arms inviting a cuddle from her little brother who bounced down the corridor showing off his new school shoes.

Rosa walked into the living room; Nana was knitting and watching the evening news.

'Evening, Nana,' she said, slumping on the sofa next to her.

'Evenin', Mercedes,' Nana replied, not turning to look at her.

Rosa pulled Toby, who had followed her over to the sofa, up onto the pillows between them.

'Let's have a look at these, then,' she said, admiring the shoes. 'Very nice!'

'Mercedes, nuh let 'im put his outside shoes up on di sofa,' Nana said with a scowl.

'But I haven't worn these shoes outside,' Toby protested.

'Toby, mi nuh—' Nana's sentence was interrupted by sudden heavy coughing.

'Toby, feet down, or go and take your shoes off and put

149

them in your room ready for school. Come on now.' Rosa pointed him towards his bedroom and Toby left the room, dragging his feet.

'Nana, your cough, have been back to the doctor about it? It's getting worse,' Rosa said. She heard her mother's voice in her head, telling her that Nana thought it was cancer.

'Mer-ce-des,' Nana struggled to say her name in between coughs. 'Mi need yuh fi guh to Toby's parents' evening pon di 2 October.' Nana paused for breath. 'It clashed with when mi have mi next appointment.'

'Yes, of course,' Rosa said but was cut off by her phone ringing. It was Craig – she had the conference she'd requested with Emmett this coming week but wondered what could be so urgent.

'Sorry, Nana, one second, I need to get this.'

Rosa answered the phone. She could hear from Craig's tone that he was upset, though the signal was weak. She stood up from the sofa and walked into the kitchen, where the signal was slightly better, and Craig's complaints were clearer. It appeared that Joyce had contacted Craig and asked why Rosa had turned up at her church saying she wanted to help Emmett.

She listened, stunned by her own bad decisions. Craig asked her if it was true, and she confirmed that it was.

'Rosa, I don't need to tell you this, but I will, so that there is no doubt in your mind. I put you on this case, but I can just as easily take you off it. There's a conference this week and we both know I don't have time to get someone else, but don't get too comfortable: this case would be snapped up in seconds.' He paused and let Rosa's guilt sink in. 'Anyway, can you let Emmett know that the police are doing forensic testing on the knife.' He ended the call abruptly.

Rosa felt a lump growing in her throat.

CHAPTER 23

The skin on Mohammed's face was now uneven, red blotches marking his once brown skin. While exactly a week had passed since his attack, some pus-filled blisters still coated his right cheek. His lips, which were pursed due to years of smoking, moved unevenly when he spoke with the weight of his forming scars. He was sitting on the bottom bunk, which Emmett had moved to in his absence, but he agreed to switch bunks immediately following his return to the cell in an attempt to avoid any further trouble.

In the few days that they'd properly got to know each other as cellmates, Emmett had warmed to Mohammed. Unsurprisingly, he was a lot more reserved than when Emmett first met him and made clear that he much preferred spending time in the cell than outside. Emmett wasn't entirely sure what had brought Mohammed to prison in the first place, and had learned that it wasn't the sort of thing that people discussed.

Emmett was doing sit-ups on the floor of the cell and

Mohammed, or Mo as he preferred to be called, sat in silence watching him.

'I don't fink that you're gonna get out, bro. It's gonna be a mad one for your lawyer. You got a barrister, yeah?' Mo said.

'Yeah, I do,' Emmett replied as he reached the top of his sit-up. 'What makes you say that?' Asking a question was the best way to avoid saying something wrong. He lowered himself backwards again, with his hands behind his head.

'Well, the evidence they 'ave on you.' Mo winced as he shifted himself backwards to bring his feet up onto his bed. 'I heard that they 'ave witnesses what saw you do it,' he said, peeling open a banana.

'Heard from who?' Emmett said, trying to disguise the surprise in his voice as breathlessness.

'Mmm.' Mo bit a chunk of banana. 'Mmhmmm.' He chewed a few times and swallowed. 'You know how it is. Being stuck in that prison hospital, there ain't much to talk about.'

Emmett pulled himself up again.

'People have been talking about me?' he said, again trying to conceal his surprise. He hadn't been in this prison long and had done everything in his power to keep himself to himself.

'You see me, yeah.' Mo chomped on another bit of banana. Again, he delayed while he chewed and swallowed. 'Me, I've got friends everywhere.'

The skin on Mo's right hand was peeling upwards, exposing the raw flesh underneath. It was hard to reconcile the kettle incident just one week ago with the idea that Mo had a lot of friends in prison. Nobody had visited him in the prison hospital, and nobody had passed by the cell. Emmett was certain that he was the only person Mo spoke to. He lay on his back for a second, looking up at the ceiling and tracing the cracks in the paintwork with his eyes. 'So, you're saying people think I'm guilty?'

'Yep. Course they do, mate.' Mo tossed the banana skin across the room, aiming for the bin, but missing by quite a few inches. 'Don't matter, though, does it? We ain't the jury. Just wanna prepare you if you are in here longer than you hoped.'

A minute passed, and then another. Emmett got up and began sharpening a razorblade he'd detached. Since the kettle incident he'd realised that he needed to protect himself.

'Don't look so down, bro,' Mo continued. 'You get used to it in 'ere. It really ain't so bad. But a message from the outside: *Don't snitch. People will always find out.*' He stared at Emmett in a threatening way.

Emmett wasn't entirely sure what Mo was talking about. He didn't know whether Mo was describing his own experiences or actually conveying a message from someone outside. He didn't want to enquire further; didn't want to appear vulnerable.

Moments passed and the men lapsed into silence. Mo leaned back on the lower bunk and scraped the dirt from his fingernails and flicked it onto the floor. Emmett sat at the desk chair and bent down to slip the sharpened blade into his sock. Eventually, Mo stopped and itched his side before lying down.

Emmett swivelled his chair to properly face the desk, grabbed a pen and retrieved some blank paper he'd left sitting there for days.

Dear Granny,

I keep meaning to write you this letter. I'm sorry it's taken me so long, and I'm so sorry I haven't called.

The truth is, I can't deal with the fact that you are disappointed in me. I hope that I can accept that in time.

Everyone here thinks I'm guilty. I'm worried the jury will think the same. I'm starting to struggle to remember all of the details of that day, which terrifies me.

Anyway, this is my goodbye. I'm so sorry, Granny.

He read the letter again and went to sign his name. His pen hovered in the air, and wouldn't connect with the paper, like magnets repulsing.

The pen fell from his fingers. On an impulse, he picked up the piece of paper and tore it in half, and then ripped it again into quarters.

'Hey, Mo.'

Mo snorted or snored; Emmett wasn't sure which.

'Mo, I'm not guilty. I'm going to go home. I won't be here forever. I'm innocent.'

'Yeah, so am I, mate,' Mo said with a smile. 'Keep fighting the good fight.'

CHAPTER 24

'Hi, you must be Rosa, I'm Kathryn but you can call me Kate. Craig said he told you that he couldn't make it here to the prison today and so I've come along to take a note.' Craig's bright-eyed paralegal bounced into the prison entrance where Rosa had been waiting.

'Hi, Kate. Yes, he said. We just can't afford to miss this conference. I hear it's impossible to get a con at Pentonville at the moment. Thanks for coming along.'

Both women retrieved their identification documents. Rosa handed over her small pink driving licence and Kate passed along her green provisional licence. The prison officer scanned both documents and handed them forms to complete and sign.

They emptied their belongings into a locker, taking only their laptops and paper notes in with them. Worryingly, the search by the officers was more relaxed than Rosa was used to in Crown Courts. They passed through a metal detector and were ushered through into a private conference room. Minutes passed and eventually Emmett was brought in.

His appearance had changed again, despite only a week or so having passed. Instead of looking gaunt, he seemed to have gained some weight and his facial hair looked overgrown. The pores on his skin were enlarged and small spots had spread sporadically across his cheeks.

'It's lovely to see you, Emmett, you're looking well,' said Rosa.

Emmett barely looked up, other than to locate his seat and plonk himself in it.

'This is Kate, she is here today instead of Craig. She will just be taking notes.' Kate flashed her shiny white teeth at Emmett, who briefly looked at her and then moved his eyes away, as though her smile was blinding.

Rosa opened up her laptop and entered the password. She clicked into her files and opened up her conference notes.

'OK, Emmett. Let's get started. I have received correspondence from the Crown Prosecution Service. They have confirmed that the two prosecution witnesses have now provided their witness statements about what they say they saw that day.'

'What have they said?'

'Well, it isn't great news, I'm afraid,' Rosa cut straight to the chase. 'They both identify you as the murderer.'

'What? How? By name? Who are they? What have they said?'

'Give me just a moment, I'll read the relevant parts out to you. Hang on . . . here it is . . . OK.' Rosa paused and waited for the PDF document to open on her screen.

'OK, so the first prosecution witness is called Mark McEvoy.

He is a teacher. He says he saw "the lighter-skinned man" with a knife. He said the other men were darker skinned?'

'Yeah, I'm the only light-skinned one.'

'And that you were hiding the knife in your jumper?'

'Well, no one would walk around a park in the middle of the day with a knife just openly in their hand.'

'So, you *did* have the knife?' Rosa shot Kate a look, making sure she was taking a note.

'No, I'm just saying. Who would carry a knife around during the day, just in their hand?'

'I understand,' she said, although she was increasingly sure he wasn't being truthful. 'And he says he saw you stab the victim. And he tried to grab the knife off you, causing you to drop it.'

Emmett looked stunned. 'That's a whole lot of bullshit. It isn't true. What is he talking about? He didn't grab any knife off me! He must be confused, it wasn't me! I was wearing a jumper, yes, but I didn't have a knife. It wasn't me. I didn't stab anyone! I'm not guilty, honestly, you have to believe me!'

Rosa skimmed once more over the rest of the statement. She still couldn't work out why this person would have any reason to lie – at worst Mark McEvoy might be mistaken, but he was so sure in his account. She closed the document and opened the next witness statement.

'The next one is from a woman called Claire Smith. She's not currently working, and says she was walking with her young child in a buggy through the park. She says she didn't see the stabbing.'

'Well, that's good, no? She can't help,' Emmett said.

'She also says that she saw a lighter-skinned man with a knife. She says you were wearing a thick winter jumper, which was unusual for the weather.'

'Why do they keep mentioning my jumper? So what if I was wearing a jumper? That doesn't make me a murderer!'

Rosa was surprised that it was the mention of the jumper that had irritated Emmett.

'Also, how did the woman with the baby see anything?' he went on. 'I didn't even know it was a woman she was so far away. There was someone with a baby but they were honestly not close enough to see anything. That's literally a lie.'

'You *can* remember some things about that day then, can't you?' Rosa said, finding her temper rising. 'Can you remember who *did* do the stabbing?'

'I don't know,' Emmett mumbled in defeat.

Kate had paused typing and pre-emptively handed Emmett a tissue. He took it and placed it on the table in front of him, slowly unfolded it and then began to refold it. He repeated this motion while Rosa and Kate sat silently.

'Emmett, the CPS are going to make sure that the knife is tested for fingerprints,' Rosa continued, more calmly. 'If your fingerprints aren't on the knife, that could really help your case.'

Emmett continued to fold and unfold the tissue slowly and carefully, without responding.

'And if they do find my fingerprints, what then? I'm guilty?' he asked.

Rosa looked at him startled. 'Well, no, not necessarily. Is

there any reason they might find your prints on the knife?' Joyce's confession about hers going missing was at the forefront of her mind.

Emmett shook his head and sighed. 'Are we done now? I feel really exhausted. I don't want to talk about this anymore.'

Rosa sat back. She'd hit a brick wall. She needed to get him on side again.

'OK, so have I understood this right? You say that on 4 September, that was a Monday, you left your house at around midday to go and get some fresh air with your friends. You decided to go to Walthamstow Park, where you met . . . let me see, two friends?'

'Yes, that sounds about right.'

'And how did you decide where to meet these friends? Had you planned to meet up with them in advance or is this somewhere that you normally hang out at this time?'

'I've told you already, I'm not talking about my friends.'

'Right, OK. And just to check one more time then, you planned to be in that particular park?'

'Correct,' Emmett said. He'd reduced his answers to just one word. Rosa knew that the questions were tiresome, but she needed her instructions to be crystal clear.

'You didn't take a knife? Nor did you ever touch the knife?'

'Exactly,' Emmett said.

'Did you know the victim, Thomas Dove?'

'No. Not even. Exactly why would I kill someone I don't even know?' Emmett blurted out.

'Well, yes, and most importantly, you say you didn't kill him?'

'Correct. That's all there is to it,' Emmett said.

Rosa looked at her note of his account. If only it were that simple.

'Do you have any idea why these two witnesses would make up that they *did* see you bring a knife into the park? Or why one witness says he saw you stab the victim?'

'I have no idea,' Emmett said in an intentionally calm voice. The calmer he seemed, the more likely it was that Rosa would believe him.

Rosa looked to Kate to see if she too had registered his tone. Kate remained focused and expressionless, her long, polished fingernails tapping away at the keyboard.

'Do you remember anyone else? Aside from these two and your friends.'

'No.'

'Are you sure? Was there anyone else around, anyone who might have seen what happened?'

'I don't think so.'

'And, sorry to ask again, your friends, you don't want to talk about them *at all*?'

'No, I don't.'

'But if everything you're saying is true,' Rosa paused, only now feeling like she'd hit the jackpot, 'they're the witnesses we need. They could corroborate everything you're saying.'

'No,' Emmett said. 'They had nothing to do with this.'

'Is there something you're not telling me, Emmett?'

Kate looked up, peering over her laptop screen, finally watching the unravelling of Emmett's account.

161

'I'm not telling you anything about my friends. I've said that multiple times,' Emmett said coldly.

'Are you covering for someone?' Rosa asked.

'No,' he said, now meeting her eyes with a hardness that sent a shiver down Rosa's spine. For the first time she genuinely thought, is this man capable of murder?

'Are you sure?' she asked again.

'I'm done with this,' Emmett said, slapping his palms down on the desk and standing up. 'I've told you what you need to know. I'll see you at the next hearing.'

'Not so fast, Emmett. As always, I need to remind you that it's not too late to consider pleading guilty. You'd still get a considerable amount of credit, which could make a big difference in your case.' Rosa hated how pessimistic she sounded.

'Oh, so you've given up on me too?' he said. 'Goodbye, Rosa.'

He stood up and tapped on the window and the guard entered to collect him.

CHAPTER 25

Rosa stripped off her suit and stood over the puddle of black clothing on the grey linoleum floor. She didn't have much time to get changed and the court toilet cubicle was small. Using the tips of her fingernails she nudged the toilet lid closed, hiding the small droplets of urine on the unclean seat from sight. Something buzzed – a text. Reaching for her bag on the hook of the door, she retrieved her phone.

> I meant to tell you, I saw his granny H at church again at the weekend. Supposedly she remembered something else that's important– she said she'll be at the hearing next week and will speak to you then. I don't really want to keep passing messages on, Rosa – can I give her your number? Xxx

Rosa felt a wave of fear wash over her; she'd got herself into enough trouble the first time she'd spoken to Joyce with Orissa's help, she was in no rush to do it again.

She switched off her phone to save the small amount of battery power she had left and began to dress speedily, heaving her navy outfit over her head. The dress fitted a little tightly, but she concealed her gut with a chunky black belt.

Rosa squeezed out of the confined cubicle, dumping her bag on the side of the sink and pulling out her make-up bag. She massaged the foundation into her skin and flicked mascara over her lashes. Her fingertips worked with speed as they painted her lips a deep rouge. She pouted in the mirror to assist, admiring her own reflection, and blew herself a kiss.

Time to get some answers.

The Underground station was as hectic as usual, with people darting in random directions like ants. Rosa slowly clambered down the escalators in her heeled shoes. She tripped at the end of the escalator.

'Are you OK, miss?' A tall man with soft lips and deep green eyes cocked his head towards her and stretched out his arms. He looked at least ten years younger than her and was incredibly handsome.

'Yeah, yeah, I'm OK. Thank you.' Rosa felt embarrassment wash over her as she clutched his forearm. Her eyes slowly followed her hands and she saw the shiny gold band decorating his ring finger.

'Oh, I really am sorry,' she said, surprising herself that her thoughts were aloud.

'No, it's fine.' He chuckled kindly. 'I never understand how women walk around in those things anyway.'

Rosa attempted to grin back, but her face was more of a grimace. She regained her balance and scurried with the other people to her platform. Without hesitation, she pushed herself onto the train, hearing the sighs of people who had been waiting there long before her.

A few stops passed and then the train jolted. A voice sounded through the carriage.

'This is a customer service update. There are severe delays on the Victoria line. Passengers are advised to disembark at this station and try to seek an alternative route.'

The doors opened and a number of disgruntled passengers stepped back on to the platform. Others waited impatiently, muttering under their breath.

Minutes passed and the train didn't move. Rosa checked her phone but had no signal – she still hadn't worked out how to connect her phone to the Wi-Fi underground – then switched it off. The same announcement was repeated a few times, and each time a few more passengers stepped off the train.

Glancing up at the different coloured lines of the tube map above her head, Rosa tried to figure out an alternative route back to Walthamstow, but without internet access she found it a laborious task. She decided to just wait.

More minutes floated by.

'Customer service announcement. We should be back on the move shortly.' Excited bodies hovering on the platform shuffled back on to the train.

'This train is now ready to depart, please stand clear of the doors . . . mind the closing doors.'

Eventually, daylight crept into the carriage as the train

emerged above ground. Rosa exited at Walthamstow North station. The platform was busy with commuters clad in dark suits, mostly fixated on their phones. The exit gates bleeped repetitively as each person tapped to leave. Rosa shuffled through, with the crowd, until she reached the pavement outside. Instead of turning left and then left again, as she normally would to go home, she continued straight out of the station, in the opposite direction. Reaching the end of the road and turning left onto the main high road, she headed uphill, passing multiple adjacent roads until she reached the fourth, Calpol Road.

It wasn't difficult to spot which house Thomas had lived in. The nurse hadn't exaggerated when she said that the flowers outside gave it away. It had been almost a month since he had been killed, yet there were still at least three bouquets of fresh flowers just outside of the front gate, and a small laminated photo of Thomas had been affixed to the lamppost in front of the house.

Without hesitation, Rosa flicked the loose handle on the front gate and stepped up the three tiled steps to the door. She rang the bell and waited. A young man with unbrushed dark brown hair came to open it, rubbing his eyes as though he'd just been woken from a nap.

'Hi, I'm Rosa Higgins,' she said, extending out her hand.

The man looked at her with a blank expression.

'I'm a lawyer in the murder case of Thomas Dove. Can I come in?'

'Er, yeah sure. Sorry, yeah, come in,' the man said, scratching his scalp. 'Let me just get Li to come down too.'

He called upstairs and opened the door widely to invite Rosa inside.

'If you just walk ahead and go through that door, that's our living room. Sorry it's a bit messy.'

Rosa heard footsteps as Li came downstairs. There were whispers in the corridor before both Li and the man with messy hair joined her in the living room. Li had a pale, unblemished complexion with jet black cropped hair, which she parted evenly in the middle and tucked behind her ears. Her cheekbones protruded, which made her face look elegant, and her ears were decorated with a number of stud and hoop earrings. As she walked towards her, Rosa noticed that Li's baggy clothes masked her skeletal frame.

'Sorry, who did you say you were?' Li asked.

'I'm a lawyer. I'm working in the murder case for Thomas Dove.'

'Oh, OK, right. How can we help you?' she said, with a slightly uncomfortable expression.

'I just wanted to learn a bit more about Thomas. What life was like for him before he, erm, passed,' Rosa said.

'You mean, before he was murdered?' Li replied.

'Um, yes,' Rosa murmured. 'Were you all friends?'

'Yeah, good friends,' the man replied. Rosa still didn't know his name but realised it was probably too late to ask now.

'I don't know about *good* friends,' Li added. 'I don't like to speak ill of the dead, but he and I didn't get on all too well. Especially since Mae broke up with him. I didn't like her much either but at least his life was a bit more . . . organised, let's say.'

'Li, come on. He wasn't that bad!' the man responded.

'He wasn't that bad? We nearly lost this flat because every single month there was another reason why he couldn't pay the rent.'

'He just wasn't great with money,' the man said.

'That's an understatement.' Li suddenly turned to Rosa, apparently realising that she was still in the room. 'Sorry, what is it that we can actually help you with?'

'Did he ever indicate that anyone was chasing him for money? Was there anything strange in the lead-up to his death?'

'I remember one day he told us that someone had turned up at the hospital and was really aggressive with him. I don't know what that was about, though. That could have been a crazy patient, or maybe it was about money. I don't really know. Like I said to the police, there is nothing that made me think that there was anyone out to murder him.'

'Yeah, I agree,' Li added, 'I didn't think he had any real enemies. We told the police this already, did they not tell you?'

'Yes, of course, I just wanted to follow up,' Rosa said.

'I didn't realise prosecutors did home visits,' Li said. 'I'm actually studying to be a solicitor at the moment – but not criminal, I want to go into housing.'

'Oh, I'm not the prosecutor,' Rosa said.

Both Li and the man looked at Rosa with surprise.

'You said you're the lawyer?' Li replied.

'I am. I represent Emmett Hamilton. The man accused of murdering Thomas.'

The man remained still, as though he still hadn't fully woken up. Li's expression changed; she scowled at Rosa.

'What on earth are you doing in our house?'

'I just wanted to ask some questions. I think I have enough, thank you for your time,' Rosa said, standing up and readying herself to leave.

'Since when do defence lawyers visit victims' homes? That doesn't seem right,' Li said.

'I really didn't mean to cause any alarm. I just wanted to find out a little bit more about him, and what was happening before he died. I'm so sorry if I've caused any upset.'

'No, you haven't caused upset,' Li said. 'Just leave before we consider reporting you. You shouldn't be going to people's homes. It's intrusive.'

Rosa nodded in acknowledgement but said nothing, to avoid making the situation any worse. She stepped outside and darted down the road.

She held her phone's power button and the bright Apple logo appeared. After a few seconds, her home screen appeared. Her phone showed a number of missed calls from Nana. There was also a text.

Rosa, you have let me down again. It was always strange reading Nana's messages, written in perfect English. She read the rest aloud under her breath, in Nana's voice.

'Mi pan mi way tuh Toby's parents' evening. Tank yuh fi nuttin.'

Rosa suddenly remembered that Nana was supposed to

have another hospital appointment today, which she must have sacrificed to attend parents' evening with Toby. She scrambled some words together to reply to Nana but realised she had none.

The flat was empty when she got home and so she shut herself in her room and pulled out her laptop, revisiting her conference notes. It was as clear as day: Emmett had no defence other than saying he was in the wrong place at the wrong time, and had somehow then been wrongly accused of a terrible murder. She knew the jury wouldn't buy it.

The prosecutor would say that the jury could be sure that Emmet Hamilton killed Thomas Dove. Not one, but two separate witnesses identified him and distinguished him from his friends as the lighter-skinned male, a description Emmett had agreed with. He had no good explanation for being in the park that day. He refused to divulge any information about his friends, the only other possible witnesses that could provide an alibi. His freedom was on the line and, the prosecutor would say, the only logical explanation was that Emmett was the killer.

The evidence was mounting against him at an alarming speed. Rosa had to speak to his grandma again – it was her only hope.

The strong smell of saltfish wafted around the flat. It was 8 p.m. and Rosa slipped away from her desk and tiptoed into the kitchen.

'Nana, do you want any help with that? I could rinse the ackee?'

Nana stayed focused on breaking the pieces of saltfish into a pan, barely acknowledging that Rosa had entered the room.

Toby interrupted the awkward quiet with his joyful booming voice. 'SADY! I had such a good report, I'm the best in my class at PE.'

Rosa turned and high-fived him.

'Well done, little man. Good job.'

Nana silenced the celebration. 'Gud at PE but wah else, Toby?' Her voice sounded unkind. Toby glanced at her, confused, and shrugged. 'Gwaan tell yuh sista, yuh nuh doing well inna any of yuh oddah subjects.'

Rosa looked at Toby with disapproving eyebrows but a kind smile. Toby appeared to understand the facial expression and smiled back at her but then turned to offer Nana regretful eyes.

'I'm sure Toby knows that we won't be doing anything fun at the weekends if he doesn't start making sure he is working hard at everything. That's right, isn't it, Toby?'

Toby's confusion grew. He wasn't entirely sure whether Rosa was on his side or not, which was fair given she wasn't entirely sure herself. With all joy having been sucked from him, he sloped back into his bedroom leaving Rosa and Nana in silence.

'Nana, look, I'm really sorry about earlier. I really have been overwhelmed with this case and I just honestly lost track of time. It's been all-encompassing. I'm worried that I'm going to be responsible for a young man being wrongly convicted of murder. I really didn't mean to miss Toby's parents' evening. I know you had the hospital too. If you can reschedule it, I promise I will book the day off work and come with you.' Rosa's apology was rambling, and she didn't know whether to keep going.

Nana stopped her.

'Mi need your money fuh rent.'

Rosa nodded, deflated; the legal aid agency was slower than ever to pay her. Her debt was growing every day. But worse still, she was losing her grandmother's respect.

CHAPTER 26

A month had passed since Rosa first met Emmett and had taken on his murder case at Leytonstone Magistrates' Court. As she approached the Old Bailey, she felt a slight rush of nerves. Today was the last formal opportunity for Emmett to change his mind and plead guilty, and the court would be setting directions for the trial.

The temporary metal railings segregated the queues at the entrance to court. As Rosa approached the door, she was stopped by a member of the security staff.

'Morning, miss, the entrance for members of the public is around the corner, this is the entrance for lawyers.'

Rosa paused, slightly startled.

'I am counsel in the case of Emmett Hamilton.'

'Oh, sorry, miss,' he replied, seemingly unembarrassed, and stood aside to let her pass.

As Rosa emptied her belongings into a plastic tray, she noticed Craig bouncing in behind her. Of course, the security guard didn't stop and question him.

'Rosa, sorry, I'm running a tad late, trains are a nightmare. We ready to go straight down to the cells?'

'I'll just need to robe up, Craig. Give me five minutes. I'll meet you back down here.'

Emmett's weight gain was now obvious. His cheeks were full, and his belly protruded through his top as the security officers brought him into the conference cell. His oily forehead glistened under the bright lights.

He joined Craig and Rosa at the small desk which was fixed to the floor.

'It's good to see you again, Emmett. How are you doing?' Rosa asked. It hadn't been very long since she'd last seen him with Kate, but she was trying to rebuild their rapport.

'I'm OK. I'm OK.' He sounded as though he was trying to convince himself.

'Today is your PTPH, that's your plea and trial preparation hearing. Now, I know what your instructions are, you've been very clear in telling us that you did not kill that man. I do have a duty, though, Emmett, to make sure that you understand that after today, any credit that the court might give you for a guilty plea will continue to reduce.'

She looked at Craig, who chimed in.

'Yeah, look, it's merely a formality Emmett, but we have to tell you, the judge will ask us. OK?'

Emmett nodded and Rosa continued.

'If you pleaded guilty today you would be afforded up to twenty-five per cent credit on the sentence a judge would have given you after trial. In a case like this, that can make a substantial difference.'

'So, what are you saying?' Emmett interrupted. 'Shall I plead?'

'No, not on the basis of what you've told me,' Rosa replied.

'No. Absolutely not,' Craig added.

The air in the cell was stagnant and the only sound was the slight whirring of Craig's laptop. They all sat there, as still as statues, while seconds drifted by.

Emmett opened his mouth to speak, and a broken croak came out. He closed his mouth and swallowed and tried again.

'D-d-d-o you ...' Emmett stuttered. Again, he paused, swallowed, and started again. 'Do you really think that I have any chance of proving that I didn't do this?'

Craig responded calmly. 'Well, that's what we're here for, so I bloody hope so.' He was trying to lift the mood, but no one smiled. Emmett gathered up the energy to speak again.

'If you think I'll be found guilty, I'd rather just plead and save myself years. Everyone already thinks I did it. My name is all over the news every week.'

'Look, I know it's difficult inside,' Rosa said with sympathy, 'I can imagine it's tough but if you ...'

'TOUGH? Miss, you don't know a thing about prison. Have you ever been in prison? Who are you to say it's difficult? You don't know a single thing!'

Rosa went to protest but caught a glimpse of Craig in the corner of her eye. He seemed unphased by Emmett's upset. She stopped herself and settled back into the wooden chair.

'Oh, there we go! You have nothing to say, do you? You privileged people come in here and think that we owe you something. This is your job!'

Rosa's mouth responded before her mind had a chance to catch up. 'I know more than you think, we really aren't so different.'

'WHAT? What are you talking about? Because we're Black?' A vein bulged through his forehead and spittle escaped his mouth furiously. 'You honestly have NO IDEA!' His voice was growing louder, and Rosa felt herself sinking further into her seat.

'YOU'RE MORE LIKE THEM THAN ME!' He took a deep breath and collapsed, exhausted, against the wall.

Rosa, for once in her life, had very little to say. Was she more like them? Had this job changed her? She closed her eyes as though at peace with Emmett's comments, but her blood boiled with anger. She was in an impossible position. How could she possibly explain how much she understood Emmett and not be judged by Craig? Slowly, she twisted out of her chair and stood up to face the door. She tapped on the glass.

'Emmett, we will see you upstairs,' Craig's voice trailed behind her as he stood and joined her at the door, and the security officers came to release them.

The judge, His Honour Judge Douglas KC, caressed his gown delicately and pressed his glasses firmly against his sharp nose. His face was cold, and his front two teeth slightly bucked over his bottom lip like a hare. His expression was a stern smile, perhaps inappropriate for the gravity of the room.

'Are you Emmett Hamilton?' the court clerk called out.

Emmett stood up and nodded.

'You need to speak out loud!' The judge's voice rang peculiarly high through Rosa's ears.

'Yes,' Emmett said begrudgingly.

'Ms Higgins, is he ready to be arraigned?'

'Yes, My Lord. He's ready.'

The judge's face remained neutral. 'Very well.'

The clerk stood up and shuffled through her papers.

'Mr Emmett Hamilton, you are charged with murder.'

An eerie stillness danced between the clerk and Emmett, as though no one else was in the room.

'The particulars of this offence are that you, Emmett Hamilton, on 4 September of this year, murdered Thomas Dove. How do you plead?'

There was no answer. Rosa turned her head slightly to try and catch Emmett's attention. He was staring blankly at the court clerk. She thought she could see a single tear rolling down his cheek.

'Do you plead guilty or not guilty?' the clerk repeated in a harsher voice.

'Erm . . . '

The judge turned to Rosa.

'Ms Higgins, your client appears to be unable to speak. Do you want to have a moment with him?'

'N-n-not guilty. I plead not guilty,' Emmett whispered, only just loud enough for the microphone to pick up.

'Oh, I see,' the judge repeated, apparently surprised. 'Very well.' He took a moment to make a note.

'Mr Hamilton, I have no doubt that you have been properly advised but it is my duty to remind you that any credit you would be given for a guilty plea depreciates as time goes on. Do you understand?'

'Yes, sir.'

'It's *My Lord*.'

'Sorry, My Lord.'

'You can sit down,' the judge said bluntly and turned to the prosecutor, Mr Pankhurst. 'Which witnesses are we expecting?'

'My Lord. There is a slight issue that I wanted to raise with the court. There are two witnesses required by both the prosecution and the defence.' The prosecutor hesitated for a moment and scrambled to find his note of their names.

'Mr Mark McEvoy, and Ms Claire Smith.'

'Right. What is the issue?' The judge dropped his pen and waited.

'Well, this morning Ms Smith arrived at court. I told her that she must not come into the courtroom, as a witness. I told her to go home, but I believe she is still waiting in the corridor, outside of this courtroom.'

Rosa narrowed her eyes at Mr Pankhurst, who had failed to inform her about this encounter before they'd entered the courtroom, but quickly decided to rise above it, knowing she had to pick her battles.

'Mr Pankhurst, thank you for keeping her out of my courtroom. I would suggest briefly explaining to her that her presence is required only at the trial. After this hearing, please feel free to inform her of the date. Ms Higgins, if you want to join her in that, that is a matter for you.'

Rosa met the judge's eyes and assented with a bob of her head.

'My clerk has just retrieved a date from the list office. This trial will be listed as a fixture. It will be listed for two weeks commencing on 30 October of this year.

'Mr Hamilton, stand up. You will continue to be remanded in custody until the date of your trial. Officers, you can take him down. Counsel, is there anything else?' the judge enquired, already closing his laptop, and packing away his papers.

Both advocates shook their heads and stood.

'Very well.' The judge stood up.

'Court rise,' called the court usher.

Outside the courtroom, Rosa hovered as Mr Pankhurst, the prosecutor, approached Claire Smith. Claire was a slightly overweight lady and strikingly attractive. Her large blue eyes stood out against her tanned skin. As she spoke, she swished her silky brown hair dramatically.

'So, you're telling me that I came all this way today for no reason?'

'Yes, I'm afraid so,' Mr Pankhurst said. 'The trial will be starting on 30 October, unless you hear of a change of date. You won't need to come to court otherwise. I'm sorry you had to travel here today.'

'Well, yeah, this all feels like a big waste of time – for some little Black kid who killed someone. Why do we need a trial anyway, we all saw it was him?'

The prosecutor looked uncomfortable, and Rosa pretended to be reading something on her phone. *Some little Black kid.* She tried not to be offended but it stung. Her little brother was a little Black kid. She, herself, was once a little Black kid. She knew this shouldn't affect her view of the case, but it made her even more determined to win.

'I am afraid I have to excuse myself now,' the prosecutor said. 'I need to discuss something with defence counsel, who has been patiently waiting for me.' Claire Smith looked over at Rosa, then back to Mr Pankhurst. 'If you have any further questions, please speak to a police officer; just explain who you are and they'll be able to pass anything on.'

Claire Smith took a step towards Rosa. 'You defend him? Why don't you just tell him to plead guilty and save us all some hassle?'

Rosa bit her tongue.

'I think you should go now,' Mr Pankhurst said firmly. 'You know that we can't talk to you about the evidence. We will be in touch, sorry again that today was such a waste of your time.'

The woman huffed. 'Right, well, I guess October it is. Let's hope everyone can see what a murderous young man he is.'

Claire Smith stormed down the corridor; Mr Pankhurst waited until she had disappeared and then told Rosa he would email her. He too then marched down the corridor to leave, just as Craig emerged from the bathroom.

'Everything OK?' he asked.

'Fine, absolutely fine,' Rosa said in a hush. 'Shall we go and see Emmett?'

A grey-haired woman with her back to Rosa and Craig shuffled in her seat upon hearing his name. She turned her head slowly to face them. Rosa caught her eye – it was Joyce.

'Ah, I'm afraid I really can't today. I have to rush off. Wife needs me to babysit. Shall we book another conference soon?' he replied.

Joyce shook her head slowly at Rosa, indicating that she did not want to be seen, and cowered her head again. Rosa looked away.

'I think we need to see him today, at least one of us.' Her eyes unintentionally wandered back to Emmett's grandmother, and she quickly diverted her gaze. 'It's OK, I'll go. Your wife needs you.'

'Thanks, Rosa. Let me know if there's anything important.' He seemed genuinely grateful and entirely oblivious to Joyce's presence.

Rosa waved him off and stood lingering in the hallway to be sure of his departure, before turning to Emmett's grandmother.

'Shall we grab one of these rooms?'

Joyce didn't answer but stood slowly and followed Rosa inside an empty nearby conference room.

The space was decorated like a shabby living room. The walls were yellow, and a medium-sized sofa lined one of them. The only other chair was a single bare wooden one, which Rosa helped Joyce lower herself onto. She then took a seat on the low sofa and rested her bag on the coffee table between them. There was a brief moment of quiet.

'Orissa said that you had something to tell me,' Rosa said, interrupting the calmness of the room. 'Something you think might help with his case?'

'No. Not just help,' Joyce said slowly. 'Something that will prove his innocence.'

CHAPTER 27

Rosa had no doubt that Joyce's information was unlikely to prove his innocence, but she did want to know more. A white plastic clock ticked mechanically on the wall in the otherwise silent room. She squinted to see the time but realised the hands were stuck at thirty-nine minutes past six, the second hand clicking repeatedly in place.

'Yes, please do tell me.'

'I spoke to my grandson on the telephone,' she started. Rosa nodded, encouraging her to continue. 'Please bear with me.' Joyce stopped and wiped a tear from her eye.

'Would you like a tissue?' Rosa reached into her handbag and pulled out a small packet of tissues, which she handed to Joyce. She took them gratefully.

'My grandson, you see, he told me that he did not kill that boy.'

Rosa lowered her head, recollecting many similar conversations she'd had with Emmett over the past few weeks. If this was the extent of her 'proof', this meeting was a waste of time.

'Look I might be old, but I'm not stupid,' Joyce continued. 'I know children lie, even us adults, we lie sometimes.
Emmett has told me lies, some important lies, too, but he
didn't kill this boy. He swore *on my life* that he didn't do it.
I am the only real family he has. My boy Emmett would not
swear on my life if he was telling a lie.'

There was no doubt that Joyce believed him. Small tears
trickled down her cheeks, and her eyes widened to stare
firmly at Rosa, awaiting her response.

'I see,' Rosa said, not giving much away. This information
was useless. She believed that Joyce felt sure of his innocence, but that didn't prove anything. All of the evidence
seemed to be pointing to Emmett having murdered Thomas.

'Do you?' Joyce asked. 'He wouldn't lie to me about this.
If he killed that boy, he wouldn't be swearing on my life.
Do you understand?'

Rosa thought about her own relationship with her
grandmother; she couldn't ever imagine swearing on
Nana's life about anything that wasn't true. She didn't
consider herself to be particularly religious or spiritual, but
didn't think it was worth taking a risk. Emmett seemed as
close to his granny as she was to Nana. She did understand,
completely.

The difficulty was, it wasn't her that needed to understand; it was the twelve members of the jury who would
be listening to the evidence in this case in just a few weeks'
time. Emmett's freedom rested in their hands and this oath
sworn on his grandmother's life was unlikely to mean anything to them. She needed something more concrete.

'Is there anything else? Anything else that he said, or anything that you remember happening in the weeks leading up to the incident?'

'There's one more small thing,' Joyce said softly. She looked long and hard at Rosa, assessing whether she could trust her with this information – this was what they were really here for. 'It's probably not relevant but I received an envelope a few weeks ago.'

'Addressed to you?'

'Yes, it was posted through my letterbox. There was no address on the front and no stamp. Just my name. Well, no, not my name. It said "Emmett's grandmother" on the front. That was it.'

'Was there anything in the envelope?' Rosa asked.

Joyce let almost a minute pass before answering.

'Yes. There was.'

'A letter?'

Joyce remained silent.

'Something else? What was inside, Mrs Hamilton?'

Rosa wasn't sure if she was being led down a long path to a dead end, but she knew that right now the evidence was weighted so heavily against Emmett, that he needed any contrary evidence she could find.

'It was money,' Joyce said quietly.

'Money?' Rosa said, failing to mask her surprise. 'How much was it?'

'About £500.' She stopped and glared at Rosa. 'Rosa, you mustn't tell anyone. Please. I've only trusted you with this information.'

'Mrs Hamilton, this could be important information in your grandson's case. We probably ought to tell the police.'

'We can't!'

'They might be able to trace who sent the money. They might even be able to do fingerprint analysis on the envelope or the notes themselves.'

'They won't,' Joyce said gloomily.

Rosa was about to question her answer but stopped herself. Emmett had made clear to her that he was the person who financially provided for his grandmother before going to prison. Since being inside, she was no doubt struggling for money and nobody could blame her for spending it.

'Did you keep the envelope?' Rosa asked, trying to avoid embarrassing Joyce.

'No. That was the first thing to go.' She closed her eyes again and took a deep breath. 'You don't need fingerprints to work out who sent the letter.'

'What do you mean? Do you know who sent it?' Rosa asked, edging forwards as if she could pull the answer from Joyce's lips.

'I have my suspicions.'

'Who do you suspect sent it?'

'There are two boys, the only two of his friends that would know exactly which flat we live in.'

Rosa was leaning so close towards Joyce that she nearly fell off the sofa. She sat back slightly.

'Do you know their names?'

'Tyrone and Jayden. They went to primary school with Emmett. I used to know their mothers. Well, Tyrone's mother was a drug addict and so we haven't seen her for a while. Jayden's mother was doing a fine job until her husband started to be quite physical with her. I always tried to keep Emmett away from them.'

Rosa pulled a pen and notebook from her bag and scribbled down the two names. She looked at her watch and realised she needed to head down to see Emmett. Joyce watched her carefully.

'Rosa, please. You must not say anything. Don't tell Emmett I gave you those names, and definitely don't tell him about the money.'

Rosa put her notebook and pen back in her bag and stood up, swinging her bag over her shoulder.

'Mrs H, I understand. I completely understand. I'm going to see him in the cells now. We will speak soon.'

Rosa hurried down to the court cells, on the way checking her phone. Tristan had sent her a WhatsApp message.

Hey, fancy a drink later?

He was acting like nothing had happened. They'd not spoken since she'd turned up and then left his house last month. He hadn't even texted her to check how she was. This text appeared to suggest she could just snap back into it. She ignored the WhatsApp and shoved her phone into a locker.

The officer guided her to the cell, and another officer brought Emmett in.

Emmett sat down at the table and Rosa noticed that his right hand was slightly shaking. He removed it from the table and sat on it in an attempt to disguise his nerves. His eyes remained low, and he appeared to be biting his lip.

Rosa reached her hands across the table and placed them over Emmett's left hand, which was clenched in a fist. He looked up and locked eyes with her.

'I'm sorry I got so angry before. This is so scary. I honestly still don't know if I made the right decision saying, "Not guilty".' His voice was shaking.

'You did the right thing, Emmett. Apology accepted. Look, I want to help you. I really do.'

Emmett looked at her disbelievingly.

'Emmett, I know you don't want to discuss your friends, but they were with you in the park, could they give evidence on your behalf?'

'No.'

'We could talk to them. I know court is terrifying, but this really could make a difference in your case.'

'I said no. I don't want my friends involved.'

'They'll just be witnesses, Emmett.'

'Look, I don't want to get anyone else into trouble.'

'Why are you protecting Tyrone and Jayden?' Rosa knew that she needed to push him a little bit further. She hadn't thought about how she would explain knowing their names, but she needed him to open up.

Emmett's big brown eyes widened, and he rubbed them before a tear could escape. His jaw dropped slightly ajar before his eyes narrowed into a frown.

'How the fuck do you know those names?'

'Emmett, that's not the main issue here. I need you to focus on answering my question. Why are you protecting them? Do they have something over you?'

Emmett's expression remained perplexed.

'I don't understand. Have they spoken to the police or something? Did the police find them? How do you know their names?' Emmett said, evidently panicking.

'As far as I know, they haven't spoken to the police,' Rosa said calmly, trying to reassure him.

'You didn't get their names from me. Whatever happens, they need to know that!' Emmett exclaimed.

'Can I speak to them?'

'NO! Are you crazy? Do you want me to die?'

A shiver ran down Rosa's spine. Emmett was scared for his life.

'Is there *anything* else you can tell me, Emmett? Anything at all that might help us help you?'

Emmett shook his head.

'I didn't tell you their names.'

CHAPTER 28

Dear Craig,

Please find attached my attendance note for today's PTPH hearing. I have included a record of my conference with Mr Hamilton. I'm not getting much out of him. I think it's important that we find out why he was in the park that day. Perhaps his phone records might tell us something?

I've seen that his phone was seized by the police, and they've presumably taken a download by now. Could you please chase the disclosure of the downloads? This could be crucial evidence.

I've also had another quick look at the Schedule of Unused Material; the police noted the victim had a letter about a loan. I'm wondering if we can get a copy of that. I know it seems like a long shot, but could we have a look into what his financial situation was like?

Sorry, there's so much to chase.

All the best,

Rosa

She clicked send and closed the lid of her laptop, and then placed it into her overnight bag at the end of her bed. She hadn't paid the loan letter much attention until now, assuming that it was just a letter he'd opened on his way out of the house that day, not knowing it would be his last. Having spoken to his flatmates, she realised that it warranted further explanation, she just couldn't tell Craig why.

Rosa slumped on the bed, mentally exhausted, and pulled out her mobile.

Tristan, are you free this evening?

She hadn't replied to Tristan's earlier text. She didn't need him to be her boyfriend, she just wanted to have sex and he was an easy option right now. Plus, the sex with Tristan was good. On any other day Rosa would have deleted his earlier message and forgotten about it, or forwarded it to Orissa to laugh about. But today was different. She needed some relief. She needed an escape.

Tristan had attempted to prepare for Rosa's visit. He had a bottle of red wine breathing and had set out two slightly different-sized wine glasses on the kitchen sideboard with a bowl of crisps that he clearly had begun to nibble.

'Rose, sorry, er, Rosa, I just wanted to say that I'm really sorry for what happened a few weeks ago. It really wasn't wha—'

'I don't care,' Rosa replied curtly. She just wanted to spend a few hours there and then get back home in order to get back to Emmett's case. 'Shall we take the wine upstairs?' she said, beckoning him to the staircase.

Tristan looked pleasantly surprised as he emptied half of the contents of the bottle into the two glasses and handed one to Rosa.

Without much further conversation, they walked upstairs; Tristan caressed the bannister, sliding his long fingers along the shiny wood and Rosa took the familiar first right into his bedroom. He glugged his wine and rested the empty glass on the windowsill.

Rosa sipped her wine and then placed her glass next to Tristan's. She lifted her dress.

'Whoa, whoa, whoa. Now where is the fun in that? Let me do *something*!'

Rosa released the hem of her dress from her fingertips and stood still like a guard at the window. Tristan pounced forwards with his glass in his hand, splashing droplets of red across his cream carpet. Unbothered, he placed the glass on the windowsill too, knocking Rosa's slightly to the side. He wanted to be the star of this show.

They clambered onto the bed. Tristan's now-free hands crept up the underneath of Rosa's dress and fumbled with the top of her lacy knickers until he gripped them securely. Then he yanked them down, slightly scratching Rosa's thigh, then her calf. She didn't move, not even to kick her knickers off from around her ankles. His hand returned to her groin, and he rubbed gently as she relaxed into his mattress. He tried to maintain eye contact, but she closed her eyes and allowed him to explore her with his fingers. It felt good, *really* good.

She wasn't thinking about work, she focused on the physical pleasure increasing in intensity. Those few minutes ended too soon as she let out a loud moan and let her body jolt as she orgasmed. His hands were still engrossed between her thighs.

She opened her eyes and looked down the bed at Tristan who looked pleased with himself. Her eyes wandered beyond him and towards the remains of the worn nail polish glittering under the spotlights, her knickers still loosely clinging to her right ankle.

Tristan unbuttoned his jeans, released the zip, and wiggled his slim buttocks out of the denim. The waistband of his boxer shorts was a slightly discoloured white, but the designer lettering still remained. His erection was visible through the cotton, and he stroked himself admiringly. Rosa closed her eyes and spread her legs while he removed his boxers. His chest pressed down towards hers and his hand dipped between her thighs.

Tristan repositioned himself and entered her body. One. Two. Three. Rosa noticed herself counting each thrust, with a detached objectivity. Again, she opened her eyes and saw Tristan's were now closed. His lips were pursed, and little droplets of sweat gathered on his forehead. Her eyes shut again. She recalled how she'd historically really enjoyed knowing that she'd pleasured Tristan. Now she knew that she was just using him for her own pleasure.

Her thoughts were interrupted by him finishing loudly, almost as quickly as he'd started.

He heaved himself off her and retrieved his boxers from the floor. Rosa reached for her knickers and pulled them up.

'The wine must have really got to me. Sorry, that was so quick.' Tristan clambered into the bed next to her. 'Did you enjoy that? Short but sweet.' He laughed nervously.

Rosa nodded and leaned into his shoulder. She still craved his affection. She lay still for a while, trying to keep Emmett's case out of her mind.

They lay next to each other, and Rosa mindlessly rubbed her hand across his thigh. Her mind revisited her conversation with Emmett's grandmother. She replayed the conversation repeatedly in her head.

A soft snore reverberated next to her. He was asleep already.

Minutes floated by and while Tristan fell into a deeper sleep Rosa gently slid out of the bed. The dress was crumpled on the floor, but she pulled it over her head. Without wasting another second, she crept out of the house and into the darkness.

CHAPTER 29

Tyrone sat nervously in the family and friends visiting area of the prison. There were multiple cameras affixed to the ceiling tiles and the seats were all firmly fixed to the floor. Where he was sitting, the seats aligned in a neat row from one end of the room to the other. They were all blue and plastic. Opposite every three chairs or so, there was a white plastic table and a single orange seat on the other side. The layout suggested that each inmate could have three visitors each. At this white table, the other two blue seats remained empty.

The orange seats were slowly being filled as inmates entered the room and found their loved ones. Tyrone sat and watched as partners reunited, and family members brought chocolate, crisps and other snacks from the tuck shop.

Eventually, Emmett was brought through and invited to sit at the orange seat opposite him.

The two boys barely greeted each other, and a minute passed before either of them spoke. Emmett was still surprised, and slightly worried, that Tyrone had booked this visit. He still didn't know how Rosa knew Tyrone and Jayden's names.

'Why haven't any of you come to see me? It's 4 October. I've been here a month!' Emmett asked through gritted teeth. He was trying desperately hard not to reveal his upset.

'I'm here now, aren't I?' Tyrone smiled, and then stopped when he realised it wasn't reciprocated.

'What do you want?' Emmett asked coldly.

'I'm just here to check you're OK,' Tyrone lied unconvincingly.

Emmett sat back in his chair and crossed his legs in front of him. He folded his arms and narrowed his eyes. They both knew that wasn't why Tyrone was here.

'OK, look, bro,' Tyrone continued. 'You know how it is. I need to make sure that you aren't going to mention us to anyone. No snitching. Not sure if you got my message.'

'Your message? What are you talking about? You're sending me threats in prison?' A security officer glared at Emmett, who was now visibly upset. He lowered his volume, 'You're my brothers, my longest friends. Or so I thought . . . ' Emmett's voice trailed off.

'We are, we always will be. But I'm serious, bro. You cannot mention us, not even to your lawyer.' Tyrone leaned in so close that Emmett could smell his candy-like cologne. His voice was almost menacing. Again, Emmett mentally questioned what he knew – that this was someone he would have trusted his life to just a couple of months ago.

Despite his anxiety, Emmett glared at him. The one thing

he knew not to risk was being deemed a snitch. He'd had enough problems at the old prison, he didn't need those problems here, or when he got out. He hoped it was *when* he got out, not *if.*

Tyrone could sense that there was something different about Emmett. He seemed less fearful, less vulnerable.

'Look, you know I don't want to make threats and that, but just remember we know where Mrs H is.' He spoke with less conviction than he intended.

'You wouldn't dare!' Emmett scowled.

'Nah, bro, look. If you make sure our names are kept out of your mouth, then there won't be any problems. Orders from above.'

The boys returned to sitting quietly. The tension was suffocating.

'It wasn't supposed to happen like this, bro,' said Tyrone, placatingly. 'Why didn't you run?'

'Because there was a man dying on the floor.'

Both boys sat stiffly. A prison officer hovered nearby, and then walked on.

'Look. I don't know what happened, bro. I just know that knife wasn't meant to be used,' Tyrone whispered. 'We were only supposed to be scaring him.'

'Scaring who?' Emmett asked. 'The man who is now dead?'

'If it makes you feel any better, I've heard that the man – Thomas Dove – was a dealer, he owed the wrong people money. He was trying to sell on the estate.'

'He was a drug dealer? And that's supposed to make me feel better?'

197

'Keep your voice down!' Tyrone snapped. 'Look, that's all I know. I wish I could be more help.'

'Be more help? Bro, my life is ruined. You've ruined it.'

Tyrone unexpectedly chuckled to himself, as though Emmett's suggestion was funny. 'Bro, I saved your life. Don't ever forget it. You owed me.'

He stood up and indicated he was ready to go. He walked towards the door.

'And so, what, now I just do your dirty work for the rest of my life?' Emmett called out angrily.

CHAPTER 30

I t had been exactly four weeks since Rosa had visited the hospital with Nana. Rosa was still struggling to process it, and Nana refused to talk about it. She'd prepared breakfast for Nana and Toby, knowing that Nana often now felt too tired to prepare meals, and she'd noticed that Nana had barely eaten any of it.

Over the past few weeks, Rosa had tried to just dedicate herself to preparing for the trial, which was at the end of the month. She didn't feel ready. There were lots of missing pieces.

Emmett had no explanation for why he was in the park that day, but he was clearly covering for his friends – Tyrone and Jayden – about whom he still refused to talk. She'd spent weeks trying to track them down, looking on social media for people with the same name from the same area with Emmett as a mutual friend, but it was futile. Emmett appeared to rarely use social media, and both Tyrone and Jayden proved to be popular names. Rosa knew she had to be discreet, and a failure to do so might compromise Emmett's safety. That made the task of finding these two men even more impossible.

Most nights she worked on her case theory, trying to nail down the story she'd be inviting the jury to accept. She'd stayed up late, trying to piece together a possible link between Emmett and the victim. She'd got nowhere. She couldn't understand what possible link there could be between a nurse and Emmett. Rosa had requested his medical records to be disclosed, and she'd received them. He hadn't been in hospital or received any medical treatment that would have led to their paths crossing. The closest link was that they both lived in Walthamstow, but their addresses were on opposite sides of what was essentially a fairly big suburb, and Rosa could not see them coming into contact with one another.

'Why is Nana not taking me to school anymore?' Toby asked, as Rosa helped him pull his school jumper over his head.

'She's just feeling quite tired at the moment,' Rosa replied, not knowing what more she could say. The advantage of focusing mostly on case preparation was that she had the time to help Nana out with dropping Toby to school and picking him up. 'Go and give Nana a kiss, it's time to go.'

Rosa decided to take Toby on a longer route to school; they'd left earlier than usual, and Rosa wanted to walk through the park. She'd walked through the park many times since Thomas had been murdered and was yet to think of anything new, but she hadn't given up hope.

Toby clutched Rosa's hand as they walked down the path across the park. As they reached the middle, where Thomas was murdered, Rosa slowed the pace and looked around as though searching for missing clues. Toby let go of her hand and sprinted ahead.

'Sady, look at how fast I am!'

'Very fast but come back here, please!' she called out after him. Obediently, he sprinted back.

'Can you record me, Sady? I want to show Nana how fast I am now.' His eyes lit up as he spoke and tried to catch his breath.

Rosa pulled out her phone and pressed the camera on. She recorded him sprinting twenty metres ahead and then spinning around and returning to her. She saved the video and put her phone away. She remembered that the last video she'd seen from this park was on the news when Thomas had died, and she had seen Nana's block of flats in the background. She'd not actually seen any mobile phone video footage, which she suddenly realised was strange, given how many people were likely to have been in the park that day. Emmett had asked her to check CCTV, but she hadn't checked for videos that the public might have made.

Having returned home after dropping Toby at school, Rosa sat at the kitchen table, conscious not to disturb Nana, who had gone back to bed. She began to search social media posts, limiting her search to the day of the murder and subsequent days, and looking for geotagged videos in the vicinity of the park. She added search words and phrases such as 'murder', 'police', 'Walthamstow Park' and 'stabbing'.

After an hour of searching, there didn't appear to be much.

Most of the videos were related to other things entirely. Rosa had only found two that appeared to be relevant in some way. One was a two-minute video of a man speaking to a camera saying that he was just in the park where a man had been stabbed. It had thousands of likes, but as Rosa read the caption on the video, it became clear that the man hadn't seen anything at all but had walked into the park once the paramedics had already arrived.

The other video was longer, about thirty minutes. It appeared to show the immediate aftermath of the incident until the paramedics arrived. It was posted from an anonymous account with the handle @PinkFairyTeeth3481. The creator of the video had also added to the caption that they hadn't witnessed the incident but heard screaming, and when they came over, they saw a man lying on the ground bleeding. The video was mostly a moving image of the grass, where it appeared the creator had just held their phone in their hands, with no effort to ensure the quality of the footage. There were only two moments in which the footage showed something more substantial.

One was of when the paramedics arrived, one of their faces caught on camera in a very unflattering pose. The second was during a small flurry of activity very close to the beginning of the video. There was a lot of screaming and a woman appeared to be running away from the camera, covering her eyes. It was impossible to properly make out her face. Rosa took a screenshot of this image and tried to zoom in. Her hair was dark and curly, and she was wearing a distinctive bright yellow and orange outfit.

This could be a potential witness.

Rosa's phone began to ring.

'H-h-hello,' she answered in a stumbling whisper.

'Rosa. It's Craig. Everything OK?'

Rosa scraped Nana's uneaten breakfast into the bin, holding her mobile phone between her head and shoulder.

'Craig. Hello! Is everything OK with you?'

'Yes, sorry, I meant to call yesterday but you know how it is, I have a million and one things on my to-do list.'

'No worries at all.' Rosa's voice conveyed the confusion she felt. She tried to rinse the plate as quietly as possible.

'Look. I'll be quick. There's some new evidence.'

'They've served the phone downloads?'

'Not yet, no. Sorry. But there's going to be a case-management hearing on Friday to chase them. We've finally got the forensics on the knife! Not sure what took quite so long. Apparently the officer in the case has been away long-term sick, and they've had to find a replacement. Anyway, luckily, I've managed to get us a video conference today, there's been a cancellation. I thought we might as well snap it up, we need as much time as we can with him. I'm praying you can be free for it?'

'OK, yes, sure. I'm off today. I'll head to the offices.' She heard relief in Craig's exhale. She could tell him about the possible witness in person.

CHAPTER 31

Rosa arrived at the door of Craig's office building at 11 a.m. on Wednesday 11 October, clutching two coffees. The building was glass-fronted but the door to the left was wooden and painted in pale green paint that had chipped over the years. The buzzer on the intercom rang loudly and she was invited inside.

'Good morning. Can I have your name, please?'

'It's Rosa, Rosa Higgins, I'm here to see—'

'Ah Rosa, you're here!' Craig's familiar voice bellowed down the hallway.

The receptionist shuffled some paper labels through a printer, which rattled and hissed and then stopped. She nudged it and it whirred again. Then stopped.

'Don't worry about a label, Lisa, she'll be fine with me.' Craig had reached the front desk and was peering over at the little machine. 'Speak to Max in IT. He should be able to help you fix it.' Lisa blushed pink.

'Rosa. Great to see you. Thanks for coming here. It's a result we managed to get a video con with the prison.'

Rosa nodded in agreement and handed him his coffee.

'Ah, thank you.' He placed it on the reception counter. 'Shall we get cracking? Let's get set up.'

He led the way to his personal office, abandoning the coffee. Well, that was a waste of money, she thought. His name was engraved into a small metal plaque above the door.

Craig's paralegal, Kate, was waiting for them. She was clad in a black pinafore and crisp white shirt, which reminded Rosa of her old school uniform. Her black loafers were freshly polished.

'Rosa, here we go.' Craig diverted Rosa's gaze to a small pile of paper on his desk. Rosa glanced at the top page – it was the forensic report.

'I printed a copy this morning, to read it proper—' he began to explain.

'What does it say?' she interjected.

'All sorted, it's just dialling in the prison now,' Kate interrupted chirpily. Without waiting for a response, she grinned and left briskly.

Rosa scanned the report as Craig positioned himself around the desktop computer to that they were both visible in the webcam preview image. She stopped at the findings.

Emmett's prints were on the knife.

'Good mornin', it's HMP Pentonville. How can we help?' A chubby-faced man wearing a security uniform greeted them.

'Yes, good morning. Have you got Emmett Hamilton there, please?' Craig shouted at the screen.

'Yeah. Gimme two seconds and we'll grab him for ya.'

The man exited through a plain windowless door. The room remained empty for a few seconds. The walls and floor were icy white and blended into one. The only thing that gave depth to the image was the school-like desk bolted to the middle of the floor and the plastic chair behind it.

Rosa reread the report's findings. There was no doubt that they had found Emmett's fingerprints on the knife. They'd also found another set of fingerprints, but they were of too poor a quality to be matched to anyone. Probably Joyce, Rosa thought.

Emmett was brought into the room; the security guard left and locked the door.

The room, and hence the screen, was bright, and Emmett's soft brown complexion stood out as he walked to the seat. He pulled out the chair and the screech of the metal legs against the floor rang through the speakers. None of his actions were rushed: he moved cautiously and slowly as though time was dictated by him. His body folded into the chair and over the desk. His head fell heavily into his palms. Sluggishly he lifted it and clasped his fingers together on the desk.

'Emmett, good morning, I'll cut straight to it.' Craig retrieved the paper copy of the forensic report from Rosa. 'There are two things we need to talk about today. There has been a significant update, and you have a hearing this week.' Craig spoke quickly, as though battling Emmet's earlier pace.

Emmett stared blankly at the camera, awaiting the revelation.

'OK. First, the forensic report on the knife has come back. Your prints are on the knife.'

'What does that mean?'

Craig looked at Rosa in disbelief. Rosa tried to assist.

'Emmett, did you touch the knife?'

'Well, I must have if my fingerprints are on it,' he said sarcastically.

'Did you take the knife to the park?'

'Nah.'

'So, someone else brought it to the park?' Craig chimed in.

'Well, they must have,' Emmett replied. His tone was unrecognisable. There was an arrogance in his voice Rosa hadn't heard before. 'I had the knife. That doesn't mean I killed him.'

Craig took charge, recognising Rosa's disappointment. 'Shall we talk about the hearing? I think we need to perhaps have a separate conversation – without Rosa.' He glared at Emmett.

'Why?' he responded, concerned.

'Emmett, the forensics are what they are, and we don't have much time. There's still the hearing this week. We're chasing your phone records, which the Crown Prosecution Service still haven't provided us.'

Rosa's mind had wandered into the various ways in which Emmett might have been more involved in this murder than he had initially presented. He had the knife in his hand, the knife that killed an innocent man. He wouldn't discuss his friends Tyrone and Jayden. What else was going to come out? She felt taken for a fool.

'Rosa?' Craig said loudly. 'Rosa? Is there anything else?'

Rosa's thoughts were clouded and troubling, but she packaged them into a box and put them to the side. She had to remain professional, for both Craig and Emmett.

'Yes, actually, there is,' she replied. 'Emmett, do you remember there being a woman in the park that day, dressed in a very bright yellow and orange outfit? Maybe a uniform.'

Craig cocked his head, confused about the line of questioning.

'I don't think so, er ... I don't know. I can't really remember.'

'She had curly hair?'

'Not sure, do you have a picture?'

'Hmm. Only this I'm afraid.' She unlocked her phone and retrieved the screenshot from her photos. She held it up to the camera, hopeful that the picture could be seen on his screen.

'I really can't see much.'

The silence hung in the air eerily as he squinted at the screen.

'Anything, Emmett, anything at all that could help you? A new witness might help to prove that you're inno—' Rosa stopped herself, remembering that his prints were on the knife. 'It might help to show your version of events.' In her mind she pressed down on the packaged box of distracting thoughts, holding it shut.

Emmett tapped on the table impatiently.

'So, what if I did remember her?' he said between taps. 'You clearly don't believe what I'm saying anyway.'

Rosa inhaled, paused, and exhaled softly. 'It's not about what I believe, Emmett. My job is to represent you in the best way I can.'

They looked at each other through the screen. They were physically miles apart but that look created an intimacy between them, as though they were sitting just centimetres from each other.

'Right, OK?' Craig said loudly. Rosa half held her hand up to acknowledge his presence and returned to Emmett.

'Do you know anything else, Emmett?' she repeated.

Emmett shook his head and completely shut down.

'Wait, let me have a quick look,' Craig said. Rosa handed him her phone and he squinted at the screen. 'Look I wouldn't be too sure, but it looks like some kind of cleaning uniform to me. That or catering. There's a little apron at the front. Rosa surely you'd recognise a—' Craig stopped himself but it was too late. Of course, she should recognise a cleaning uniform. Nana was a cleaner after all.

'Mmm,' she murmured through gritted teeth. 'Well, perhaps Kate starts calling local cleaning companies and catering companies to try to get a match for the uniform?'

CHAPTER 32

I t was Friday morning, nearly the weekend and just a week before the trial, and the court usher was inviting everyone into the courtroom. Rosa had woken up feeling terrible on Orissa's fairly uncomfortable sofa. They'd had a wonderful evening in to celebrate Orissa's birthday, and while most of Orissa's friends had left by midnight, Rosa had drunk too much and hadn't wanted the night to end. Apparently, however, she didn't quite have the stamina for all-night drinking anymore and was currently in the robing room suffering from a throbbing headache.

For once there didn't appear to be much public interest today. Perhaps the press hadn't advertised this hearing, or perhaps they just didn't know. Either way Rosa was grateful to not have to put on such a performance today.

She entered the courtroom and took her place closest to the empty jury seating. Her opponent, Mr Pankhurst, also took his seat.

The courtroom was quiet and Rosa embraced the few minutes of silence, giving herself a moment to think through some of the discrepancies in the case. She still could not figure out how Emmett and Thomas were connected. The only loose connection she could make out was that Tanya Williams, Emmett's school teacher, distantly knew Mark McEvoy, one of the witnesses, but that didn't have much bearing on the case. They both lived locally, after all.

The familiar rattling sound of the jailor's keys filled the quiet as the back door of the dock was unlocked and Emmett was brought in.

Mr Pankhurst pulled out a bottle of water. Anticipating that the judge was about to enter, he tipped the nearly full contents of the bottle into his mouth, glugging down the liquid at an alarming rate. His cheeks bulged with the last mouthful as the usher knocked at the judicial door.

'All rise!' the usher bellowed unnecessarily loudly. Mr Pankhurst swallowed and tried to subtly put the plastic bottle on the floor. Both he and Rosa stood, and the fold-up chairs flipped up behind them.

The judge strode theatrically into the courtroom in his ancient robes and sat down, Rosa and Mr Pankhurst followed suit.

'Calling on the case of Emmett Hamilton – are you Emmett Hamilton?' the clerk's voice boomed through the courtroom.

'Yes, miss,' he replied. Emmett was the only person in the room still standing.

'You may be seated,' the judge, HHJ Douglas KC, said. 'Mr Pankhurst, where are we?'

'My Lord, well ... erm ... I appear for the prosecution and my learned friend, Ms ... erm ... '

'It's Ms Higgins. Yes, I know who everyone is, please let's just get on with it. I asked a very direct question, where are we?' The judge raised his eyebrows mockingly.

'Well, yes, of course. Sorry.'

'Please don't apologise, just *please*, Mr Pankhurst, get on with it.'

'Yes, yes, sorry, I mean.' The prosecutor fumbled with his laptop and switched between multiple tabs on his browser. 'Sorry. Just one second.'

'Ms Higgins, can *you* help me?' the judge asked impatiently. 'I have an extremely busy list today.'

Rosa stood up, feeling like a teacher's pet.

'Yes, My Lord, this is a case management hearing listed to deal with the Crown's non-disclosure of the telephone records and the—'

'One thing at a time, Ms Higgins!' the judge shouted. Rosa's warm feeling slipped away as quickly as it had arisen. The prosecutor sat down. 'Mr Pankhurst, don't sit down yet, have you got yourself together now? Where are the telephone records?'

Rosa sat. They were up and down like yo-yos. Mr Pankhurst stood back up and wiped sweat from his forehead. He jiggled the wig on his head into place. What *was* up with him this morning?

'My Lord, the telephone records were uploaded to the digital case system by the CPS at, erm ... 9.57 a.m. this morning.'

212

The judge scowled at the prosecutor. His lips wrinkled as he pushed them outwards into a pout.

'And does the CPS think that uploading documents three minutes before a hearing is due to start is acceptable?'

'No, sorry, My Lord. I will pass it on.'

'Yes, you most certainly will. It's simply not good enough.'

The judge shook his head and his fountain pen twitched in his hand as he wrote a note.

'Right. OK. What's next? I'll ask Ms Higgins, shall I?'

Rosa stood back up and the prosecutor see-sawed with her, returning to his seat.

'Also we haven't received the previous convictions of the witnesses in this case,' Rosa said politely, hoping not to upset the judge any further.

'Mr Pankhurst?' The judge's eyebrows were raised so high that Rosa thought they might blend into his hairline.

The prosecutor appeared to have regained some confidence.

'They were also uploaded this morning. I appreciate that my learned friend may not have seen that yet,' he responded calmly.

'Well, of course not,' the judge snarled. He flicked his pen up and down in his notebook. 'Ms Higgins, is there anything else?' he asked, as though exhausted already by this hearing.

'No, thank you, My Lord.'

'Mr Pankhurst, anything else?' The judge did not look up from his notebook as he addressed him.

'Yes, the Crown has made an application for special measures for the witnesses.'

The judge nodded. 'Yes, I've seen those.'

Mr Pankhurst seemed unsure as to whether to continue. The judge turned to Rosa.

'And the application is opposed, isn't it, Ms Higgins, for the reasons you've set out in your response?'

Rosa rose to her feet again. 'Yes, My Lord.' The prosecution had asked for screens in court for the witnesses – screens always made a case slightly more difficult. Witnesses always seemed a little more convincing when they received the protection of a screen. And it made a defendant look a little more dangerous.

'OK, anything else either of you would like to add, bearing in mind I've read both documents.'

Both advocates shook their heads and resumed a seated position.

'Right, well, I'll be granting the special measures applications. Both witnesses will have screens while giving their evidence.'

Rosa clenched her jaw.

'Thank you both. That concludes today's hearing. The defendant remains remanded in custody.'

CHAPTER 33

Rosa left the courtroom; unusually, she was by herself. Craig hadn't attended court today. He'd emailed her this morning, sending her a short update on Thomas's loans – they had totalled almost £10,000 but had all been settled, by him, shortly before his death. There was nothing else that he was able to find out.

Kate, the paralegal, had been sent along in Craig's place, but for some unknown reason she had crept out of the courtroom before the hearing concluded. Rosa snuck into an empty conference room and opened her laptop.

She typed her username and password into the Digital Case System and scrolled to the recent uploads. A short summary document was uploaded as well as the raw data. It highlighted the text messages the Crown hoped to rely on. She scrolled through them with a rising sense of panic and fury.

These messages were going to destroy her case.

She slammed her hands against the table in frustration.

'Rosa! I've been looking for you!' Kate said, bursting into

the conference room. Rosa exited the document. 'Sorry, I was late this morning. I don't know if you saw me come in, but I was sitting at the back for most of that and I think I've got a decent note.' Her apology was genuine. 'Shall I come with you to the cells?'

Rosa nodded politely, packed away her laptop, and they walked out of the room towards the locked door.

The familiar stale odour of the cells permeated their noses and Kate crinkled her face. They took a seat in the cells' interview room, both pulling out their laptops. Kate was ready to take a note and Rosa opened up the phone downloads.

Emmett was brought in and took a seat on the other side of the desk.

'As you will have heard, we have the phone downloads,' Rosa said slowly as she closed and reopened the document, which wasn't loading.

'What, so you know what calls I made?' He paused. 'Can you read my text messages too?' Emmett asked nervously. Apparently, Craig hadn't told him that this would be happening.

'Yes, we can,' Rosa replied in a dry voice. 'Did you provide your pin number to the police?'

'Yeah, they told me that they'd charge me with another offence if I didn't.'

Kate tapped away, recording every word of the conversation.

'Well, they might have,' Rosa said. 'In any event, they have your unlocked phone, and we now have the messages.' She locked eyes with him. 'Is there anything you want to say?'

Emmett looked like he was trying to ascertain whether she was bluffing. 'Like what?'

'Emmett, why were you in the park that day?'

'I told you already,' he said. 'I just was. There was no reason.'

'Are you sure?' Rosa said, wishing that she wasn't slightly enjoying this game of cat and mouse.

'Er, yeah. I think so. I can't really remember,' he said, his position slightly shifting.

'Well, shall we try? It's important that you're honest with me. I'm trying to help you.'

'I'm being honest!' His voice was raised, and he sounded increasingly anxious. 'What am I lying about? I just was there. There was no reason. I've told you that.'

Rosa knew that she shouldn't be cross-examining her own client, but she needed to get to the bottom of this.

'So, no one told you to be there?' she asked.

'No.'

'And you're sure about that?'

'Yes, I'm sure,' Emmett said, now fidgeting with his fingers. 'What *is* this?' He looked to Kate for assistance, but she kept her head low behind the laptop and continued to type.

'So, if we look through your phone, we won't find any messages telling you to be at the park that day.'

Emmett narrowed his eyes and kissed his teeth.

'I've answered the same question so many times. Just get to the point if you have one.'

She pulled up the relevant message on her laptop screen. She twisted her screen to face Emmett.

I don't want to be involved in this. *Outgoing message to number ending 738. Sent at 06.03 a.m.*

We could get into so much trouble Ty. *Outgoing message to number ending 738. Sent at 06.17 a.m.*

She scrolled further down the page.

You gonna bring it yeah big man? *Incoming message from number ending 738. Received at 05.55 a.m.*

It'll be a quick in and out. Don't stress bro. *Incoming message from number ending 738. Received at 06.14 a.m.*

We got you bro. Will text you where to go. *Incoming message from number ending 738. Received at 06.19 a.m.*

Don't let us down. *Incoming message from number ending 738. Received at 06.20 a.m.*

Emmett read the final message a few times but said nothing. He barely moved.

Rosa tapped her fingers on the desk, which was the only

sound in the room since Kate had stopped typing. Emmett let out a huge sigh.

'Emmett,' Rosa said after a minute or two. 'Emmett, you said nobody told you to be at the park.'

'OK,' Emmett said softly.

'It's not OK, Emmett. This is serious. You've been charged with murder. I'm your lawyer. Your trial is in ten days!' Rosa tried not to overplay her importance but knew that she was the best bet Emmett had of regaining his freedom. 'Emmett, you're not being honest with me.'

'OK,' he said again, this time more rigidly.

'Who told you to be at the park?' Rosa leaned in and whispered the question, as though inviting Emmett to share this secret with her.

'I don't know.'

'Emmett, that's not true. You do know.' Rosa's voice became more agitated as she started to lose her patience.

'Do I?'

Rosa pulled her laptop back towards her and clicked on the string of messages she'd read moments earlier. She enlarged them on her screen and turned it back to face Emmett.

Emmett stared blankly at Kate, who was oblivious to his gaze. Eventually she looked up and smiled awkwardly but then returned her attention to her note.

'Look here!' Rosa demanded. 'Is Ty referring to Tyrone, your friend?'

Emmett stood up. 'Fuck this. Who the fuck are you talking to?' He crashed his hands down on the table and both

219

laptops bounced upwards, then he stepped towards the door and banged on the glass.

'Guard. Guard. We're done here. Let me out.'

Kate continued to type, recording every little detail.

CHAPTER 34

Emmett's block was long and rectangular, with pale blue cell doors running along each of the long sides. He slid his hands along the bright yellow railings that ran parallel to the cell doors and walked towards the only two small windows at the end of the walkway. Stopping outside his cell, he ran his fingers along his waistband, feeling for his concealed razorblade.

'You good, bro?' Mo asked as Emmett entered the cell.

'Been better,' Emmett replied. He dropped his body to the floor dramatically and began to do some press-ups.

'That's all you can do, bro,' Mo said. 'I heard people saying you're fucked if you don't buss case because they'll go hard on your sentence. Your case is all over the new—'

Before Mo could finish his sentence, Emmett had jumped to his feet and pushed him up against the wall.

'Bruv, don't you ever come at me with that shit again! You don't know shit about my trial and I don't want to fucking hear it.'

'Uh, uh, OK, bro,' Mo said, panting. 'I'm sorry, bro, what the fuck. I'm sorry.'

Emmett felt his waistband for the blade again, rubbed his forefinger over it. But then he froze. *What was he doing?* He released his grip on Mo and stepped back.

'I'll be going home,' he said, as though trying to convince himself.

Emmett could already feel his stomach rumbling, despite having eaten only a few hours ago. The prison meal schedule included an early breakfast, a cold lunch at 12 p.m. and a hot meal at 4 p.m. It was 3 p.m., which meant it was time to exercise, but all he could think about was the chicken and onion pie that he knew was on the menu tonight. The food was poor quality, but he'd surprised himself how quickly he'd grown accustomed to it.

He approached one of the metal pull-up bars stationed in the concrete yard. For forty-five minutes every day he and the other men on his block were entitled to roam around in a grey, lifeless cage – and told they should be grateful for the privilege of getting some fresh air. Emmett tried to use the opportunity to work out. There was no way to properly work out in his cell, but out here they'd put equipment in place – a few pull-up bars and dip bars and even a sit-up bench.

Emmett placed his hands in a firm grip over the bar, clenched his eyes shut and pulled the weight of his body up until his chin was above the bar. This motion was a lot easier now than it had been two months ago when he'd first arrived.

Something felt strange about their recreational time today. It was as though everyone was whispering, planning something. He didn't know what, but the feeling wasn't good. His biceps bulged as he pulled his head up above the bar again – this time with his eyes wide open.

Within seconds, the calm of the yard erupted into commotion. One man knocked another to the floor and thumped him repeatedly. The perpetrator was bald with a huge tattoo on the back of his scalp. He went by the name 'Cutz' and he ran the drugs supply on Emmett's block. Although Emmett hadn't ever spoken to him directly, he and everyone else knew not to mess around with him. The man on the floor, who Emmett couldn't properly make out, had spindly, thin legs and writhed on his back like a cockroach trying to escape being killed.

'Emmett! Help me, please!' the man on the floor called out. Emmett questioned whether he had heard that right. *Was the person calling out for him?*

He dropped down from the bar, stepped forwards and squinted, trying to see who was cowering, calling for him like a frightened child. He didn't have any friends in this place.

'Emmett! Please,' the man screamed, wheezing in between words.

It was Mo.

People were now turning to look at Emmett. He glared back at them.

Very slowly, he stepped back and reached for the push-up bar, closed his eyes, and heaved himself up. His body felt heavy this time, and his eyes remained firmly shut.

An alarm sounded and guards approached Mo, stopping the other man from beating him to a pulp.

Emmett, arms quaking, realising he'd been holding himself up for far too long, let himself drop back down and followed everyone else back to their cells.

CHAPTER 35

Rosa woke up on Saturday morning in a foul mood. Emmett had lied to her face. She'd spent the week trying to perfect her case but felt as though there was little use. Everything he was saying could be a lie, and in just a few days she'd be trying to defend him in a murder trial. She couldn't imagine a less desirable position.

She sat up in bed and tugged her duvet closer to her waist, forming a mermaid-like skirt. It was duck-egg blue and faded, having been washed too many times. Lever arch files were sprawled over it like large ships in a small sea, and she was careful not to knock them to the floor as she pulled. She reached forwards and to the right, robotically, balancing carefully as she outstretched her arms to pinch her laptop from her open handbag. Like a skilled fisherman she pulled it slowly upwards and on to her lap, collapsing backwards into her headboard.

She opened the laptop; the dark screen flashed white, and then flashed again, displaying a photograph of her, Nana and Toby at Christmas. The laptop screen was dusty, which she worsened as she smeared her fingertips across the screen to clear it. Her fingers darted across the keypad as she entered her password and then hit the enter key. The screen flashed again.

The text message downloads had been left open on her browser. It was peculiar, reading a person's messages; most were mundane. She'd learned so much more about Emmett by reading them, so much more about who he really was. Unsurprisingly, she'd confirmed that he was particularly close to his grandmother, who he messaged regularly to tell her he loved her. Almost every single day, in fact – the only day she could see where there wasn't an outgoing message to his grandma was on the day of the murder.

Emmett also didn't appear to have many friends, something else Rosa felt they had in common. He played football every Sunday, which was organised by a group text and cost £5 to play – she was finding out things that she didn't even need to know. It was a draining process, trying to filter the messages into what was relevant and what was not when she didn't really know what could be useful in the quickly approaching case.

'Rosa, yuh wan breakfast?' Nana called out from the kitchen. Nana was apparently feeling energetic this morning.

'I'm OK, Nana, thank you,' she called out back. 'I'm just working.' She hoped her response would indicate that she didn't want to be disturbed.

Returning her attention to the screen, she focused on the messages highlighted by the Crown.

There was something odd about the messages from 'Ty',

who must be Tyrone. All of the messages were sent and received on the same day. Either they hadn't exchanged any messages before this day, or they had all been deleted. Rosa sensed that it was more likely to be the latter but couldn't work out why he'd delete these messages unless he was worried someone might read them. Perhaps he intended to delete these ones too but, being arrested at the scene, he hadn't had enough time. She scrolled to the highlighted sections.

I don't want to be involved in this.

We could get into so much trouble ty.

Emmett was undoubtedly involved in whatever 'this' was. He'd lied to her, to Craig, clearly also to his grandmother. He knew more than he was letting on.

You gonna bring it yeah big man? *Incoming message from number ending 738. Received at 05.55 a.m.*

That must be the knife. Tyrone had asked him to bring the knife to the park that day. The tone conveyed superiority, as though the question were more rhetorical then actual. Or, Rosa considered, was she still trying to persuade herself that Emmett was innocent in the face of damning evidence? He'd explicitly told her that he hadn't taken the knife to the park.

It'll be a quick in and out. Don't stress bro.
Incoming message from number ending 738.
Received at 06.14 a.m.

What would be in and out? A cold shiver trickled through Rosa's spine as she pictured the knife plunging into the man's flesh, in and out, quickly. Surely not ... she shook her head and tried to ground herself. She was thinking like a police officer or a prosecutor and felt slightly disappointed that she'd leapt to such a conclusion. There were multiple innocent explanations: it could just have meant that he was planning on arriving and leaving quickly, and she reminded herself that she didn't even know that these particular messages were related to the murder in the park.

Rosa stretched out her legs and flexed her toes. They poked out of the bottom of her duvet, she noticed the chipped nail polish and quickly withdrew them back underneath the cover. Her back was beginning to hurt, sitting perpendicular against the headboard. She tilted her neck to each side and lowered her shoulders down and back to stretch each of the muscles. Slowly, she tilted her head backwards and let out a low moan of relief as the pain temporarily subsided. She turned her attention back to the messages.

The three black letters of 'bro' now stood out against the white screen. *Don't stress bro.* It struck her that the familiar address would be something the prosecutor would lap up. In the face of an ignorant jury, 'bro' might signify a close relationship – a brotherhood. Rosa knew better, but that rarely mattered. Memories of her teenage years floated through her mind, as she recalled how almost everyone that she went to school with used 'bro' as a pronoun for another male. Sometimes she'd even heard it being used for women – she'd been called 'bro' a few times. The word didn't symbolise great affection in Rosa's eyes. She'd done multiple cases where 'bro' was used with hostility. 'What you got for me, bro?' was something she'd heard repeated in street muggings, as if scripted.

Why wouldn't Emmett speak to her about these men? It didn't make any sense: if he wasn't guilty then the most obvious thing to do would be to tell her what situation he'd got himself into so that perhaps, just maybe, she'd be able to help him out of it. But, by staying silent, he was making this trial so much more difficult. It wasn't going to be hard for the jury, with these messages, to reach the conclusion that Emmett was the person who took the knife to the park – the knife that murdered this man – and that was only one small step away from deeming him the murderer and finding him guilty.

Even if he wasn't the person who physically put the knife into Thomas Dove's chest, he'd clearly played a significant part in his murder. He'd been party to the murder plan. He brought along the weapon. If he was willing to take a weapon, he might have even been capable of using it. Rosa tried to slow down her thoughts but was struggling.

We got you bro. Will text you where to go.
Incoming message from number ending 738.
Received at 06.19 a.m.

'We got you bro' – yes, he was involved as much as they were. She was certain that there was an undertone of trust. These men were friends.

Don't let us down. *The incoming message received on Emmett's phone at 06.20 a.m.*

'Emmett. Come on, come on. Give me something. If you didn't do it, help me help you. Don't let *me* down!' Rosa whispered to herself with exasperated breath.

Her phone began to ring. Rosa scrambled through the files on her bed in search of it.

'Hey Ro—, just want— to che— in. The CP— have just email— and want to know if—met is consid—ing plea—' Craig said.

It sounded as though he was jogging while talking and it was difficult to hear him as the wind gushed around his phone. Rosa tried to piece the words together.

'Craig, Craig, I can barely hear you!'

'T— t— sec—' The line fell silent, as the call ended. Rosa waited patiently. The phone rang again.

'Hello, hello, can you hear me?' It was much clearer now. The wind was a distant purr.

'Yes, thank you.'

'Did you catch what I said? The CPS have asked whether Emmett is considering pleading; they want to know whether the trial is going to be effective.'

'I see. Well, right now I'm really not sure. Craig, to be honest, I am a little concerned. Have you seen the messages?'

'Oh yes, no doubt our kid probably did it – but that's not our job to decide, is it? I think we go ahead with the trial. We've got to give him a good shot.' Rosa allowed silence to consume the space in Craig's pause. 'Oh, Rosa, come on! You know as well as I do that if we were upset every time that we had a gut feeling our client was in fact guilty, we'd never sleep at night.'

She imagined Craig's chirpy eyes and mocking grin, but it was quickly replaced in her mind by Emmett's desperate eyes and hardened frown.

'Have we taken instructions on whether anyone else had access to his phone?' she asked.

'No, but come on, let's be realistic. Do you really think that's the journey we want to take the jury on?'

'No, you're right.' Rosa sighed heavily, embarrassed by her desperate attempt.

'Ha, I know I'm right! Honestly, the trial is due to start in just over a week, and he's refused to have any more video conferences with us. The phone download really does change things, but look, we can only do so much!'

They ended the phone call with polite goodbyes and Rosa flicked her phone across the bed, just as it began to ring again. She retrieved it – an unknown number. Her finger hovered over the red decline button, but she suddenly and unexpectedly changed her mind, and swiped to answer.

'Er, hi!' she exclaimed, more enthusiastically than she intended. An automated voice informed her that she was receiving a call from HMP Bronzefield. She waited, giving her consent for the call to be connected.

'Rosa. It's me, Mum.'

'Oh – oh right – Mum.' The word still sounded strange on her tongue. 'Is everything OK?'

'Well, don't sound too enthusiastic to hear from me,' her mum chuckled to herself, her hoarse voice grating in Rosa's ears. 'I'm calling about Nana.' Her laughter stopped immediately.

'What about her?' Rosa felt herself becoming defensive. There was a slight draft from her bedroom window, which was cooling the warmth of her bed.

'Rosa, she doesn't want to have chemotherapy. They've told her that it's the only treatment available. She doesn't wan—' The line fell quiet. Then Rosa heard a soft sob.

'Wait, what?' Rosa replayed her mother's words in her head. 'Chemotherapy? She doesn't want it . . . ' Her voice broke as she uttered the final word.

Her mother continued to weep; it was the softest sound Rosa had ever heard from her. 'Are you crying?' She hadn't meant to ask so bluntly but struggled to hide her surprise. In her thirty-five years of life, she couldn't recall ever having heard her mother cry.

'Will you talk to her?'

'I'll try.' Rosa was barely following what she was being asked. Nana hadn't told her that the hospital had offered her chemotherapy, and she certainly hadn't told Rosa that she wanted to refuse it.

'You know I would if I could,' her mum added. Rosa very much doubted this.

A moment of silence passed awkwardly, and Rosa's mum

hastily offered her goodbye. The call ended but Rosa's mind remained fixed. *Nana didn't want treatment.*

Rosa switched the phone to silent, dropped it onto the bed and retrieved her dressing gown from the back of her bedroom door, wrapping herself up tightly like a gift. She tiptoed into the living room and rested her weight against the window, gazing at her nana, who was sitting in her armchair with the *Jamaica Gleaner* spread open between her hands. The heavy curtains tickled Rosa's arms and she scooped them into the tieback. A stream of light flooded into the room.

'Nana, I spoke to my mum again.' She paused, trying to gauge Nana's reaction. There wasn't one. 'She's worried about you.'

She scoffed. 'Tell 'er tuh worry 'bout 'erself before she worries bout mi.' She lifted the newspaper to shield her face from the sun. 'An' Rosa, it too bright!'

The armchair was once floral but had worn over time and the flower petals were indistinguishable; it had begun to look like an abstract art installation. Nana's legs were outstretched, and her feet supported by a cushioned footstall, which still had discernible flowers in its pattern and didn't match the armchair. The television murmured in the background. Rosa found herself imprinting the whole scene on her mind, her Nana, her life, scared that these memories would one day disappear.

'Rosa!' Nana's voice was sharp.

Rosa lifted the curtains out of the tieback and released them.

'OK, OK, but Nana, please. Can we talk about this?'

'Chat 'bout what?'

Let's talk about the fact that you have cancer and were offered chemotherapy but didn't want to tell me. Not only that, but you don't want to undergo chemotherapy treatment and didn't tell me that either. No wait, to add insult to injury, you told my mum. Of all people.

No, that sounded self-centred.

Let's just talk about why you're telling my mum you won't have chemotherapy.

Again, no. It was too selfish.

She thought she was closer to Nana than anyone in the world, but Rosa found it difficult to separate the anger and upset at having found out something so important through her mother. Nana saved her from the silence.

'There's nuttin tuh chat 'bout. Mi know wah chemo does tuh yuh.' Nana spat the words.

'Do you want me to come and speak to the doctor with you?' Rosa asked. She began to regret having agreed not to go into the consultation at the hospital.

'No.'

'Do you want to talk to me about what they said?'

'No.'

'There might be other options. We could talk to the doctors about whether there was anything else. We could think about the positives and negatives.' Rosa's voice was heating up in intensity. 'Remember you always would tell me to weigh the positives and negatives up whenever I'd get a crazy idea. Not sure I'd be doing my job now if it wasn't for your positive and negative tables.' There was desperation in her voice.

'No, Mercedes,' Nana said.

'Is there anything I can do?' she pleaded.

'No.'

Nana took a deep breath and tried to hold in a cough. It didn't work and she spluttered for a few seconds. Rosa grabbed the tissues on the table and passed two to Nana.

Eventually, once the coughing stopped, Nana said, 'Mi a old 'oman, Rosa. Let mi guh wen God ready fi mi.'

Rosa dropped the packet of tissues back onto the table and stepped clumsily towards Nana. No words would be adequate. Nana stared at the blank wall in front of her. Rosa took another step towards her, now hovering just inches from the armchair, and embraced her grandmother. Nana sat stiffly but allowed Rosa to hold her. The rigidity of Nana's pose contrasted with the softness of her body, which melted into Rosa's arms. She cried small wet tears on Nana's back. Nana's eyes stayed dry but for just a short moment she relaxed, and her head fell into Rosa's chest.

CHAPTER 36

Mo returned from the prison hospital after a few days. It appeared that while the beating in the yard might not have caused him a lot of internal damage, it had certainly caused him a lot of external damage – he looked extremely fragile. Mo entered the cell without acknowledging Emmett's presence.

The men sat in silence for what felt like days. Emmett wanted to say something, but he didn't have the words. Guilt smothered him.

Some time later, still with nothing being said, Emmett left the cell to get his dinner, closing the door behind him. Tonight's hot meal was a chicken leg with mashed potato and white cabbage. His food looked like a beige paint wheel as it sloshed around on his blue plastic plate. He grabbed some plastic cutlery and made his way back to the cell.

As he approached, he noticed that the door was ajar. That was unusual. Why would Mo leave the door open after what had happened to him?

Emmett felt for the razorblade in his waistband. He'd

never used it, but it always made him feel safer knowing it was there. Slowly, he slipped it free and held it loosely in his free palm, while balancing his plate of food in his left hand. He approached with caution. As he grew closer, he could hear Mo's muffled screams.

Emmett had everything to lose, his trial was starting tomorrow – but he couldn't stand by and watch again. Not again. This wasn't the Emmett his grandmother had raised.

He dropped his plate of food and burst into the cell brandishing the small blade.

A small man with squirrel-like features was holding a pillow down over Mo's face. Seeing Emmett, he jumped back and dropped it. Mo locked eyes with Emmett for a brief second. Emmett gave the tiniest nod, and charged towards the man, slamming him up against the wall, as he had done with Mo just weeks earlier. This time, though, his fury rising, he tightened his grip on the man's throat and flashed the razorblade in his face. The man looked genuinely terrified. He was either following someone else's orders, or had just tried to take advantage of Mo in his injured state. Emmett didn't care which. He pressed the blade against the man's cheek, drawing a small amount of blood, which dropped down his freckled face.

'I'm so sorry, I'm so sorry. I wasn't going to hurt him,' the man pleaded.

'You had a pillow over his fucking head!' Emmett bellowed.

'Yes, yes, but jus—' he spluttered, struggling to breathe as Emmett's grip tightened again around his neck. 'I just had to scare h—' The man struggled to finish his sentence and his face turned a bright red. Emmett, panicking, unclenched his hands. The man hobbled forwards and then tried to regain his balance. Emmett tried to reach out to grab him again, but he sprinted out of the cell.

Mo and Emmett stared at each other, neither of them sure how to break the tension in the room.

'Thank you,' Mo said softly.

'I'm sorry I didn't act before,' Emmett said, defeat washing over him as he collapsed to the floor.

CHAPTER 37

Emmett was woken early on Monday by the prison officers and bundled into a van with the other prisoners being taken to court today. Mo had wished him luck, which had felt good. Every fibre of his body was twitching with anxiety.

He'd scrubbed his body clean, knowing that every little detail might matter to the jury. In the van he fiddled with his hair, which had grown considerably over the past few months and was knotty. He tried to comb it into a little topknot, but even pulling the strands backwards tugged at his scalp and hurt.

Although Emmett was terrified about the start of the trial, there was also an underlying sense of calmness that comforted him. Whatever happened, he'd soon be out of this nightmare period of limbo. He didn't know if he was coming or going and had been haunted for months with nightmares. His memory of that awful day was fading all the time, and he had to try to revive his recollection. He wasn't sure now whether he'd successfully kept his memories alive, or had slowly built a fictional mental video of what had happened in the park.

The van pulled into the court and the prisoners were led off into the cells. He felt like he'd been through this before, this exact moment a dim echo of his arrest, but he still didn't know what was going to happen next.

A cell officer offered him something to eat but he wasn't hungry. He refused water too, knowing that it would run through his body almost immediately. He just needed space.

Someone in the cell next to him was screaming. He was cursing and shouting that he didn't want to go into court today and said he would not be leaving his cell. The cell staff seemed unconcerned about the noise and just left him to it. It was relentless, didn't stop no matter how much Emmett willed for him to be quiet. He considered saying something but decided he didn't need the confrontation. He pressed the palms of his hands against his ears in a desperate bid for some quiet.

The door unbolted again, and a young, dark-haired woman stood in the doorway. She was clad in the cell-officer uniform but looked a similar age to Emmett. She was pretty and when she smiled her eyes lit up. In another life, he thought, they might have made an attractive couple.

'Come on, Emmett, your barrister is here to see you,' she said calmly. He stood up and followed her out obediently.

As they walked down the corridor, Emmett could hear the man from his neighbouring cell still screaming.

He was led into one of the conference rooms where Craig and Rosa were sitting, separated from him by a large wall of glass. He walked into his part of the room and sat down too. The door closed and the sound of his neighbour faded into a distant murmur.

'It's your big day today, son,' Craig said in a strangely chirpy voice, muffled by the glass wall between them.

Rosa, who was much more sensitive to Emmett's nerves, sat there quietly and offered Emmett a look of reassurance.

'There's nothing much we need to talk to you about this morning, kid,' Craig continued in an upbeat voice. 'We just wanted to make sure we said hello. Don't be too nervous, not much will happen today.'

That was easy for Craig to say, Emmett thought. As if telepathic, Rosa caught his eyes and they looked away in sync.

'Anything else you want to say to us?' Craig asked, the enthusiasm dropping from his voice. 'No pressure, we aren't expecting anything. Just want to check?'

Emmett looked at Rosa again and they held eye contact. He wanted to talk to her in private but didn't know how to ask for that and hoped that his eyes would give it away. They didn't.

'Emmett?' Rosa now asked.

'No, nothing,' he said flatly.

'OK, great, well, we'll be called on soon,' Craig said, standing up. 'We'll see you upstairs.'

He knocked on the door. A cell officer came and opened it. Rosa and Emmett's eyes stayed locked. She turned away, breaking the magnetism, and followed Craig out of the door, but then stopped and stepped back inside.

'Emmett,' she whispered, just loud enough to be heard

through the glass. He looked up, surprised. 'I'm doing everything I can.'

To Rosa, it seemed that Emmett's face morphed into Toby's for a brief second, and he looked like a young child. His eyes began to well up, and he quickly wiped them.

'Thank you,' he said quietly.

Rosa exited the cell and caught up with Craig.

'What was that about?' he asked.

'Nothing,' she said. 'I just thought I'd left my pen in there.'

Rosa took her place in the courtroom, with Craig just a row behind her. The hearing was already starting late because the judge had to deal with another matter before Emmett's. Mr Pankhurst looked slightly less flappy today, dressed in a well-tailored suit and with his hair neatly combed back. He looked more prepared than Rosa had ever seen him before. Rosa tried to smile in his direction, but he looked straight through her.

On the desk in front of her, Rosa laid out her laptop and set up a pile of lever-arch files. Mr Pankhurst, or a paralegal at the CPS, had dropped a copy of the jury bundle on her desk, which Rosa picked up and put on top of the other folders.

And they waited. The big clock in the courtroom ticked. It was a quarter past twelve and Emmett still hadn't been brought into the courtroom. Rosa's stomach tightened with every passing minute.

As if on cue, keys jangled, a door slammed open in the dock and Emmett was brought inside. Rosa looked at his grey sweater and tracksuit bottoms, both worn and tired. His hair stuck upwards in a little pigtail of afro. Rosa bit her lip. She didn't want the jury to see him like this every day.

The judge, HHJ Douglas KC, entered and everyone in the room rose to their feet. HHJ Douglas KC sat down, and as always, everyone followed suit.

Emmett was identified and the judge turned to Mr Pankhurst first. He checked whether it was expected that the trial would last any longer than two weeks.

'No, My Lord. In fact, if I might say so, it may last far less than that.'

'Let's not get carried away, Mr Pankhurst,' the judge said. 'Ms Higgins?'

'No, thank you, My Lord,' Rosa replied.

'No need to thank me, I'm just asking a question.' Rosa noticed that this judge took everything very literally, as if purposely trying to humiliate the advocates.

'Phil, can we bring in the potential jurors?' he said to the usher. 'Let's get this show on the road. Mr Pankhurst and Ms Higgins, are there any questions to be put to the jury? I assume you'll read out the list of names and I can just tell them where the stabbing took place?'

'Yes, My Lord,' Mr Pankhurst said, answering the latter question but ignoring the first. He was careful not to say anything that the judge would latch onto.

Phil, the usher, returned with a group of potential jurors behind him.

'Good morning, all,' the judge said, surprisingly cheerily.

'In you come, that's right. Please do shuffle in, it doesn't matter at the moment where you sit. Just there is fine.'

The group shuffled in. Rosa started to cast her eye over each of them. In the top left of the two-row jury section was a short, plump man with a balding head and red face. He was wearing a plain T-shirt and looked sweaty and hot, despite it being chilly in the courtroom. Next to him was a man of the complete opposite build. He was tall and thin and had a head of shaggy, wavy brown hair. He too was wearing a T-shirt but it had a picture of a rock band on the front. The third person in the back row was an incredibly tall, stocky woman, who was almost the same height as the lanky man to her right. She was wearing a fluffy pink jumper and had similarly fluffy blonde hair.

Most of the jurors had settled into their seats and the judge began to address them.

'Good morning, ladies and gentlemen. Thank you for joining us here today.' His tone was so different when addressing the jury. He was friendly and had a kindness to his voice that Rosa had not heard before now.

'You are members of a jury panel and from your panel of ... let's see,' the judge started to count with his pointed finger. 'Fourteen or fifteen of you, twelve of you will be selected as jurors to try the case in this court today and for the next two weeks.'

Rosa continued to examine the jurors. Fourth in line, next to the blonde fluffy-jumper lady was another man, Asian with a full beard. He was wearing a light grey tracksuit jacket and appeared to be chewing gum. Beside him was an olive-skinned woman, who looked as though she'd joined the courtroom from another, much more sophisticated decade. She was wearing a yellow and pink polka-dot dress with white gloves and had far too much blusher on her cheeks.

The judge's voice continued in the background.

'There are several guarantees of the fairness and independence of any jury. One of them is that no one on the jury should have any connection with the person being tried or anyone who is a witness in the case. This case, the one you are about to hear, involves a murder which happened on 4 September in Walthamstow Park, in Walthamstow.'

Rosa watched the faces of some of the jurors drop. The juror with the tracksuit jacket stopped chewing and sat up in his chair. The lady with the polka-dot dress let out a small gasp. One woman, with dyed red hair, looked nonchalant.

'Because a jury must decide the case only on the evidence given in court, it is essential that no one on the jury has any personal connection with, or personal knowledge of, the case or anyone associated with it,' the judge added.

Rosa looked at the last two people in the back row. They looked oddly alike but nonetheless unremarkable, two mousy-haired plain women in their late thirties.

'I am now going to give you some information about the case. If you know any of the people personally, or you know anything about the case, please indicate that by raising your hand or by writing a short note explaining this and handing it to the usher.' The judge pointed to Phil. 'The defendant's name is Emmett Hamilton. He is the person standing in the centre of the room in the dock.'

All of the jurors turned to face Emmett, who stood there like an abandoned toddler in a shopping mall, on the brink of tears. His childish little topknot didn't help.

'Next, Mr Pankhurst, who is prosecuting this case, will read out the names of the people who may be called as witnesses or who are connected with the case. Please listen carefully to the names and think about whether you recognise any of them.' The judge turned to Mr Pankhurst, who rose on cue.

'Thank you, My Lord. The names are ...' he fumbled with the pieces of paper on his desk. 'Oh, got them. Here we go,' he muttered under his breath.

The judge turned to the jury and smiled.

'Thomas Dove, the victim.' He paused and waited. There was no movement from the jury area.

'Mark McEvoy.' Again, nothing.

'Claire Smith.' For the final time he stopped. There was no movement. He nodded at the judge and sat down.

'One particular place which will feature in this case is Walthamstow Park, in Walthamstow,' the judge declared. 'I'm not expecting anyone to tell me if they know it. I'd hope most of you do. It's quite a nice park in that neck of the woods. Just please let us know if you were there, or in the vicinity on 4 September 2023. Anything that you think might be relevant to your impartiality.'

A juror in the front row raised her hand. Rosa hadn't noticed her before. She had short, relaxed hair, which she wore in a neat bob. She was a slight woman, perhaps in her fifties. Her fair skin was freckled with dark brown moles. She was the only Black person in the jury pool.

'I see that the lady in the front row has raised her hand in relation to that last question. Would you step up to my learned clerk's desk for a moment, where you will see there is paper and pen. Would you write me a short note to say why you raised your hand, and please put your name on the piece of paper?'

The woman stood and approached the clerk's desk. She bent over slowly, looking fragile, and scribbled a note. She folded it and handed it the clerk, who passed it up to the judge. The judge unfolded the piece of paper and read the note.

'I see, madam, that you ride past Walthamstow Park on the bus on your way to work and may have that morning, but have never spent time there. I don't suppose that will be a concern for anyone?' The judge looked at Mr Pankhurst and Rosa. They both shook their heads. Rosa was glad that the only Black person in the jury pool was still eligible to be selected for the case.

'Would you please return to your seat?' The lady with the straight bob followed the judge's instructions. The man seated next to her had placed his bag on her seat when she'd stood up; he picked it up again and returned it to his lap. He was middle-aged and dressed very smartly, with a neat tie and ironed shirt. Rosa got the impression that he felt there were more important things that he could be doing right now than sitting as a juror in a murder trial.

Another juror raised her hand. It was another elderly woman sitting in the front row. The judge invited her to step forwards to the clerk's desk. She whispered something to the clerk, who picked up the pen and started to write for her. Once again, the piece of paper was folded and handed to the judge. He unravelled it and read it, humming to himself.

'Hmm,' he said, after a short pause. 'I see you, madam, do not know the victim Thomas Dove, but since the murder you have become friends with Mr Dove's mother.' The judge glanced at the advocates. Rosa made it clear through her expression that she was disapproving.

'In those circumstances, you should not sit on this particular jury. Please stand to one side.'

After confirming that there were no other issues, the judge thanked the jury for their patience.

'We can move on to the next stage. Another guarantee of a jury's fairness and independence is that each member of the jury is selected at random. You will see that the clerk in front of me is shuffling the cards that have your names. That is the process called the ballot. The clerk will now call out the first twelve names. If your name is called, please say "yes" and then take your place in the jury box.'

The clerk called out a sequence of names. The first was the tall, curly haired, fluffy-jumper woman. She strode up to the jury box and took her seat. Rosa predicted that she would be the jury foreperson. The second name belonged to a small, thickset man whose glasses took up most of his face. He squeezed in next to fluffy-jumper woman. Third was one of

248

the two brunette women – Rosa couldn't tell them apart, let alone which was selected. Fourth, the woman in the polka dot dress. Fifth, the tall, lanky man with shaggy hair. Sixth, the gum-chewer in the tracksuit. Half of the jury members had been selected.

Rosa nervously fixed her eyes on the woman with the bob. They needed her but she knew that the jury selection was random. The courtroom was still while the first half of the jury settled into their seats and adjusted themselves. The clerk then resumed calling out the names.

The clerk struggled to pronounce the seventh name; it transpired that it belonged to an elderly white woman sitting in the corner. The eighth was called, but it belonged to the woman who'd been taken aside. Another name, and this time a small, athletic woman stepped up, dressed almost entirely in gym gear, save for the flip flops she wore on her feet. Ninth was another woman Rosa had not noticed initially, with jet black hair and facial piercings she looked like she'd only just turned eighteen. Tenth was a young man of around the same age, well-presented, in polo top and chino trousers. There were only two more jurors to be chosen and the Black woman was still waiting patiently. Eleventh was the woman with red hair. Finally, the twelfth juror was selected: the short, stocky man. His bald head was shiny with sweat as he heaved himself into the last seat.

These twelve people would be deciding the fate of Emmett Hamilton. There were no Black jurors. And there was absolutely nothing that Rosa could do about that.

*

249

At 2 p.m., after lunch, the court speaker system demanded their return to court.

Various bodies shuffled into the courtroom and waited patiently for Emmett to be brought upstairs. Rosa started to unpack the contents of her work handbag, pulling out her laptop and positioning her tablet on her portable stand. She reached for the electronic cable chargers and fiddled with the plug sockets trying to slot them in.

'Ms Higgins, I really wouldn't waste time getting too comfortable,' the judge bellowed, startling her. Rosa abandoned the laptop charger and let it fall softly onto the desk.

Emmett was brought into the courtroom and then the jury followed. Once they sat down, the judge immediately commanded the attention of the room.

'I am sorry to be the bearer of bad news,' the judge began, directing his gaze towards the jurors. Mr Pankhurst clambered to his feet awkwardly and knocked his cup of water onto the floor on the way up, which he pretended not to see. The judge ignored him and continued to address the jury.

'An extremely important personal matter has arisen over the lunch break, which means that I cannot sit beyond 2.30 p.m.' The judge tried to be matter of fact but the regret in his voice was obvious.

'For that reason, and because our trial has not yet started, I'm afraid I have had to make the decision that this case will not begin today. In fact, it will not start this week at all. I am releasing you for the rest of the week but will require that you attend at 9 a.m. sharp next Monday morning.' The judge nodded once at the jurors, as if to check they understood, and then turned to the advocates. 'I can only apologise profusely and assure you all that I have not made this decision lightly.'

'I apologise to the advocates,' he turned his head to Emmett and nodded towards him, 'and of course, I apologise to the defendant. Mr Hamilton, this will have no bearing on your trial. I just want to make sure that we have enough time to give it the proper attention it deserves.'

It might not be true to say that it would have no bearing on his trial, the judge couldn't possibly know, Rosa thought. The people left in charge of determining whether or not Emmett killed Thomas Dove were the twelve jurors who looked irritated and frustrated at having been made to wait around all morning only to be sent home. This was not the start to the trial that Rosa had envisioned.

CHAPTER 38

Rosa woke up in a panic, with sweat dripping from her forehead. She reached over to her bedside table and looked at her phone – it was only 5 a.m. For the second night in a row, she'd dreamed that she had woken up late and the trial had started without her. She wiped the sweat from her forehead with the corner of her duvet cover.

The sun poked at her through a gap in the curtains, preventing her from getting back to sleep. Eventually, she dragged herself out of bed.

Nana was in the kitchen chopping some strawberries for Toby's lunch box. He was watching cartoons on a small screen in front of him while tilting his bowl to his mouth and messily slurping the leftover sugary milk from his cereal. Nana discarded the small green leafy tops into a small pile as she scooped the chopped fruit into a plastic container. Rosa watched her, leaning in the doorway. As her grandmother clicked the container closed, she noticed Rosa's silhouette.

'I'll drop Toby to school today,' Rosa said once Nana

locked eyes with her. 'It'll give you a chance to put your feet up.'

'Mercedes, we need to talk about yuh brudda, at school,' Nana said, without acknowledging Rosa's offer.

Nana spoke about Toby as though he wasn't there, albeit he seemed oblivious.

'What about him?' Rosa croaked quietly. Her throat was dry from sleep, but it had the added benefit of not allowing Toby to hear their conversation.

'Toby's new teacha, Ms Goodwin or Goodchild or sup'm like dat, she seh him ave bin distracted inna class.'

Rosa tried to focus on what Nana was telling her, but her mind wandered. What were the jurors doing now? They'd been warned not to look into the case outside of the courtroom but no one monitored that. What if they were googling Emmett now? What if they'd made their mind up before the trial even started?

As Rosa buttered her toast and swirled the spoon in her black coffee, her phone began to ring. She apologised to Nana, who looked affronted at being cut off, and took the call in the hall. It was her clerk, Steve.

'Rosa, we've got someone on the line who wants to speak to you. He won't give us his name but says it's urgent, he says it's about your case with Emmett Hamilton.'

'He won't give his name?' Rosa asked, not masking the surprise in her voice. 'Is he a journalist? A member of the public?'

'I don't know. He won't tell us anything. He just says it's urgent. Do you want me to get rid of him?' said Steve.

'No, no, no. Let me hear what he has to say. Yes, connect the call, please.'

A dial tone sounded for a few seconds and then stopped as a strangely familiar voice spoke on the other end of the phone.

'Hello, Ms Higgins, you don't know who I am but there is something that I think you need to know.'

She'd heard this voice before, but she couldn't figure out where from.

'Right. Go on?'

'Well, it's about Tom, Thomas Dove. He had got himself into a right mess.'

'This is probably something you need to speak to the police about. Can I take a name?'

'No. I'm not speaking to the police, Rosa! Sorry, Ms Higgins.' His voice was intensifying. 'Please just listen.'

Rosa fell quiet, unsure of what else to do.

'I heard him threatening someone.'

'Threatening someone? What do you mean, to hurt someone?'

'No, no. Just threatening to expose someone. I think it probably had something to do with work. I'm not too sure. I just remember hearing him ask for money, blackmail. I think he did it to a few people.'

'Do you remember when this conversation took place?'

'A few months ago, I'm not sure of an exact date. I thought it was weird but obviously I didn't write it down,' he said defensively.

'I'm not sure I'm quite making sense of this. You're saying

254

you heard Thomas Dove asking someone for money and threatening to expose someone?' Rosa was beginning to suspect that this was a prank call.

'Yes, look I'm not a detective or a fancy lawyer. I just thought it might help. When you came to our house, I wanted to tell you, but she said not to trust you. Then she told you about his money problems anyway.'

'When I came to your house?' Rosa's memories flickered momentarily. 'You're Thomas's flatmate?'

The speaker paused, realising what he'd said. 'Oh shit, I just said when you came to our house. Oh fuck. Oh my fucking God, I am a moron.'

'Look, please calm down,' Rosa whispered, trying to lower the volume of the telephone conversation. 'I can't force you to speak to the police, or anyone else for that matter. Thank you for what you've told me. Was there anything else? Did you work out who he was talking to?'

'No. Nothing else, and I have no idea who he was talking to. I need to go.'

'Wait ...'

The call ended.

Nana was cleaning up after Toby and readying him for school when Rosa returned, which left her about ten minutes to get some more work done. She had no idea of the relevance of the alleged phone call, if any, and knew it would be impossible to identify the call from the information they had.

She checked her emails; there was a new one from Kate.

Dear Rosa,

Following our conference, I have called a number of cleaning companies in the area, as you suggested. I found one company that appears to require staff to wear a uniform matching the one seen in the video you sent over. It's bright yellow and orange. They're called CL3AN Ltd and I've just spoken to the acting manager who says that they are a commercial company who outsource their staff to other businesses. He explained that most of their cleaners are contracted on a long-term basis to different businesses in the area. I'm going to make enquiries today to local businesses and I will keep you updated on the progress.

Kind Regards

Kate

Paralegal

CHAPTER 39

Thursdays were the day Toby had football practice, and so he trotted down the road next to her looking like a tortoise, with his huge school backpack and drawstring PE bag and football boots looped over the top.

'Rosa, my friend Casey ... his nana died,' Toby said, as they stopped at a zebra crossing. 'But he doesn't live with *his* nana.'

'I'm sorry to hear that, Toby. It's important to be extra nice to Casey, I'm sure he's feeling very sad right now.'

'No. He's not sad. He said his Nana always used to shout at him,' Toby said innocently. Rosa tried not to raise her eyebrows and said nothing. She reached for Toby's hand and clutched it as the green man flashed and they crossed the road.

'What would happen if Nana died?' Toby asked. 'Would you look after me?' His big brown eyes awaited her response.

'Of course!' she said before she even had a chance to think about the practicalities. 'But let's not worry about that, Toby. You've got an exciting day at school to think about.'

'School is boring.'

She bent to kiss him at the gate but to her surprise he wriggled and squirmed in disgust. She'd clearly forgotten what it was like to be young and have family members plant a sloppy kiss on you in full sight of your friends. She was worried that with all the time she was spending on the case, she was drifting apart from him.

The walk back from Toby's school was strangely lonely. Rosa felt an inexplicable emptiness as she headed home, and the dark grey clouds loomed over her. She crossed next to Walthamstow Park and imagined Emmett's friends calling out to him as he lay there cradling a dying man. A woman barged past her speaking loudly on her phone and pushing a huge pram, bringing her back into the present.

She walked into the estate and stopped abruptly, sensing someone behind her. They were so close that she could smell their sickly sweet fragrance. As she turned to look, the person also turned and walked in the other direction. They were of a slim build and wore dark clothing, with a hood pulled over their head. It was impossible to tell whether it was a woman or a man – but the lingering smell resembled aftershave more than perfume. Her instinct told her to call after the person, but were they actually following her?

Shaking, and feeling a little foolish, Rosa climbed the steps to Nana's flat and slowly slotted the key into the lock. She twisted the handle and edged the door open. The flat was unusually silent. She tiptoed in, closing the door softly behind her.

'Nana?' Rosa called out, as she walked towards the living room.

Nana lay outstretched on the living room carpet, still.

'Nana!' Rosa yelped and dropped to the floor. She tried to shake her. Nana was not responsive. She scrambled for her phone and dialled 999.

As she waited for the emergency services, Rosa embraced Nana's limp body and prayed under her breath. In a moment of desperate need, she texted Orissa, who replied instantly and said she was on her way.

After what seemed like hours – Rosa had no idea how long it actually was – the paramedics arrived. They didn't provide Rosa with much reassurance, but suggested she join Nana in the ambulance as they took her to hospital. She climbed into the back, and texted Orissa to meet them there.

They arrived at the Accident and Emergency department of Whipps Cross Hospital, the paramedics working at speed to transfer Nana on to a bed before wheeling her away. Everything seemed to move in slow motion and Rosa felt like a leaf in a storm, swept around by forces beyond her control.

'Are you related to this lady?' a bright-faced woman in a light-blue uniform asked.

'Yeah, she's my nan,' Rosa said with a tremor in her voice.

'I'm so sorry, darling, our team will just need to spend some time working out what's going on and we just ask that you wait here in the meantime.' She pointed Rosa towards a room, which had a colourful sign above the door reading FAMILY AND FRIENDS.

Rosa nodded, although hardly listening, and obediently entered the room and sat down.

'If you need a tea or coffee, or even a bite to eat, there's a little café down the corridor, OK?' she added with genuine kindness.

Within half an hour Orissa had arrived and was sitting beside Rosa, wrapping her in her arms. Rosa remained cold and stiff.

'I've organised for Annie, the childminder my sister uses, to pick up Toby from school,' Orissa said, still gripping her tightly. 'I've spoken to the school, they said they'll call you to check that's all OK, but I can tell them to wait until a bit later?'

As if on cue, Rosa's phone began to chime.

'It might be the school, do you want me to get it?' Orissa asked, reaching for Rosa's bag.

'It's OK,' Rosa said, grabbing it herself. It was the first time she'd spoken since calling the ambulance, and words felt unfamiliar on her tongue.

Without looking at her phone screen she answered. It was Kate.

'Hi, Rosa, it's Kate. Sorry to call you so soon after emailing.'

'Hello, Kate. Now isn't really a good time.'

'Oh, I'm so sorry, I can call back later. I just wanted to update you on the search. I thought it might be quicker to just call.'

'What have you found?'

'Well, I've spent all morning calling businesses in the area

260

and I basically asked whether they use any cleaners from CL3AN. Sorry, I don't know why I'm telling you how I did it, you don't need to know that. I just wanted . . . no, never mind,' Kate rambled nervously. 'Anyway, I narrowed it down to three companies locally. The DIY store on the high street, the—'

'Sorry, Kate, I don't mean to be rude, but have you found anything positive? I'm quite busy at the moment,' Rosa said, trying to be kind but failing.

'Oh, I'm so sorry. Shall I call back later?'

'No, please just tell me what, if anything, you've found.'

'Oh, yes, of course, sorry. OK, well, I think Devilz is our winner. They have a long-term cleaner from CL3AN and it sounds like she matches the physical description, according to the bartender I spoke to.'

'Devils?' Rosa repeated.

'Yes, Devilz with a z. It's a strip club.'

'And the woman matching the description is a cleaner?'

'Yes, apparently.' Rosa heard the sound of shuffling papers. 'The woman I spoke to was called Sharon, who was on shift this morning. I said that I would need to run everything by you. Or Craig, I guess.'

'Have you told Craig about this yet?'

'No. I wanted to tell you first. Just in case you wanted to try to meet her.'

'Now? Now isn't great.' Rosa looked around the busy family and friends' room. No one had moved in almost an hour, and she figured that was unlikely to change imminently. 'Actually, I'll be there shortly, but I can't stay long.' She looked at Orissa who stared at her wide-eyed.

261

Rosa looked at her smart watch. 'Let's meet there in, say, thirty minutes.'

'Where? Devilz? Erm, yes, definitely,' Kate replied enthusiastically.

Rosa ended the call and looked back at Orissa. She opened her mouth to explain but the words weren't coming to her.

'It's work?' Orissa said flatly, not really expecting an answer. 'Rosa, your Nana is in hospital. Can't you take a break for just one day?' But Orissa knew there was no point trying to persuade Rosa to do anything she'd already made her mind up about.

'I won't be long,' Rosa said. 'It will only be an hour, and look, nothing is happening here.'

'But it's your Nana, Rosa.'

'Don't guilt trip me, please. I know what's at stake here. There's a young man's life on the line, and if I don't act quickly, he may not be able to prove his innocence. Look, I'm going to leave my number with the nurse and I'm going to be back in an hour . . . ' Rosa's voice started to trail off as she marched away to the nurse's desk and scribbled down her number. Orissa stayed seated, bewildered.

CHAPTER 40

Rosa looked up at the strip club and was almost disappointed in how plain the building was. The name 'Devilz' had made it sound far more exciting. The club was in a row of other buildings, between a supermarket selling only frozen food and a shop flogging phone accessories. It hardly seemed like the best location for a strip club.

Given it was lunchtime, Rosa was not surprised that the front door was locked, but she was slightly unnerved by the thick rusting chain that looped through the door handles as an additional safeguard. As she pulled the handle, the chain rattled loudly but the door remained closed. She slumped against the door, again knocking the rusty chain, and pulled out her phone.

'Can I help you?' A ragged female voice made Rosa jump slightly and her phone fell from her hands onto the concrete. Rosa crouched down on the pavement and picked it up. The shattered glass screen sparkled in the sunlight.

'For fuck's sake,' Rosa muttered.

As she stood up, she examined the woman who'd

addressed her. She was wearing battered Converse with fishnet tights. Her legs were long, but the skin hung loosely, as though she'd lost weight or aged quickly. As Rosa lifted herself out of a squat, her eyes travelled up the woman's body accordingly. Her legs ended in a denim skirt, and although she was slim, her tight-fitting top highlighted a small hanging bulge of her stomach.

'Can I help you?' the woman repeated, evidently noticing Rosa's full body examination. Rosa, feeling slightly embarrassed, stood up quickly. She noticed that they were a similar height as she directly looked the woman in the eyes. Her stare did not make the woman uncomfortable.

'I'm just trying to find someone who works here at Devilz, called Sharon, I think,' Rosa spluttered.

'You've found her. What do you want?' The woman's face was as harsh as her voice. Her thin, wrinkled lips shot each word at Rosa.

Kate appeared, as if from nowhere, and stood by Rosa's side.

'My colleague here spoke to you on the phone. I'm here to talk to your cleaner. We think she might be able to help us.'

The woman's small green eyes scanned Rosa's body up and down, which Rosa found considerably more uncomfortable than Sharon clearly had. Her examination was much quicker, and her eyes stopped on Rosa's face.

'Are you a police officer? We aren't causing no problems, so I don't know why you're here.'

'Oh, no. I'm not a police officer!' Rosa replied, a little too defensively. 'I'm a barrister, a defence barrister.'

Sharon looked sceptical.

'I am currently instructed, I mean, I'm currently dealing with a case – it's a murder case.' Rosa stared hard into the woman's eyes, pushing her shoulders back. 'I have a murder case. Your cleaner might be able to help out.'

'How is *she* going to help?'

'Well, we think she might have been there.'

Sharon shook her head, and her wispy, straw-like hair blew into her eyes. She used the back of her hand to sweep it behind her ears. 'Well, she's not said anything to me.' She paused for a moment to think. 'Wait, is this the one that happened round here. In Walthamstow?'

Rosa nodded.

Without saying anything else, Sharon led Rosa and Kate into Devilz. It was a windowless building with small neon lights flickering over the entrance, attempting to spell 'Devilz' but the 'v' having apparently dropped off. Stepping into the strip club felt like entering into a shadowy underworld. The air was thick with the smell of stale alcohol and sweat. The walls were painted a tired shade of red and the worn-down tables were paired with torn leather sofas. Rosa sat down and Kate copied her. Sharon indicated that she would return shortly, and the two women waited in silence.

After just a few minutes, Sharon came back with a shorter, stockier woman following behind her. The woman had brown skin and thick curly hair that was tied loosely into a ponytail at the back of her head. Just like in the video, she was wearing a distinctive bright orange and yellow uniform.

'This is Bouba,' Sharon said.

Rosa thanked her and smiled with a small sense of relief. She explained to Bouba that she represented Emmett and was here to see if she could help at all.

'Bouba, can you tell me a bit about yourself?'

Bouba hesitated. She lowered her head and spoke quietly into her hands.

'What do you want to know? I am from Cameroon, and I 'ave a little boy. I have a son. 'Ee is still livin' in my country. I want a better life for 'im and for me.'

Rosa nodded slowly. 'Do you know why we are here?'

'Yes. I am so scared. I want to help this boy, your boy. I would want someone to 'elp my son. I know 'ee didn't do it, but I am so scared.'

'*You know he didn't do it?*' Rosa repeated, trying to hide her astonishment. Silence flooded the room. 'Tell me, what are you scared of?'

'I don't 'ave legal status here. I don't want ze police to ask me questions and to send me back to my country. I need to keep my head down low. Ze most important thin' for me is to make sure that my son 'as a bright future ahead of 'im. I risked everythin' to be 'ere.'

Rosa sat and listened, not yet responding. Silence was a powerful tool for getting more information from people than they often wanted to give.

'I risked everythin'. I cannot lose it all. I really want to help but I cannot lose everythin',' Bouba said, and tears began to roll down her face.

Rosa tried to explain that the police were not likely to be concerned about her immigration status in these proceedings, as their primary focus would be whether or not Emmett killed Thomas Dove, but she knew she couldn't make any promises. She hadn't done any immigration law since her pupillage training many years ago, and didn't know much about how the immigration authorities and the police would coordinate on a case like this. The problem was that this case had drawn national attention, and if it came to light that a witness did not legally enter the UK, the government wouldn't want to be seen to be soft on immigration.

'Can I just write down what I saw? I don't want to go to ze police. I don't want zem to know anythin' about me.'

'I can't promise that will be enough,' Rosa replied reluctantly. 'All I can say is that this young man needs your help. Like you said, Bouba, you'd want someone to help if it was your son.'

Bouba sat quietly for a few moments.

'What do I need to do?'

CHAPTER 41

The conference room in Craig's office was large but was consumed by a huge, long table surrounded by chairs, leaving little room to walk around. Rosa and Kate sat down, but Bouba hesitated over one of the chairs, the space seemed to squeeze her into nothing.

It was getting late. Rosa checked her phone. Orissa had messaged.

> No news yet. Annie has Toby. You've been gone
> nearly 6 hours ... You really need to sort out
> your priorities, Rosa.

'Please all sit down,' Craig commanded as he took a seat at the top of the table. Bouba slowly sat at last.

The sun penetrated the room's large windows, making it very warm, and Rosa shuffled uncomfortably in her thick jumper. Craig explained that Rosa would be in the room but merely as an observer because of how little time they had.

Craig would be asking the questions. Bouba looked nervous and said something in French.

'She said – well, asked – whether you can give her some kind of immunity from deportation if she helps this young man out?' Kate said, translating.

'No,' Craig said firmly, aware that this didn't need interpreting. 'Can we stick to English, please, from now on?'

Bouba looked down into the palms of her hands and shook her head. She stood up and glanced at Rosa.

'I can't do zis,' she said in English and left the room.

Craig glared at Rosa, who clambered to her feet. He sighed and tapped his pen. Rosa didn't wait for his sarcastic remark and followed Bouba out.

'Wait, please, Bouba—' she said, jogging down the corridor to catch up with her.

Bouba stopped to look at her. Rosa unlocked her phone and showed Bouba a picture of Emmett that Joyce had sent. His hair was short and neat, and a small slit had been shaved into his eyebrow. Sporting a Leyton Orient football shirt, he faced the photographer grinning from ear to ear.

'The police have said he murdered Thomas Dove. If you know something that we don't know, we really need you to tell us. If he is found guilty, he might go to prison for the rest of his life.'

Bouba cupped her hands over her eyes and cried softly. Rosa embraced her, inhaling her sweet powdery smell, and letting Bouba's head rest softly on her shoulder.

At that moment, Rosa's phone lit up. The hospital.

*

269

Nana looked weak. Wires poked out of her body in several places, octopus tentacles holding her down to the bed. The nurse explained that the doctor had just visited, and that Nana was recovering well. They had concluded she had fallen and knocked herself unconscious. They emphasised that Nana was not at all well. The nurse said Rosa finding her and calling the ambulance may have saved her life, which Rosa suspected was an exaggeration, but nonetheless it made her feel a little better.

She approached Nana's bed and lifted her hand. Nana's long fingers, with her overlong and unpolished nails, fell limply over Rosa's palm, and Rosa squeezed them tightly. With her other hand she lightly fiddled with Nana's hair, brushing it away from her face. Rosa closed her eyes and listened to Nana's soft snoring. She softly mumbled a prayer, thanking God for her grandmother's life and asking him to watch over her. Then, from somewhere, a little voice in her head made her continue, asking God to look over Emmett too.

Rosa sat with Nana for over an hour, gently rubbing her hand as the old woman slept next to her. Rosa had begun to nod off when she was woken by her phone alerting her to a text message from Craig.

We've got a statement. She says she saw him with the knife, but somebody snatched it. The usual caveat of it happened very fast, but she seems pretty sure.

Rosa sent a single word in reply.

Who?

Her phone buzzed again instantly. It was Steve, her clerk.

Rosa, I've had Matthew Weisberg calling
chambers. He's a journalist from the Daily Mail.
Apparently, your case might be front page news
and he wants a comment from you. Let me know
if you're interested.

A reply came through from Craig, and Rosa switched to
his message.

She doesn't know who. She's not sure she'd
recognise him again. She closed down when
I pressed on it. She's nervous about this
immigration stuff.

This is good, right? Rosa replied, hopefully.

I think so. It's not perfect but we have a
statement, and she says it wasn't him. I'll speak
to the CPS now.

CHAPTER 42

The following morning, Rosa ushered Toby into the shower while she prepared his breakfast. She sat down at the kitchen table with her own bowl of frosted cereal and tipped in a small amount of milk. She planted her laptop beside her and opened the screen. A flurry of emails popped up. The first was an email from Jeremy Pankhurst, the prosecutor.

Craig and Rosa,

Thanks for the update. I've had the officers try to visit Devilz to contact Bouba and they brought her in for questioning early this morning when she finished her shift.

Anyway, she's not saying much. I'm told she seemed 'confused' and didn't want to speak to the police officers. We've checked her PNC, no convictions, and so no real issues.

We don't object in principle, but it seems you may have issues getting her to attend because she was pretty adamant with the officers that she wasn't going to give any evidence in court.

272

Rosa sighed softly and archived the email, and then clicked on the next email, from Craig.

Rosa. I've tried calling her this morning, her phone goes to voicemail. She's now unreachable. This might be why. [LINK]

C

Anxiety began to seep through Rosa's veins as she dropped her metal spoon back into her cereal bowl, drowning the flakes of cereal under the milk. She clicked on the *Daily Mail* link and an article popped up. It was by Matthew Weisberg.

Illegal immigrant set to be the star witness in male nurse's murder.

Rosa was astounded. She'd only located Bouba yesterday and already her presence had been leaked to the media. She had no idea who had leaked the information. Her instinct was to think that it was someone internally within the police, or perhaps even the CPS, trying to sabotage Emmett's case. Realistically, she knew that it could also have been anyone in Devilz who had overheard their conversation, or anyone Sharon might have told – or even Sharon herself.

She clicked on the next email, which was another forwarded message, this time from the Court.

Rosa – see below.

Rosa slapped her laptop closed and discarded her cereal bowl by the side of the sink. She called Toby out of the shower and instructed him to get dressed and ready for school, before jumping into the shower herself.

'Where's Nana?' he called through the door as Rosa started the water. She pretended not to hear his question.

Minutes later, as Rosa buttoned her blouse and unlocked the bathroom door, Toby appeared at the doorway, with a milk moustache decorating his face.

'Where is Nana?' he asked again.

'She's not feeling very well, Toby.' Rosa wiped the milk from his face with her thumb. 'Aunty Annie is going to pick you up from school again today. OK?' Rosa looked into his warm chocolatey brown eyes. He gazed back at her perplexed.

'What's wrong with her?'

'I'm not quite sure yet,' she said, lying through her teeth.

'When's she coming home?'

'I'm not sure of that either.' She was desperate to put an end to his questioning. 'We can go and visit her this evening together, if you'd like?'

'Yes. Instead of school?' Toby said grinning.

'No, I said *this evening*, Toby. That means after school.' She saw his joy evaporate. 'Come on, school isn't so bad.'

He shook his head ferociously to show that he didn't agree with Rosa.

'Come on, get your things together. We don't want to be late!' Rosa said hurrying him into his room to collect his school bag.

'What will happen if Nana dies?' Toby asked. The question caught Rosa off guard, and she took a moment to catch her breath.

'Don't think like that, Toby. Nana will get better. Where's this coming from?'

'Casey at school, his Nana died.'

'Yes, you told me, but Nana hasn't died, she's just unwell,' Rosa said reassuringly as she straightened out his jumper.

Toby put his small chubby hands on his head as if in contemplation. 'Casey said it would be sad for me if Nana dies because my mum is in prison.'

Rosa stopped fiddling with his outfit and her face grew solemn.

'He said what?'

'That my mum is in prison. Is she?'

Rosa wasn't sure if Toby even understood what prison was, nor how 'Casey' seemed to know so much about her family. She'd dreaded the day that she'd have to explain to Toby that their mum wasn't just on an extended holiday, and had always secretly hoped that Nana would be able to take on that task. She imagined Nana smirking about the

275

fact that Toby had planted that question on Rosa while she was away.

'Toby, darling, we really need to get you to school. Don't listen to what Casey has to say. We'll talk later on.' She knew that this wouldn't buy her much more than the school day, but she needed some time to think about it. Without giving Toby a chance to respond, she picked up his school bag and ushered him through the door.

Having dropped Toby at school Rosa walked to the nearby bus stop. The bus was due in three minutes, which was good news given the weather was uncomfortably warm. She peeled her blouse away from her armpits and tried to subtly raise her arms in an attempt to aerate her underarms.

She failed to cool herself down, and a few minutes later was grateful to climb aboard the air-conditioned double-decker. She went to head for the upper deck, but something stopped her; the sensation of feeling followed the other day still played in her mind, and instead she found herself turning around and plonking herself on a seat close to the driver. Only seven stops until she reached the hospital.

Her grandmother looked small lying on the bulky hospital bed, she seemed to have shrunk, trapped inside its white plastic bars. Wires remained attached to her and a small thick-bordered screen beeped quietly above her bed. The woman in the opposite bed on the ward, who talked constantly to herself, stared intensely. At first Rosa thought it was at her, but after a few minutes of listening to the woman mutter 'I can see your feet', she realised that she was preoccupied with Nana's sock-covered feet poking out of the end of the bed.

Nana remained asleep through the noise. She snored more than Rosa remembered, which was probably due to the tubes poking out of her nostrils. Rosa, trying to create some privacy on the busy ward, stood up and pulled the duck-egg blue curtain around Nana's bed.

Rosa flicked through her phone as she sat there holding Nana's hand. She had a message from Orissa, checking in on her, which she bookmarked to reply to later. There were no other messages. She tapped on her call log and scrolled. She stopped at Sharon's number and her finger hovered over it.

Slowly and carefully, she slipped her hand out of Nana's and tiptoed to the break in the curtain. She walked down the centre of the ward, between each of the beds, and past the nurses' desk until she reached the corridor. Rosa pressed the small buzzer, squirted some hand gel on her hands and pushed the door to enter the empty hallway space. As she re-entered her passcode, her phone screen still displayed her call log and Sharon's number stood out. Her thumb hovered for a few seconds before she pressed it and let the dial ring.

'Hello, Sharon, it's Rosa, the barrister.' Sharon clearly had saved her number because she didn't sound surprised. 'I'd really like to talk to Bouba. Is she at work?'

'Did you hear the police came to our club? That ain't really good for business, is it? You didn't say you'd be sending the police round.'

'Oh, I heard about the police,' Rosa said. 'They didn't visit because she's in any trouble. It's just protocol. The

277

police will want to speak to her and ask her questions about what she saw.'

'Well, you didn't tell us about that otherwise I would have said Bouba definitely ain't gonna help you. My manager is on my back now. To be honest, Bouba don't want to do it now anyway. Just thought I'd tell you.'

'Believe me, I know it didn't help. But honestly . . . ' Rosa could hear the desperation in her own voice. 'My client's life is on the line here. His freedom. Everything.' Rosa stopped herself from going on any longer.

'That's sad to hear but Bouba can't help you. I heard the press have got hold of it too, we both know there's no chance she'll want to help now.'

'Was that you?' Rosa exclaimed.

'Do you think I'm gonna go to the press when I work at the same place that employs her? Let's not be stupid. Just saying. All the best, because she don't wanna help.'

'Please, just tell her that her evidence is so important,' Rosa said finally.

Toby looked sad as he trailed out of the school gates, ignoring his teacher waving goodbye. Rosa tried to greet him with a hug, but he remained aloof and cold. He refused to talk to her and once they eventually got home, he went to his bedroom and shut the door.

Rosa wasn't quite sure what was wrong but suspected it was either related to Nana or their mum, and she still didn't feel ready to address either conversation with him. It had begun to dawn on her that Toby was likely to be her sole responsibility one day. Her mind was otherwise preoccupied with Emmett's trial – on which she'd been working for most of the afternoon – and the fact that she hadn't yet received a telephone call from either Sharon or Bouba.

She walked into the kitchen and made Toby a small cup of hot chocolate with lots of marshmallows on the top. On a small side plate, she put two chocolate-covered biscuits, his favourite type, and despite their usual house rule of no food in the bedroom, she took both to his door. She stood outside and inhaled deeply. Knocked gently and called his name. There was only a child-like grunt. Rosa twisted the handle and slowly opened the door. Toby was curled up in bed, still in his school uniform.

'What have I told you about getting changed when you get home, Toby?'

He grunted again and sat up to look at her. He pulled his school jumper off, above his head, and lay back down, still clad in his uniform.

'Toby, I've brought you your favourite.' She held the hot chocolate and biscuits awkwardly out in front of her, but Toby didn't acknowledge them and just crossed his arms and narrowed his eyebrows.

'You lied to me,' he said eventually.

'What are you talking about?'

'Casey said his mum said that our mum is definitely in prison. He says he's seen *proof.*' Toby spat out each word.

Rosa was speechless and didn't know what else to say. Toby filled the silence between them.

'You and Nana told me that she just worked away. You

told me that she loved me!' His high-pitched voice grew even higher, and he struggled to hold back his tears.

'She does love you, Toby!' Rosa protested.

'No, she doesn't. If she loved me, she wouldn't be a bad person and go to prison!' he said, frustration and anger in his voice.

Rosa stepped closer towards him.

'Sometimes people just make mistakes, Toby. I was angry like you once. She does love us, though, I promise you. She does.'

Toby burst into tears and Rosa cradled him as he cried into her chest.

'Toby, I promise you that it's nothing to do with how much she loves us,' she whispered as he continued to sob. And suddenly she realised she was beginning to believe it, too. 'Come on, let's get you changed, you can drink the hot chocolate and then we'll go and see Nana. I think she's missing you!' And she rocked him gently.

CHAPTER 43

Monday morning crept round quickly, and Rosa headed to court having dropped Toby at his school's breakfast club. It was a warm day, and the streets were busy with parents and school children. As she walked, she sensed footsteps walking closely behind her. She turned but there was no one out of place. She continued walking, but yet again she had the creeping feeling of a presence behind her. She swivelled her head, guts churning, but again, no one. Was she losing it? She was stressed, tired and nervous about the trial – it was hardly surprising her mind was playing tricks on her. But she had to get her head straight.

She desperately refreshed her text messages and call logs, hoping to have something from Bouba but there was nothing.

Arriving at Court, Rosa headed down to the cells and buzzed to be let in.

'Who you here to see, miss?' a large cell officer asked. His shoulders were broad, and his torso seemed never-ending.

'Emmett Hamilton,' she replied.

Eventually she was let inside, with less than five minutes to spare. It was instantly obvious that Emmett wasn't hopeful. His face was gloomy, and his tone despondent.

'Emmett, today's the big day,' she said, as though it was his wedding day or the birth of his first child. She instantly regretted it, but Emmett didn't appear to notice, merely shrugged in acknowledgement.

'We have a witness who says she saw someone snatch the knife from you.' Emmett's eyes snapped up to her face. 'Unfortunately, this has all been happening very quickly and we don't exactly have much time.'

'Well, if she's written a statement, can't you just use that as proof?' Emmett said, bewildered.

'It's not quite that easy. A statement wouldn't be very persuasive to a jury. We really do need her to come to court.'

'And what, you can't just force her?'

'We've discussed whether to apply for a witness summons but honestly, Emmett, it could backfire. She might turn into what we call a "hostile witness"; she might refuse to give us the evidence we need.'

Emmett sank back into his chair, dug his elbows into his thighs and rested his forehead in the palm of his hands.

'We haven't given up, Emmett. I keep waiting for that message or call.' She wasn't sure why she was encouraging him to hold out hope, when right now she knew that Bouba wasn't coming – and that Emmett was still hiding so much from her.

'I just want to get on with it,' he said, and stood up to leave. 'If they find me guilty, that's it isn't it. It is what it is.'

*

282

The court clerk called the case on as everyone settled into their seats. The public gallery was full, as were the seats for the media representatives. Rosa spotted Matthew Weisberg who lifted his palm to say hello. She ignored it, still angry about his article, and shifted her gaze. Nerves crept through her body. She opened her laptop and stroked the touchpad to wake it.

An hour flew by as Mr Pankhurst gave an opening speech. Rosa barely paid any attention. She restarted her phone repeatedly, turning it on and off airplane mode. There were no new messages. She sent a 'test' message to herself to check it was working. She received it instantly.

Mr Pankhurst finished his opening speech and called the first prosecution witness to give evidence.

'Could you please state your full name for the court?' Mr Pankhurst said.

A red-haired man shuffled in the chair of the witness box. His head was square, and his eyes were far too small for his face. The tie around his neck was a sickly green and his crisp, white shirt was perfectly ironed. He reached for the plastic bottle of water that had been left for him and Rosa noticed how thick and pink his fingers were, like raw pork sausages.

'My name is Mark McEvoy, that's M-A-R-K, space, M-C-E-V-O-Y.' He spoke calmly, perhaps *too* calmly. In all the years she'd done this job she'd never had a witness voluntarily spell out their name. Onlookers would have been forgiven for thinking that he was in Court today to give his evidence on a professional corporate transaction, not somebody's murder.

He didn't appear to be even slightly moved by the prospect of giving his evidence in front of so many people.

Mr Pankhurst invited him to confirm his statements, which he did willingly.

Mark McEvoy was invited to tell the jury a bit about himself. He was a teacher who worked in a school nearby, although he explained that he hadn't been able to return to work since the murder as he had been suffering from post-traumatic stress disorder. As he spoke, Rosa noticed how glimmering white and unnatural his teeth were. They looked odd on an average-looking man standing in a witness box, more befitting a Hollywood movie star.

He explained that he had been walking through the park on a long lunch break – his lesson preparation time had fallen just before lunch and so he had more time than he usually would. Mr Pankhurst asked one of Rosa's intended questions: why he'd chosen to go to that park when there was one much closer by. He said he just fancied walking somewhere different, given he had the time to do so.

Mr Pankhurst pushed him a little harder with a follow-up question, why he chose that particular park, and Rosa sensed an irritation growing in Mark's voice. It was obvious that this wasn't a question he'd expected, and he struggled to answer it. Rosa made a note of his demeanour. He stumbled a little bit and could only repeat that he was entitled to walk wherever he wanted.

Mr Pankhurst then asked open, broad questions, encouraging him to tell his story to the jury of what happened that day.

His account was fairly polished overall and Rosa realised her scepticism may be unfounded. He described the weather: sunny and bright. The park was busy but calm. He'd decided to take a leisurely stroll, something which, to this day, he said still haunted him. As he said this, he looked genuinely vulnerable, and the jury seemed to cling to his every word.

'What happened next?' Mr Pankhurst asked.

'The murder!'

One juror, the tall thin man with a head of shaggy dark hair, who'd not been paying much attention until now, sat up abruptly.

'Mr McEvoy, I'm afraid I'm going to need you to take this step by step. What did you see first?'

Mark McEvoy took a deep breath. He looked upset and his lips quivered as he recounted the minute details. He tipped a quarter of the bottle of water into his mouth, ignoring the plastic cup that had been provided.

'Well, I first noticed the boys because a fight was kicking off,' he said.

Mr Pankhurst remained silent, allowing him to continue.

'A bad fight. There must have been around three Black boys and one white guy.' As he said 'one', he held up his hand with a single pointed finger. Rosa caught a quick glimpse of his expensive-looking watch – although she realised that as someone who had no interest in luxurious items, she had no idea whether it was actually worth anything or just designed to look that way.

'*Around* three Black boys?' Mr Pankhurst clarified.

'I think so, yeah, it was a while ago.' He scratched his

chin, 'I think they were Black, but I don't know for certain, one of them may have been mixed-race. He was lighter than the others.'

Rosa could feel herself being sucked into Mark McEvoy's evidence. Everything he'd said so far sounded truthful. She knew that her job wasn't about what she believed. She just needed to show this jury that they couldn't be sure of Emmett's guilt.

His description of the fight corroborated the witness statement he'd provided to the police.

'What, if anything, did you do in all of this?' Mr Pankhurst asked.

'Well, I tried to save him!' Mark said warily. 'I genuinely tried. I intervened. I tried to break the fight up!'

'What did you do to intervene?'

'What do you mean?' Mark responded. Mr Pankhurst didn't respond to his question; Rosa suspected that the silence would lead him to attempt an answer anyway. She was right. 'Well, if you mean what did I physically do, I walked into the middle of the fight. I risked my life with all these boys with knives around me. I was stabbed in the leg by one of them!'

Rosa made another note in her notebook while glaring at Mr Pankhurst. Mr Pankhurst acknowledged the look.

'Mr McEvoy, I'm afraid I must ask you to keep focused on what you saw in respect of Mr Dove's death. You said just a moment ago that the "killer" was the man with lighter skin. What exactly did you see?'

Mark McEvoy looked to the ground, as if the grubby, dark

carpeted floor would help him with an answer. He wasn't enjoying giving evidence. The spotlight was on him and he had a captivated audience.

'The lighter one, the defendant, that's who it was, can I tell the jury that?' he asked disingenuously. No one answered and he continued. 'He was the person carrying the knife. As I was trying to break up the fight, I saw the defendant with the knife.'

Mr Pankhurst asked more questions. He asked Mark to tell the jury about the knife, the size of it, whether it had a handle, the type of knife it was. He went on to describe the angle he could see it from, and the fact that nothing, despite there being a brutal fight, obstructed his vision of the knife. Rosa suspected Mark was exaggerating, but she found it difficult to tell where the truth ended and where the embellishment began.

He mentioned the jumper that Emmett had been wearing. That jumper wasn't disputed, and the jury were shown a photo of the blood-soaked clothing, which Mark McEvoy confirmed was the jumper in which Emmett had concealed the knife. The weather was good, he said, and it was unusual that someone would wear such a thick jumper on a warm sunny day.

'Did you actually see the stabbing itself?'

'Yes, I saw the defendant stab him,' Mark McEvoy said loudly and clearly.

'LIAR!' Emmett called out from the dock. 'YOU'RE A LIAR!'

'Mr Hamilton, be silent at once! It is not your turn to speak.

I will not have chaos in my courtroom!' the judge roared before turning to speak to Rosa. 'Ms Higgins, please control your client! He should know far better than to be screaming out in my courtroom.' Rosa nodded and shot Emmett a look. He was in tears and his face was bursting with rage.

'My Lord, may we break for a moment?' Rosa asked, standing to address the judge.

'No, I don't think we need to, and we've hardly got started. Mr Hamilton will control himself or I'll send him downstairs, and I will hear the evidence in his absence.'

Rosa nodded and sat down.

'Mr McEvoy, please continue with your evidence.'

'Where was I?' he asked, emphasising the interruption.

'You were telling us about what you saw in relation to the stabbing,' Mr Pankhurst said.

'I saw it all, I saw it so clearly. Even now, I have nightmares about it.' His confident demeanour subsided for a brief moment, and Rosa thought she detected truth in his voice. 'Oh yes, I had a clear, clear view. I saw Mr Dove stabbed multiple times. I saw the knife go in and out of his body.'

'How many times did you actually see the knife go into his body?' Mr Pankhurst asked.

'Oh, multiple times. Four, maybe five. I lost count.' His voice slowed and he sounded genuinely distressed.

'Mr McEvoy, would you like a moment?' Mr Pankhurst said.

'No, I'm all right. It's just hard, even now all this time later. I just remember it so vividly. I tried to grab the knife off him, I really did try. I pulled the knife away until he finally dropped it bu— but,' he stopped and took a deep breath to try and calm his emotions.

The courtroom was so silent Rosa could hear the birds singing outside.

'But it wasn't enough,' he whispered. 'I should have done more. I could have saved him.' He cupped his hands over his eyes and let out a small moan. The usher walked to the witness stand and handed him a box of tissues. He took two and rubbed his eyes with them.

'I remember it all. I just tried to help save that poor man's life.'

One of the jurors, the brunette woman who had been indistinguishable from another potential juror in the jury pool, was also crying. She brushed the tears away with a small handkerchief that she pulled from her handbag. The courtroom remained eerily silent. Rosa stole a look at Emmett who stared at Mark angrily.

Mr Pankhurst moved Mark McEvoy on, to talk about what he did next. He described how he left swiftly, he saw a mother and baby and wanted to get them to a place of safety.

'I couldn't save him, Thomas Dove, God bless his soul, but I thought maybe I'd be able to save someone else.'

'Did you call the police?' Mr Pankhurst asked, returning to his flat tone.

'Yes, of course.'

Rosa reached for her hardcopy of the police report and flicked through it. She scribbled something in her notebook and placed her pen down.

'Can you remember when?'

'Erm, as soon as I could. I remember stepping away from it all and calling the police. It was straight away. I just wanted everyone to be safe and away from those boys.'

Rosa picked up her pen again and searched the desk in front of her for Mark McEvoy's statement. As she looked, Mr Pankhurst tidied up the last few issues and concluded his examination in chief. He sat down with a look of 'job done' as he looked at the jurors' captivated faces. She found the statement and combed through each page, until she found what she was looking for and placed a small asterisk in the margin.

'Members of the jury, it's been a busy morning. We are now going to break for lunch. Can you all please make sure that you are back here by 1.55 p.m. ready for a 2 p.m. start,' the judge declared. 'Thank you.'

CHAPTER 44

The lunchbreak passed quickly, and it was soon 2 p.m. The advocates returned to their seats, Emmett was brought up, the judge settled into his chair and the jury were summoned and finally, Mark McEvoy was called back to the witness box.

'Ms Higgins,' the judge said, inviting Rosa to begin. She stood, placed both hands on the lectern and turned to face the jury, before turning back to face the witness. The juror with dyed red hair had been staring at Rosa but diverted her gaze abruptly. Rosa looked at the note she'd made in her notebook and, with a leap into the dark, departed from her pre-planned questions.

'Let's start with something that you said to Mr Pankhurst not long ago. You said you called the police?'

'Yeah, I did.'

'And you said you think it was about ten to fifteen minutes after Mr Dove was stabbed.'

'I think so, maybe a bit later.'

'How much later?'

'I don't know, maybe up to thirty minutes. I'm not sure. I think ten to fifteen minutes is about right.'

'But you definitely called them?'

'Yes, definitely.'

'And what did you report?'

'I reported a murder, I assume, or an attempted murder at least. I didn't know whether he was dead.'

'The attending police officers say that they arrived just *minutes* after the stabbing occurred.'

'OK?' Mark said slowly.

'They said that they received a call about a fight. There was no mention of a knife at all when they were called.'

'Well, maybe someone called before me. I don't know how it works. I know what I said, though. Maybe the police have made an error in their statement.'

'But you are sure you called them?'

'Yes. I've told you that, like, three times now.'

'Ms Higgins, if you have a question besides whether or not Mr McEvoy called the police, then please ask it, otherwise move on,' the judge called out.

'You told the police, when they interviewed you, that you didn't call them because you were busy making sure everyone was safe.'

'I must have been confused; it was all very sudden. I would have still been shaken up that day when I spoke to the police.'

'Your statement wasn't drafted on the day of the incident?'

'Don't know ... I think maybe the day after.'

'Please turn to page seventy-two of the bundle in front of

you.' She asked him to confirm that it was his signature on the statement, and just below the signature was a date. The statement was dated two weeks after the incident took place.

'Maybe that's an error from the police, I'm sure it was a couple of days at most.'

'The police seem to have made a lot of errors,' Rosa said coolly.

'Wouldn't be that surprising, would it?' Mark said, winking at the jurors. Most of them ignored it, but one juror chuckled.

Rosa didn't let his newly flippant demeanour unsettle her; she adjusted her line of questioning.

'Did you just wink at the jury, Mr McEvoy?' she said.

He was caught off guard – it had been such a small instinctive action, that for some it may have gone unnoticed, but said aloud in this large courtroom, the inappropriateness of it was obvious.

'Erm, did I?' he stumbled, trying to brush the issue away. 'I don't think so. I mean, I don't know. I didn't intend to if I did.'

Rosa took some delight in his squirming. She paused, allowing the jury to soak up her point.

'Mr McEvoy, I ask the questions, and my question was very clear. Did you wink at the jury?' Rosa repeated.

His arrogance quickly drained away and he glared at Rosa, frustrated that he was losing his cool. He searched for an easy way out.

'Yes, maybe. I guess. I can't really remember.'

'You can't remember whether you *just* winked at the jury?'

'I, er . . . I—'

'Ms Higgins, where are you going with this?' the judge said. 'I'm not seeing the relevance here. Can you move on, please?'

Rosa nodded. She had finally got under his skin – she had him where she wanted him.

'Just before we continue, I'd like to check something with you, if I may?' Rosa asked rhetorically. 'Mr McEvoy, Mr Pankhurst took you through your account earlier. I'd like you to look at your witness statement, please. It's at page seventy-two, if you'd like to take a look.'

He picked up the huge court bundle, which had been left on the correct page.

'Yep, I've got it,' he said.

'And at the time of writing that witness statement, you say at most a couple of days after the event, can I please check whether the contents of that statement were true to the best of your knowledge and belief?'

'Yes, of course. Why wouldn't it be?'

Rosa ignored his question.

'And is there anything that you now recognise as inaccurate, anything that you'd like to change?'

'No nothing at all,' he replied. 'It's all the absolute truth, so why would I need to change anything?'

Rosa nodded.

'And would you agree that your memory at the time of writing that witness statement, two weeks after the incident, is likely to be significantly better than now?'

'Well, I guess so, but I still remember it quite well.'

'OK. Well, we're going to move on. I'm going to take you back, Mr McEvoy, to something you said earlier.'

Mark McEvoy looked uncomfortable. His eyes rolled upwards as if trying to retrieve the oral evidence he had just given to this court.

'You told this jury that you risked your life with all these *boys with knives* around you.' Do you remember saying that?' Rosa asked.

'Yes, I think so.'

'It's fairly straightforward,' Rosa said calmly. 'Either you do remember saying it, or you don't.'

'I do,' he said quickly.

'How sure are you, that the answer you gave was truthful?'

'Very sure!' Mark McEvoy said, speaking before his thoughts had a chance to catch up. 'I mean, yes, pretty sure. I did risk my life. They had knives and I didn't. That's why I was stabbed too. Sadly, I didn't do enough,' he said, looking to the jury for sympathy. The jurors remained poker-faced, with the exception of the white woman who appeared every day in athleisure, who offered Mark a sympathetic smile.

'I just want to be clear: you said all these "boys with knives" around you? So, there were multiple knives?'

'Yeah.' Again, Mark's mouth moved before his brain could process the question.

'But until today you hadn't ever mentioned that the other men were carrying knives?'

'I think I did,' he said and looked at his witness statement.

'Let's have a look, shall we?'

She took Mark to the relevant pages where he only ever

referred to 'the knife', a single knife. Rosa was confident that his evidence was falling apart; the jury must be able to see that he was exaggerating, Rosa inviting him to make bold and concrete statements, only to then be undermined by his own earlier statement. She told herself she would repeat this exercise until it was obvious that the jury had the point, and while she hadn't clearly established a motive for why Mark would exaggerate, or even lie, she felt she'd done enough to put doubt in the jurors' mind that Mark saw Emmett stabbing Thomas Dove.

'But what about on the first page?' he said unexpectedly, flipping papers to reach the beginning of his statement.

Rosa flicked the papers too and looked at the first page.

'It says, "I am writing this statement about a murder that I saw take place with a group of Black boys with knives,"' he said.

Rosa read it again, she must have missed that reference. She'd read his statement what felt like close to a hundred times. How could she have missed it?

'When I said "the knife", I was obviously talking about the knife used to kill Thomas Dove. There were other knives but "the knife" was the killing one.'

Rosa was mortified that she'd made such a stupid mistake.

She tried to move on, attempting to push Mark on the issue of why he was in that particular park that day. She forced him a little further in explaining, that he'd visited that park before and particularly liked the colourful flower beds, but it was nothing useful. It didn't undermine the prosecution's case. He was clear that he was just taking a walk. It wasn't a crime to take a walk through the park on a warm day, and while something didn't quite add up for Rosa, she wasn't sure that she'd be able to get the jury on side with this point.

There was one more thing she had left to explore – the connection between Mark and Tanya, Emmett's teacher. She didn't want to sound desperate to the jury, but she felt like she was currently walking through a maze.

'Do you have a friend called Tanya?'

'Tanya?'

'Yes. Tanya.'

'Tanya, who?'

'Tanya Williams.'

'I know a Tanya Williams. What does that have to do with this trial?'

'I have been wondering the same thing,' the judge added. His brows were furrowed, and his lips were tightly pressed together.

'My Lord, I hope the relevance of my question will become clear,' Rosa said disingenuously, knowing that she wasn't sure what answers she was seeking from these questions.

'Did you know that Tanya Williams was Emmett Hamilton's teacher at school?'

The juror dressed in athleisure cupped her mouth with her hand in astonishment, but Rosa wasn't quite sure why.

'No. How would I know that?' he replied. His eyes darted around the room, and he tapped on the desk in front of him as though tired of Rosa's questions. She tried to detect nervousness in his body language but all she could sense was impatience.

She sat down, feeling exhausted, and worried she'd ended his evidence on a bad note.

There wasn't much by way of re-examination. Mr Pankhurst focused on trying to highlight that Mr McEvoy had absolutely no reason to make any of this up. Athleisure juror nodded through this line of questioning. Whose side was she on? The other jurors continued to remain straight-faced. Rosa suspected it was because the evidence had lasted most of the day and everyone was tired and needed a break. Mark McEvoy's evidence eventually finished, and the court day ended.

There was no sign of Bouba. Rosa checked her phone, but knew it was pointless. Even if Bouba could give evidence, it wouldn't necessarily negate Mark McEvoy's, which she couldn't be sure she'd undermined.

She grabbed a chocolate bar and energy drink from the vending machine and scoffed them both quickly.

'Shall I meet you by the door to the cells?' Craig called out, as he headed down to see Emmett. Rosa agreed, knowing it would give her a small amount of time to visit the bathroom. She was going to be sick.

CHAPTER 45

Emmett was beyond irritated at that witness's evidence, the way he'd spun things and exaggerated, and he could see some of the jurors lapping it up. He was desperate to explain what really happened but knew that he couldn't talk. He punched the wall of the court cell hard in anger and pulled back his throbbing fist with a squeal. He'd barely dented the plaster, but his knuckles immediately turned red, and he was hit with a burst of pain. He collapsed on the floor and let out a low sob.

He'd seen Tyrone in the public gallery that afternoon, sitting next to his grandma. The boys had clearly arranged for someone to watch over everything, to make sure he didn't step out of line; that he didn't get anyone else into trouble. None of this was worth it. He should never have let Tyrone take all of the blame for the drugs they'd both been caught with a year ago. Tyrone had only received some kind of youth referral order for possession with intent to supply, but he dangled it over Emmett like he'd saved him from a burning fire.

He regretted everything. He regretted lifting the knife from his grandmother's kitchen drawer and hiding it in his thick jumper. He regretted brandishing it. His memory of what happened next had grown hazy, but he was sure it hadn't been him that had used it. He just struggled to remember who had, and how, and why it was him left holding Thomas Dove, a man he'd never met before, as he died. If only he'd left the knife at home that day, Thomas Dove wouldn't be dead.

A cell officer called him out of the cell, inviting him to go into a conference with his legal team.

'We haven't given up,' Rosa said, breaking the eerie silence.

Emmett didn't know how to respond to that, so he remained quiet. His anger hadn't fully subsided, and he still needed to calm down.

'I've been trying to contact the witness. I've been checking my phone all day. I'm going to keep trying.' Rosa, in that moment, decided to abandon her efforts to manage his expectations. She didn't need to make him worry or prepare him for disappointment. 'I'll keep trying.'

'It's OK,' Emmett said, despite feeling that it wasn't; he didn't know what else to say.

They sat in stillness for a few minutes. Craig appeared to be doing some other work or responding to emails because he continued tapping away, unaware of the lingering silence.

'Rosa,' Emmett said, surprising himself that his thoughts were being spoken aloud. 'Can I ask you something?'

'Of course,' she said, trying to manage a smile.

'Do you think I should consider changing my plea?'

'What do you mean?' Rosa asked, understanding the words but not why he was asking the question.

'I mean, do you think that I should plead guilty?'

Craig stopped typing and looked up.

'Why do you ask?' Rosa said cautiously.

'Well, really I am responsible, aren't I? It's all my fault that Thomas Dove is dead.' Emmett shuddered as he said his name. 'I took the knife to the park. I— the more I think about it the more I think it is possible that I—'

'Let's stop right there, son!' Craig interrupted Emmett. 'I don't think you need to say any more to Rosa without having a chat with me first.' He gave Rosa a look that stopped her prodding further. They fell into silence again.

Rosa had been in many situations like this before. She'd had clients who were keen to tell her what really happened but were guided by solicitors who wanted to make sure they didn't say anything that would make it difficult for Rosa to continue representing them. It used to make her feel really uncomfortable when she first started out, but she'd grown used to it. The justice system, she'd learned, wasn't really focused on obtaining the truth or finding out what really happened; it was just all about what could or couldn't be proved.

And she realised Emmett knew that.

'Rosa, I remember you saying something about me getting a discount, even if I plead now, at trial. Is that right?'

Craig glared at Rosa; she knew she had to tiptoe around the answer.

301

'Well, yes, Emmett. Yes, that's correct. You would be likely to receive up to ten per cent credit if you pleaded now,' she said slowly.

'So, let's say I got thirty years, I'd have twenty-seven instead?' he said.

'Yes,' Rosa said, almost tragically proud of the young man's arithmetic. 'It could be reduced to twenty-seven years.'

'Three whole years more, just for fighting it?' he whispered.

'Well, at this stage fighting it is the only logical thing to do,' Craig chimed in.

Rosa wasn't sure that she agreed but she wanted Emmett to remain hopeful. Despite what he'd just said, she was convinced of his innocence. It wasn't his fault, she just knew it. She needed to prove him not guilty.

CHAPTER 46

Claire Smith strode up to the witness box and tapped on the microphone as though about to perform a song. She flicked her hair behind her and offered the jury a beaming white smile before turning back to Mr Pankhurst.

There was a low buzz of noise in the courtroom as the judge spoke in a hushed whisper to the court clerk as people continued to file into the public gallery for the second day of evidence. They were starting late as a juror hadn't arrived until just before 11 a.m. Rosa watched Joyce lower herself into a seat at the edge of the front row, as she took her own seat in the front row of the courtroom. It felt much lonelier today without Craig; Kate had said he was feeling unwell again. She hoped Emmett wouldn't notice.

The courtroom eventually fell silent, and Mr Pankhurst invited Claire to begin. She confirmed her full name and that she was a stay-at-home mum.

Rosa remembered when Claire had mistakenly arrived at court at an earlier hearing; she had thought then, just as she did now, how attractive Claire was. She captured people's attention with her piercing blue eyes and glossy presentation. Her fingernails were perfectly polished and painted a bright pink, which stood out in the dull courtroom.

Just as she had in her witness statement, she gave a perfectly reasonable explanation as to why she was in the park that day. She'd gone for a walk with her young child, who was in a pram. She had been very unlucky that day to have ended up being a witness to such a brutal murder, while with her baby. The jury, and the judge, looked horrified.

The prosecutor invited her to explain that there were a lot of people around that morning, and she said that a lot of them were Black. Her evidence was less concrete than Mark McEvoy's; she didn't put a number on the amount of people she saw, but said it was a big group. Rosa knew this would be difficult to challenge – she couldn't accuse her of exaggerating or lying if she hadn't given any specific detail.

'Could you describe to me what happened in the park, once you saw the group?' Mr Pankhurst said.

'Well, I think the first thing that I saw that there was like a fight, like, lots of the boys – the Black boys, that is, they were in, like, a fight with knives and stuff.' Claire Smith spoke quickly and ineloquently.

'With *knives*?' Mr Pankhurst queried.

'Well, to be honest with you, I didn't see them all with knives, but I know there were lots of knives.'

Rosa had learned her lesson the day before and decided not to press this issue any further.

'Ms Smith, I need you to focus on only what you saw yourself, please,' the judge intervened.

'Oh yeah sure, your Highness,' she replied clumsily. Neither Rosa nor Mr Pankhurst acknowledged that she referred to the judge as a member of the royal family. But it was strangely endearing, and Rosa could feel the jury warming to her.

Mr Pankhurst invited her to continue.

'Well, OK, yeah, I didn't see loads of knives. I just know there was definitely at least *a* knife.'

Mr Pankhurst tried to move her on and asked her to describe some of the men she'd seen.

'There was a white man, I think he was a witness in this trial. He was like the hero. He went to try and save the guy on the floor. Well, yeah, there were actually two white men, then, weren't there?' she said.

'Can you remember anyone else?' Mr Pankhurst asked.

'Well, there were three Black boys, too, as I've said in my statement.' Her voice sounded slightly nervous, and her eyes wandered into the public gallery before quickly returning to Mr Pankhurst.

'Anything else that you can remember?' Mr Pankhurst asked, as though he didn't really want an answer.

Claire Smith flicked her hair over her left shoulder and fiddled with the ends. Again, she looked up at the public gallery and then quickly looked away.

'Erm, yeah, I remember that everyone was wearing tracksuits?' she said, looking around as though checking whether everyone found her answer helpful. 'And I saw the darker boys running away,' she added. She looked to the judge to see if more detail was needed. 'I saw the, erm, I saw

305

Emmett . . . I saw him with loads of blood on him and, like, close to him on the floor.'

'Had you ever seen Emmett, Mr Hamilton, before that day?'

'No. Sorry, *Mr Hamilton*. No, I hadn't ever seen him before.'

'Did you speak to the police?' Mr Pankhurst said.

'Sorry, what did you say?' Claire asked, apparently distracted by something in the public gallery. Rosa tried to follow her gaze, but she couldn't decipher what Claire was looking at. She locked eyes with Joyce and attempted a quick smile.

Claire Smith refocused on Mr Pankhurst. 'Did you say, did I call the police?'

Mr Pankhurst nodded and waited, without saying anything.

'I can't remember if I called them, but I definitely spoke to them in the park,' she answered. 'I was the one who showed them who the murderer was. Can I say that, sorry?'

'What you meant to say was that you showed the police where someone was – who was that person?' the judge asked.

'The man up there, Emmett,' she said. 'I mean, *Mr Hamilton.*'

Rosa noticed Claire was using Emmett's first name. She jotted her thoughts on a piece of paper beside her.

'Mr Emmett Hamilton,' the judge said aloud, also making it clearer to the jury. 'Right, let's stop here,' the judge called out. 'We can stretch our legs and we will return after lunch.'

*

Rosa found her way to the staff car park next to the court, the only place she felt she could simultaneously get a moment of privacy and some fresh air. She found a small step by a camouflaged door, a likely fire exit, and collapsed backwards against it, lowering herself down until she was sitting on the step. She breathed deeply, and suddenly caught a hint of a familiar sweet-smelling aftershave lingering in the air around her. What was *wrong* with her? It was as though a shadow was constantly chasing her. But yet again, there was no one.

Most of the lunchbreak had already passed. Despite her stomach rumbling, she didn't feel hungry. She pulled out her phone. There were no new messages. She started to type.

> Sharon, I know I'm sounding desperate now but please, if you get the chance, please let Bouba know that we need her . . .

She sent the text message to Sharon and then dropped her phone into her handbag. Within seconds she retrieved it again and clicked on the message, knowing that this time she may have gone too far. Now she'd created hard copy proof of the pressure she was placing on Bouba to give her evidence in this case. The message had already sent, and there was nothing she could do to unsend it. She deleted the message from her phone. It made her feel slightly better. She began composing another text.

Nana,

Things feel strange without you at home. I won't be gushy because I know you'd hate that. Just know, that when you get a chance to read this, I am thinking about you right now.

Lots of love

Rosa

She sent that text, too, knowing it wouldn't reach Nana anytime soon.

Rosa put her phone away. She wanted a moment to decompress, a few minutes just to be with her thoughts; without talking and without technology.

She looked at her watch, she could spare only about two more minutes on this step, out of sight from everyone else.

A car pulled up in the car park and neatly reversed into a space. A woman got out of the passenger side and started to walk towards her; Rosa lowered her head, not quite able to see the woman's face from where she was without making it obvious. The woman hurried past Rosa without paying any attention, but kept looking over her shoulder, as though worried she might be noticed. Rosa stole a quick glance at her as she passed. It was Claire Smith.

Once Claire had gone, a man stepped out of the driver's side of the car. From the back Rosa was almost certain she didn't recognise him. As he stepped closer their eyes met and they both looked away immediately. Rosa heaved herself up and walked in the opposite direction as quickly as she could.

It was Mark McEvoy.

CHAPTER 47

It was Rosa's turn to ask questions in the courtroom. She started revisiting some of the small inconsistencies she'd noticed throughout Claire Smith's evidence and tried to highlight to the jury where her account had slightly changed. The jury looked bored, and one juror intermittently closed his eyes. Even the judge looked tired. Claire looked comfortable. The cross-examination was tame. Rosa started to struggle, there just wasn't much more to ask this witness. She paused, debating whether to sit back down, but decided to pursue just a few more questions.

'You told us earlier about the other white man in the fight, the one you described as a hero?'

'Yeah, Mark, he even describes himself as that, I think I've picked it up from him.' Claire had grown so comfortable that she hadn't realised what she'd just said. Rosa dived for the gem.

'So, you know Mark?' Rosa asked.

'Sorry what? Nah, what do you mean?' Claire's face started to blush pink. 'No, I don't know him. No.'

'Ms Smith, I just want to remind you that you are under oath,' Rosa said, as Claire flushed an even deeper shade of pink. 'Let me rephrase my question so that it's crystal clear: do you know Mr Mark McEvoy?'

Claire looked mortified and then nervous. She looked up at the public gallery and Rosa followed her eyes. It looked like Mark McEvoy was sitting there guiding her with his glares, but from her angle she couldn't be sure.

'How did you arrive at court this afternoon?' Rosa asked.

'What does this have to do with anything?' Mr Pankhurst squawked, jumping to his feet.

'Ms Higgins, I cannot see how this question is relevant,' the judge said in response.

Rosa said nothing but looked at Claire and narrowed her eyebrows.

'Yes, I do know him,' she said eventually. Mr Pankhurst sat down slowly and grumbled to himself.

'How well do you know him?'

'Er, quite well.'

'Are you romantically involved with him?'

'No.'

'I'm going to ask you one more time. I just want to make sure that *you* are sure. Are you romantically involved with him?'

Claire hesitated. She was now bright red and a few droplets of sweat appeared on her forehead. In the public gallery, Mark McEvoy had stood up to walk out and both Claire and Rosa followed his movements with their eyes.

'Are you?' Rosa pressed.

'Yes,' Claire said reluctantly. 'But it's not what you think, it's just— I'm not lying about anything I've said.'

Rosa asked the next question, ignoring all the training she'd had about not asking a question to which she had absolutely no idea of the answer.

'Why on earth did you not tell this court about your relationship then?'

Claire dropped her head, defeated.

'Well, because I'm married, I've got a baby . . . '

One of the jurors gasped, as though watching a television soap, and Rosa let out a disappointed sigh. This revelation might make the jurors think slightly less of Claire Smith's moral compass, but it did nothing significant to increasing Emmett's chances of being found not guilty.

Rosa pushed a little harder.

'Ms Smith, do you think that, given you both claim to be witnesses to murder, revealing the fact you are in a romantic relationship might be more important to the court than protecting your husband from being upset?'

'My Lord!' Mr Pankhurst jumped up to object.

Claire continued despite the objection.

Her smile disappeared. 'No. You don't know what my husband is capable of.'

Rosa paused and gathered her thoughts. 'Where did you and Mr McEvoy meet?'

'Er, we met that day actually.' Her voice was surprisingly timid.

'Which day?'

'The day of the murder. We met there, in the park. He helped keep me and my baby safe.'

'Are you sure?'

'Yes.'

'Absolutely sure?'

'Yes.'

'Ms Higgins, she's answered multiple times now, please move on,' the judge ordered.

Rosa asked some more questions about the two of them working together and collaborating in their accounts of what happened, but she knew that ultimately, they both came across as pretty convincing witnesses. It was 3 p.m. and the judge decided it was time to stop for the day.

CHAPTER 48

Rosa opened the front door to her block of flats. Freddy, the homeless man, was sitting in the stairwell, and she smiled at him and said hello. She retrieved a £5 note from her jacket pocket and told Toby to hand it to him.

'Fank you, dear,' he said softly.

She held Toby's shoulders tightly and pulled him closer to her. They'd barely spoken on the way back home; he was preoccupied with a spaceship game she'd let him play on her phone.

'Miss?' Freddy called out, as they were entering the elevator.

'Yes?' Rosa replied bluntly, peering outside of the metal doors. She hovered over the door sensor to keep them open.

'A man came here looking for ya, just now. You're the barrister, right?'

'A man? Looking for me?'

'Yeah. I didn't really catch a good look at him because he had a cap on, pulled low so I couldn't really see his face.'

'Sorry, what?' Rosa said, still standing in the doorway

of the elevator. Toby had joined her in peering at Freddy, suddenly losing interest in the game.

'I don't know what he wanted, but he was only here a few minutes.'

Rosa felt terrified. Her palms began to feel sweaty. She ushered Toby back into the elevator.

'Thank you, Freddy,' she said in one quick breath, trying not to reveal her fear. She stepped in behind Toby and watched the doors slowly close.

Her heart raced as the elevator climbed through the floors. The numbers flashed in neon green. 7, 8, 9. They finally arrived at the tenth floor and the doors opened to reveal Nana's barred front door. She and Toby stepped out in unison, and she scanned the door for clues to a visitor. There were none. But she did notice one thing: the slight smell of a distinctive aftershave, slightly too sweet, hanging in the air.

She wasn't going mad. She wasn't paranoid. Someone had been following her – and that someone had now come to her home.

Her door key was a little stiff but within moments they were standing in the front hallway facing a white envelope on the floor. Rosa picked it up and sent Toby to his room to get changed.

'What's that?' Toby asked.

'Toby, go and get changed out of your uniform!'

The other person who'd received an envelope through their door like this was Joyce.

She peeled open the blank envelope and pulled out a folded piece of paper. She unfolded it carefully.

Rosa Higgins. I'm watching you. Be careful. Don't do
anything in court that you might regret. Thomas thought
he was clever too.

Was this Thomas's real killer? He thought he was clever?
Could this be the person that Thomas was blackmailing?

She needed to go to the police. This was her home. This
was where Toby lived. But what would going to the police
achieve? They couldn't protect her day in day out, and she
might even end up being pulled from the case as a witness.
No, she couldn't do that. She was petrified, but she needed
to find out who was trying to threaten her.

'Toby, change of plan. You're going to stay at Aunty
Orissa's tonight. Put your shoes on.'

'But you just told me to—'

'Toby! Just please, I don't have time to argue with you.
Please, just put your shoes on and get your coat.' She needed
him to be safe.

Orissa opened her front door slowly, surprised to see Rosa
and Toby on her doorstep.

'What's going on, Rosa?' she said, startled.

'I need you to watch Toby for a few hours, *please*.'

'Is your Nana OK?'

'It's not Nana,' Rosa said, guilt creeping through her veins,
'it's this case.'

'Rosa, no!' She stood firmly in the doorway. 'No. You're
not doing this again. You know I love Toby, but I am not
going to just be his carer while you frolic around playing

315

detective. No. This isn't right. Your grandmother is seriously unwell and all you care about is this bloody case. No, I'm sorry, but no.'

Rosa reached into her pocket and pulled out the creased letter. She handed it to Orissa without a word. Orissa smoothed it out and read it.

Orissa looked at Rosa in dismay. 'What on earth have you gotten yourself into?

'Toby, come inside, sweetheart. Come on in. You can go and sit in the living room and put the TV on, I'll be with you in a bit.'

Toby looked up at Rosa as if seeking permission to go in. She kissed the top of his head, and he tiptoed inside.

'Rosa, what the fuck?' Orissa said, once Toby was out of earshot.

'Thank you, Orissa, as always. I need to go, but thank you.' She turned her back and walked away before Orissa could ask any more questions.

Rosa was trying to solve a puzzle with a missing piece. She didn't believe that Mark McEvoy didn't know Tanya was Emmett's teacher. Tanya had told her that they'd discussed it, but she knew that this hearsay comment wouldn't be admissible evidence. Rosa needed to go back to speak to her. She might be able to help.

She rushed to Green Tree High School, hopeful to catch Tanya before she left. She arrived at 5.30 p.m. and optimistically pressed the intercom on the olive-green gates. Without interrogation, she was invited in. The car park was much emptier than the last time she'd visited, which made the brick building look grander.

'Good evening. Who are you here to see?' a receptionist with a short pixie cut called out as Rosa walked into the reception area.

'Good evening. I'm here to see Tanya Williams.'

'Is she expecting you?'

'No, but it's urgent.'

'I see.' She looked up from her computer screen for the first time and eyed Rosa. 'I'll call her, but she may have left already.'

The receptionist tapped at a landline phone, which rang loudly enough for Rosa to hear even though it wasn't on loudspeaker.

'Tanya, it's Adeola from the office. Yes, yes. Thank you. I have someone here to see you. She says it's *urgent*.'

Rosa heard a low murmuring on the other end of the line.

'What's your name, love?' the receptionist asked.

'Rosa. I'm a barrister. I'm Emmett's Hamilton's barrister. She's met me before.'

'Her name is Rosa, a barrister? Emmett Hamilton's barrister.'

Tanya must have lowered her voice because Rosa could no longer hear her responding to Adeola.

'Mmm, I see.' Adeola's eyelids closed, and she lowered her head, as though she'd just received terrible news. 'Yes, I'll make sure to pass that on.'

She pulled the phone away from her ear and placed it down in front of her.

'I'm afraid Miss Williams is unavailable. She's kindly asked that you don't return to speak to her.'

'What?' Rosa said, astonished.

'She doesn't want to speak to you and has asked that you leave. She doesn't want you to contact her again. Is there something else I can help you with?'

Rosa was speechless. What had happened?

'If there's nothing else, I am afraid I do have to ask that you leave. The school will be closing soon.'

'Just one thing,' Rosa said, looking the receptionist dead in the eyes. 'Ask Miss Williams whether she ever spoke to Mark McEvoy about Emmett, Tyrone or any of their friends.'

The receptionist scribbled a note with certain passive aggression. Rosa turned to leave. There was one more thread she had to follow up on and she was running out of time.

Rosa arrived at St Margaret's Hospital, where she'd visited with Nana months ago. Instead of going to outpatients, she headed to the maternity department. The waiting area was surprisingly busy; there appeared to be a flurry of family and friends at this time of the evening. Rosa tried to blend in as she walked to the nearest staircase with a confidence she didn't feel and climbed to the second-floor ward. She wasn't sure exactly where she was going, but she needed to find someone who knew Thomas.

Despite the chaos of the arrival area, the nurses' station looked relatively relaxed. One nurse was writing on a white-board display, while another two sat at a desk seemingly gossiping.

'Hi, hello there,' Rosa said, awkwardly interrupting their conversation. All three women looked at her. 'My name is Rosa Higgins. I am a barrister in a murder case – the murder of one of your former colleagues, Thomas Dove?' She looked at them hopefully.

One of the women sitting down was quick to excuse herself from the conversation. 'I really didn't know him. He left when I joined.' She stood up and adjusted her scrubs. 'I should be getting back to work. Karen, I'll tell you the rest of that story later.'

The other woman, Karen, also stood up. 'I don't think I'll be much help. I did know of him but I never liked him.' She looked down her nose and pursed her lips. 'I need to get back to work too.'

Rosa didn't protest, instead she waited patiently for the nurse writing on the board to finish.

'Oh, you're still here,' she exclaimed as she eventually turned around and took a seat. She was a short woman, and when she sat down her height against the chair remained the same as when she was standing. 'Can I help you with anything else?'

'I'd like you to help me with learning more about Thomas if you can?'

'I didn't know him *that* well.'

'But you knew him?'

'Yes, you could say that.'

'What was he like?'

'Erratic, unprofessional, always late. He even asked me for money a few times.'

Rosa listened carefully. 'I see.'

'I wasn't his biggest fan, I have to say. I had to discipline him on more than one occasion for "forgetting" to return drugs to the cabinet. I requested that they transfer him elsewhere. I think he went straight to Outpatients.'

'That's very helpful, thank you. Was there anything else unusual about him?'

'*He* was unusual. Everything about him was unusual. He had no friends but would try and make friends with the patients. One patient told me that he asked her for money! That was the final straw for me. I'm surprised the hospital kept him.' She rolled her eyes. 'We're just so desperate for nurses.'

Rosa smiled gratefully.

The nurse, whose name Rosa hadn't asked, apologised for speaking ill of a dead man and excused herself. Thomas was not so perfect after all.

CHAPTER 49

Rosa couldn't believe that it was already Wednesday. Both Mark McEvoy and Claire Smith had finished their evidence and this morning was the new Officer in the Case, the previous Officer in the Case having sadly passed away. His replacement, Detective Sergeant Emily Boyles, appeared to have familiarised herself with the important facts in a relatively short space of time. She was an unhelpful witness, merely reading out the statements of the two attending officers. One was unavailable for health reasons, and another was uncontactable since leaving the police force. Rosa didn't complain. Their evidence was agreed in any event and it only helped her case to have a detached witness reading the statements to the jury in a flat voice.

'Yes, one set of the fingerprints on the knife matched with the defendant's, Mr Emmett Hamilton,' DS Boyles said firmly in response to the prosecutor's question.

Mr Pankhurst paused for a few seconds and let DS Boyles's words resonate with the jury.

'One set?' Mr Pankhurst then responded, encouraging her to elaborate.

'Yes, we found two sets. The other could not be identified.'

Mr Pankhurst pushed further and asked about the blood on the knife.

'Yes, the expert report confirmed that the blood found on this knife belonged to Thomas Dove.'

The jury sat silently while the officer described the murder weapon and tried to link it to both Thomas and Emmett.

Rosa listened for inconsistencies in the evidence but there were very few. When it was her turn to ask questions, she tried to highlight the presence of the other fingerprints, a possible unknown culprit, but in the back of her mind she knew that Emmett had taken his grandmother's knife – it wasn't her strongest point and this witness had very little to offer the jury that would help Emmett. She rushed through her questions.

The morning finished with the prosecutor confirming to the jury that Emmett had answered 'no comment' in his police interview.

The court afternoon sitting also passed by slowly, with a lot of agreed expert evidence being read out by the prosecutor. There was no dispute that Thomas Dove died of stab wounds, the medical evidence was not challenged. It was agreed that the paramedics attended and found Emmett cradling Thomas's body and covered in blood; that matched his account perfectly. The jury were tasked only with determining whether or not it was Emmett Hamilton that stabbed Thomas Dove.

The most interesting thing in court, throughout all of this read-aloud evidence, was the public gallery. At the beginning of the day, Rosa noticed that Mark McEvoy and Claire Smith had attended together and were now holding each other's hands. It had nothing to do with the trial what these two witnesses got up to in their free time, but she remained suspicious. Something just didn't feel right.

'Ms Higgins, your client has his hand raised,' the judge announced.

'My Lord, thank you. May I please briefly turn my back and see if I need to take some instructions?' Rosa asked.

'Yes, of course, please do,' the judge said, evidently grateful for the opportunity to take a break from writing a note of the evidence.

Rosa walked to the dock and leaned towards the small gaps in the glass.

'Is everything OK, Emmett?'

'Can I leave?' he asked.

'What? Why?'

'It's too much in here, man. I don't want to listen to all of this. To sit here while everyone sits around judging me.'

'I really don't think it's a good idea for you to leave. You should stay,' she said firmly.

'But look up there, everyone's just watching me. It's horrible.'

Rosa looked up and saw he was pointing to the public gallery.

'I noticed them too,' she said. 'Strange, isn't it, that they now come to court as a couple?'

'What?' Emmett replied. 'No, not them, I don't give a shit about those liars. I'm talking about the boys. Nah, I've had enough.'

Rosa felt embarrassed by her own ignorance. She hadn't even noticed the boys, who were a similar age to Emmett, sitting high in the public gallery. Emmett seemed fearful of them.

'Ms Higgins, can we continue to hear this case? This isn't an opportunity for a chit chat!' the judge said.

Rosa turned her head to face him.

'My apologies, My Lord, we may continue.' She quickly flicked her head back towards Emmett. 'You really must stay,' she said, stepping back to her seat in the front row.

Mr Pankhurst continued to read agreed facts out to the jury. He confirmed that the other set of fingerprints on the knife were not of a high enough quality to provide any analysis. The report couldn't even identify whether there was more than one person's fingerprints.

Suddenly, the door of the courtroom burst open.

Mr Pankhurst fell quiet and looked to his left. A woman stood at the threshold.

The court usher rushed over and tried to explain that she must have the wrong courtroom. Rosa leaned forwards out of her chair to see the woman's face.

It was Bouba.

CHAPTER 50

'My Lord, could we please ask the jury to vacate the courtroom,' Rosa said, clambering to her feet, and trying to hide her relief. 'I'm afraid something urgent has arisen that will need to be addressed in their absence.'

The judge looked unimpressed but sent the jury out with the usher in any event. The last juror left, and the door closed behind him.

'Ms Higgins, what on earth is going on in my courtroom? There best be a very good explanation for this.'

'My Lord, there is. I'm afraid I may also need to invite the court to ask this woman to wait outside the courtroom while I address the court. She is a defence witness.'

'A defence witness?' the judge exclaimed. 'I don't think so! Are her details on the Digital Case System? I'm afraid it is not reasonable to be permitting new witnesses at this stage of the trial.'

'Her details are on the DCS, My Lord,' Rosa replied. 'I can also confirm that the Crown Prosecution Service have had the opportunity to carry out their necessary police – sorry, PNC – checks ahead of today.'

'Right,' the judge replied, scrolling through his laptop. 'Oh yes, I see. Bouba Ali. Ms Ali, can I please ask you to step outside of the courtroom?' the judge asked her.

Bouba, appearing not to fully understand, stared at him blankly. The judge pointed at the door and repeated himself, which seemed to make the instructions clearer.

'OK, Ms Higgins, I'm not impressed with the interruption I can tell you that much, but let me hear from Mr Pankhurst, please,' he said.

Mr Pankhurst made a feeble attempt to object to Bouba Ali giving her evidence but seemed to suspect that the judge was likely to grant permission. The judge listened to his brief submissions and thanked him.

'Right, I am prepared to hear Ms Ali's evidence,' the judge said. 'I am satisfied that the CPS has been given proper notice, as has the court; the CPS has also been afforded the opportunity to carry out police checks in the usual way. I cannot see any reason why the court should not hear this evidence.'

Rosa avoided looking at Emmett but could feel his smile at the back of the courtroom.

'Ms Higgins, does she need anything from the court? I seemed to sense that English may not be her first language.'

'That's right, My Lord, Ms. Ali's English is very good but we would like a French-speaking interpreter if possible,' Rosa answered.

'OK. Razia, can you organise for a French interpreter to

attend tomorrow, please?' the judge called out to his clerk. 'And then could you please kindly direct the witness to a side room. Ms Higgins will need to be in court until the end of the evidence but can speak to her at the end of the court day.'

'My Lord, may I have permission to send those who instruct me a quick text message to let them know that she's here?' Rosa asked. 'It may be that they can attend court and speak to her while I'm still in court.'

'Of course,' the judge said, and Rosa fished out her phone and texted Craig.

'OK, counsel, are we ready to get back on with the evidence?' the judge asked. 'Let's try and get the prosecution case wrapped up today if we can.'

The advocates nodded in agreement and the judge called everyone back into court.

The prosecution case had finished, and Rosa stayed up late that night working, piecing together the defence case. She'd picked up Toby from Orissa, who barely spoke to her, and taken him to see Nana – silent, unconscious. They'd bought fish and chips on the way home and Rosa now felt both full and exhausted.

Some time after midnight her phone rang loudly. She reached to the side of her desk to view the screen; it was an unknown number. Reluctantly she answered it, tiredness tainting her voice.

'Yes?'

'Good evening, I apologise for calling you at this time in the morning. This is Sister Marshall. I am calling from

Whipps Cross Hospital. Can I please confirm who I am speaking to?'

'It's Rosa, I mean, erm . . . it's Mercedes Higgins,' she said, voice breaking with tiredness.

'OK, yes, thank you. Ms Higgins, you are registered as the next of kin for your grandmother, I understand?'

'That's right, yes . . . is everything OK?'

'Well, she's become quite unwell this evening, and we wanted to invite you to come and visit, her if you'd like?'

'Is she dying?' Rosa asked.

'I'm not entirely sure, Ms Higgins, that's not something I'd be able to say definitively, but I think you may want to visit her.'

Rosa hung up the phone and woke Toby from sleep. She dressed him, his eyes barely opening as she put his socks and shoes on his feet. She called Orissa, apologising profusely but asking if Toby could stay there until the morning, one more time. Orissa, softening, replied to put Toby back in bed and that she'd come to the house to save the hassle.

'Orissa, honestly, thank you. I don't know what I'd do without you.' Rosa could hear her voice cracking and she ended the call. She undressed Toby again, putting him back into his pyjamas and tucked him back in before he properly woke up. Within fifteen minutes, Orissa arrived and Rosa set off for the hospital.

Rosa pulled into the car park and didn't bother paying for a ticket, leaving that as a problem she could deal with later. She rushed through the hospital to the ward and barged through the double doors. A nurse was sitting at the desk and her face was solemn as she locked eyes with Rosa.

She dashed to Nana's bed and saw her body, still, the machines quiet at last. The nurse from the front desk came up behind her.

'Is, is, is . . .' Rosa was breathless and unable to speak. 'Is she still alive?' she asked, looking at the nurse's kind face.

The nurse shook her head slowly and put her hand on Rosa's shoulder. Rosa shook it away and grabbed Nana's hand, holding it tightly. She began to weep and lowered her body into Nana's familiar, sagging form. She was surprised how warm she still was.

Nana was gone.

CHAPTER 51

Rosa stood outside the courtroom staring at the court board. She felt empty. Lost. She noticed everything. COURT 1 was spelled out in neat white lettering on a less tasteful dark brown plaque. Below, a blue pin board had been fitted into an alcove in the wall. There were numerous leaflets, like an off-licence window, but they weren't advertising child-minding services or a missing cat. On a large A3 poster, COURT AND TRIBUNAL RULES were listed: no mobiles, cameras or food and drink allowed in the courtroom. Everything seemed so trivial. Nana was dead. Emmett was about to be convicted of murder.

Rosa tipped the last few drops of her coffee into her mouth and tossed her cup into the bin.

She reread an email Craig had sent her from the evening before, which she barely remembered reading.

Hi Rosa,
    I finally got through to Bouba. She's said she wanted to

330

speak to you and *only you*. She refused to speak to me.
She said she'd come to court tomorrow.

I'd say, don't get your hopes up.

Let's see how tomorrow goes.

Best,

Craig.

Rosa felt a little burst of hope.

She sat in the conference room reading her case notes. There had to be something here that she could try to use to cast more doubt in the jury's minds. She'd attempted to undermine the witnesses but even she found it hard to fathom why anyone would make it up.

Rosa thought about how nervous Emmett had been about the men in the public gallery. She needed to ask him what was going on, but it was 9.45 a.m. already and court would be starting soon. Her thoughts bounced off the internal walls of her mind, and she felt a real headache growing.

'Could the parties in the case of Emmett Hamilton please come to Court 1?' a voice called through the speaker system, bringing her back into the present.

Everyone shuffled into the courtroom. Rosa could hear Emmett being brought up into the dock from the sound of the jailor's keys, but she couldn't bear to look at him.

The courtroom settled and the judge turned to Rosa.

'Ms Higgins, do we have our defence witness?'

Rosa glanced around the courtroom, suddenly remembering that Bouba was supposed to have attended first thing today. She was nowhere to be seen.

'My Lord, I'm afraid not. My understanding is that she may not be willing to speak to anyone other than me.'

'Well, I'm afraid it's your client's witness, Ms Higgins, and without a formal application to adjourn – with good reason might I add, I'm afraid that this is precious court time, and we are going to have to plough on.'

Rosa, struggling on the little sleep she'd had, the sorrow she was feeling, and her overall frustration with the case, didn't even protest.

'There is, of course, a French interpreter.' The judge turned to the interpreter who was sitting close to the clerk's desk. 'Madam, thank you for attending, please get my clerk to sign your time sheet before you leave.'

The judge invited the defence case. Rosa asked for the court to call the sole defence witness, the defendant himself.

The jailor unlocked the dock door and began to lead Emmett out.

CHAPTER 52

Anxiety cloaked Emmett as he stepped into the witness box; he felt overwhelmed and distracted, like trying to listen to every conversation in a crowded restaurant. He couldn't focus. Having sat through the evidence of the various prosecution witnesses, in his own memory the events of that day were becoming like a long-forgotten story. It didn't make any sense. He began to wonder whether he *had* stabbed Thomas and just had blocked out any recollection of it. His memory seemed to be failing him.

The courtroom felt different from the witness box. He could see everyone much more clearly, and although he still felt as though he was in the hot seat, he felt more human than when trapped behind the walls of the dock. He looked at the jurors; their facial expressions had shifted from the day before. They were no longer glaring at him like he was a vicious dog in a cage, but seemed interested in what he had to say. The public gallery was full. He spotted Tyrone and Jayden. Mark McEvoy and Claire Smith. He despised them. His grandmother, so frail and frightened. He looked away, unable to carry that weight, swivelling his neck to face the judge, who appeared disinterested, tapping his fingers on the desk in front of him. He looked at Mr Pankhurst who looked similarly restless. Then he looked at Rosa. She smiled at him but remained poker faced – he couldn't read how she really felt about him. Never could.

'My name is Emmett Hamilton,' he said, answering Rosa's first question.

Rosa asked him why he was in the park that morning, and he felt irritated at the line of questioning. He had heard Rosa, and Mr Pankhurst, ask every witness that same question but he knew he didn't have a good answer.

'I don't really want to say,' he said, realising as soon as the words left his lips that this sounded much worse than any possible explanation. Rosa's expression confirmed that for him.

'Who were you with?' Rosa asked. Again, he felt irritated. He knew that she had to ask these questions, but she also knew that he didn't want to tell the court this information. He looked up at the public gallery and his eyes met Tyrone's, who shot him a threatening look.

'I don't want to say,' he said again, this time feeling the jury's burning gaze.

Rosa tried again with her questions, but Emmett was hostile and refused to provide any detail. She tried to elicit a coherent account of what happened that day, but her attempts were futile.

Mr Pankhurst pressed Emmett on why he had never identified another person as the possible killer. He went over his police interview, his defence statement, and even his examination in chief with Rosa. Emmett had never even mentioned another person as a possible killer.

'I don't know who killed him,' Emmett said desperately. 'I just know it wasn't me.'

Mr Pankhurst looked to the jury and back to Emmett.

'You don't know? This is a criminal trial for murder, Mr Hamilton!' Mr Pankhurst shouted, his cheeks flushing a bright red.

'Mr Pankhurst. Questions only, please, now is not the time for comment, as you well know,' the judge said calmly.

'Emmett, let's look at some text messages you sent and received. We'll try and do this in order. Can you turn to page 122, er, no, page 123 of the bundle?'

'*You gonna bring it yeah big man?* A message you received from a number ending 738 at 05.55 a.m. What was that about?'

'I don't know.'

'You don't know?' The corners of Mr Pankhurst lips lifted into a wry smile.

'I don't remember.'

'Right. Well, let's look at your response and see if that jogs your memory. Page 121 please. These are your outgoing text messages. Right?'

'I think so.'

'Well, look at them. Are these messages you sent?'

Emmett's eyes dropped to the pages below and rested on the small black rows of text messages.

'I don't know. I think so. I really can't remember.'

335

'Well, that's convenient. These messages were sent from your phone, on the morning of the murder. Ms Higgins, your barrister, didn't ask you any questions suggesting you didn't send them did she?'

'Er, no.' Emmett glanced at Rosa. 'No. She didn't.'

'Right. And she didn't challenge the officer in the case who said these messages were pulled from your phone?'

'Mr Pankhurst. This is not your opportunity to make comment. I will not tell you again.'

'I'm sorry, My Lord.' Mr Pankhurst flushed pink and scribbled a note in his blue notebook.

'A message was sent from your phone, to that same 738 number, at 06.03 a.m., just a few minutes later. It said, *I don't want to be involved in this.* What did you not want to be involved in?'

'I don't remember.'

'Again, you don't remember?'

'No.'

'Right. And the next message. *We could get into so much trouble Ty.* You sent this to the same number at 06.17 a.m. What would you be getting in trouble for?'

'I don't remember.'

'Were you saying you'd be getting in trouble for planning to murder someone?'

'No!'

'Really? Well what about for providing the murder weapon?'

'No.'

'Hmm. OK. Well, there's one more message that I'd like to ask you about. Can you turn back to page 123.' He paused and let Emmett turn the pages. 'You received a message at 06.20 a.m. *Don't let us down.* Any explanation of what that meant?'

'No. I don't know.'

The prosecutor continued trying to push Emmett, but he maintained that he didn't know who had killed Thomas Dove, just that it hadn't been him. He moved on from that line of questioning and started to ask Emmett about why, throughout this process, he had failed to name any of his friends. Emmett looked up at the public gallery for a brief second and then returned his gaze to Mr Pankhurst.

'You wouldn't understand,' he said quietly.

'Why don't you help me?'

Emmett remained silent. Mr Pankhurst continued with his questions, but Emmett refused to give the court any more information.

'So, according to you, you know nothing about why Thomas Dove was murdered?' Mr Pankhurst scoffed.

'No. I don't.' He paused momentarily. 'But you know what? What I do know is that this system is so fucked up. I didn't kill that man. I had no reason to kill that man but none of you want to believe that. I'm a Black man and that's all you see. You think I must be a killer.'

Rosa felt a lump grow in her throat; she was failing him.

'Ms Higgins, do you have any re-examination?' the judge asked.

'Yes, My Lord, I do.'

'Well, shall we get on with it?' the judge asked. 'It is

a Friday and I'm sure we'd all like to go home at some point. I'd like to get speeches done this afternoon. So, let's get going.'

Rosa let the silence linger for a few more second before taking a deep breath, and asking the question she had asked so many times before.

'Mr Hamilton, why were you in the park that day?' she said.

The judge looked up and scowled, 'Ms Higgins, I think we've had that question a few times now.'

Rosa looked at Emmett in one last desperate plea. He sat quietly and stared at her blankly.

'Ms Higgins?' the judge said loudly.

'Mr Hamilton, can you turn to page 123 of your bundle? I want to ask a few questions about one of the text messages. One that wasn't read aloud.'

Emmett looked down.

'I'm on page 123,' he said bluntly.

'*We got you bro. Will text you where to go.* That was a message you received from the 738 number at 06.19 a.m.'

Emmett stared blankly, waiting for a question.

'Emmett, was someone pressuring you that morning?'

'I don't know what you're talking about,' Emmett said, scowling.

'I'm just wondering, Emmett, did someone tell you to be at the park that day?' Rosa asked, knowing she was crossing the line.

'My Lord! That is a leading question!' Mr Pankhurst sprang to his feet to object, scattering papers in the process.

'I'm well aware, thank you, Mr Pankhurst,' the judge said. 'Ms Higgins, you know that you cannot ask leading questions. Do you have any *other* questions for this witness?'

Rosa again looked at Emmett, wide-eyed and hopeful. He said nothing.

'Ms Higgins!' the judge shouted. Rosa looked at Emmett one more time, and he sat still. She looked up, leading his gaze to the public gallery, and he followed it, as if riding an invisible line with her to the top, to Tyrone and Joyce, and beyond. They locked eyes and Rosa sat, embarrassed, and defeated.

'No, My Lord, I don't,' she said sadly.

'Right, thank you,' the judge said. 'OK, Mr Hamilton, that concludes your evidence. You are now free to speak to your lawyers again. I'll adjourn for lunch now and I'm sure they'll make their way down to you.'

Rosa couldn't even look up.

CHAPTER 53

Emmett sat slumped in the chair in the small conference room by the cells. His face told Rosa that he was losing hope.

'Emmett. I know it's hard, but I need you to keep a little bit of faith in me. We still have speeches to go.'

He let out an unkind laugh. 'Right. Cause you give a shit? I honestly don't care anymore. I see how they look at me. They've made their minds up.'

'Emmett, please.'

'This ain't your fucking life, Rosa. It's mine. Don't come here and tell me to have faith in you. You don't know anything about this life.' His eyes began to well up. 'Just leave me alone.'

Rosa's desperation filled the room and it was suffocating.

'Emmett, I think your teacher, Tanya, Ms Williams . . .' Her voice was shaky, she'd not spoken her theory aloud before. 'I think she told Mark McEvoy about your friends.'

Emmett looked up. 'My friends?'

'Yes,' Rosa hesitated. 'Well, I think so.'

'Why would she tell them about my friends?'

'I'm still figuring that out. I think it had something to do with you all being told to be in the park that day.'

'I don't understand. What do you mean, Ms Williams told him about my friends? Told him *what* about them?'

'Maybe he paid them to stab Thomas?' Rosa blurted out.

Emmett scowled and slammed his fists on the table.

'ARE YOU FUCKING JOKING? YOU THINK MY FRIENDS WOULD KILL SOMEONE FOR MONEY?' He screamed so loudly that a male guard approached the conference room door. Rosa shooed the guard away.

'I promise you, Emmett, people you love can surprise you. My mum—'

'I don't give a fuck about your mum.' Emmett stood up and tried to catch the attention of the guard through the window of the door.

'Emmett, just sit down and LISTEN to me!' Rosa demanded. The authority in her voice surprised her. 'My mum is in prison too. I told you before, and I really meant it. We really aren't so different.'

A tall, slender man in uniform approached the door and opened it. He remained outside of the room but craned his neck so that his head bobbed between the door and the frame.

'Everything OK, miss? We all done here?'

'NO!' Rosa shouted. 'Sorry, no, no we're not done. Could you please just give us a moment.'

'No problem, miss. You just let us know when you're ready. Mr Hamilton, you need to remain seated I'm afraid.'

341

Emmett sat down obediently.

'Right, all good. Yeah, just let us know, miss.' He withdrew his head, like a rabbit retreating back into a hole, and left.

'As I was saying, Emmett. I get that things aren't easy for you right now. I can't imagine being in prison, no, but look, my mum is there; I don't even know who my dad is but there's a good possibility that if he's alive, he's in there, too, judging by my mum's choice of companions.'

Emmett looked at her unsympathetically.

'My grandmother, the one person who was able to hold my broken world together, has just died.' She knew she was rambling, but she couldn't stop herself. 'My little brother, he's still in school and I'm now the only person he has to rely on.'

Emmett's face started to shift; the harshness began to wash away and softness crept in.

'So, Emmett, no I don't fucking know what it's like to be in prison, but I do know what loneliness feels like. I know what it feels like to be betrayed. I know how hard it is to trust anyone except yourself.' Her voice began to crack. 'I promise you – I understand.'

Rosa paused but her words continued to pace the room.

'Why are you telling me all of this?' Emmett asked calmly.

Rosa took a deep breath and wiped a tear from her cheek.

'Because I need you to trust me. I need you to recognise that life might have handed you a pretty shit deck of cards, but you can't just throw your life away. I need you to keep fighting.'

CHAPTER 54

Rosa made it back to court just in time for the 2 p.m. start. The judge addressed the advocates before the jury were called back.

'Ms Higgins, do you still have another defence witness . . . let me see, Ms Ali?'

'My Lord, I have been trying to reach her.'

'Right, well, if she's not here by 2.30 p.m., I'm afraid we simply just won't have the time. As I said, I was hoping that we would be able to do speeches this afternoon.' He wiped a few droplets of sweat from his forehead with the back of his hand. 'Are there any objections to postponing speeches and directions to Monday? I suspect not. I can then send the jury out and get on with this other matter.'

'No, My Lord,' the advocates replied in unison.

'Right, let's bring the jury in.'

The usher dutifully collected the jury members, led them into the courtroom and stood back while they all took their seats.

'My Lord, can I say something?' Emmett said. All heads turned towards him, the judge scowling.

'Well, not really, no, we have concluded your evidence,' he said in an irritated voice.

'My Lord, it's important. It's really important.'

Rosa rose to her feet, anxiety rising. What was he playing at? 'My Lord, can I assist? May I briefly turn my back to speak to Mr Hamilton?'

'No, I don't need to speak to my barrister,' Emmett pressed. 'I want to speak to you judge, and the jury.'

The judge tutted in full view of the jury and sat back in his chair.

'Well, frankly, this really isn't how a trial works, Mr Hamilton. You don't just get to speak whenever you'd like.'

'My Lord, I just want to say that I was at the park that day because someone told me to be there. The message that my barrister asked me about earlier . . . yeah, well that person is who made me be there. I don't really want to say who that person is . . .' His voice trailed off.

'Mr Hamilton, this is evidence! It is not appropriate for you to be addressing me like that from the dock. Ms Higgins, are you seeking for your client to be recalled? This is chaotic.'

'My Lord, I'm so sorry. I did not appreciate that he wished to address the court.' She paused and reflected on what he'd just said. 'My Lord, do I have the court's permission to recall him?'

The jury were asked to leave the room while the advocates exchanged words as to whether Emmett could give more evidence. Eventually, the jury were asked to return – and Emmett asked to enter the witness box.

'Mr Hamilton, we all understand that you wish to tell the jury something about why you were at the park that day,' Rosa began. 'Could you repeat what you wanted to tell them?'

Emmett repeated his confession, that his friend had told him to be at the park.

'Who?' Rosa asked, hoping that Emmett wouldn't just shut down again.

'I don't want to say.'

'Why not?'

'Because, to be honest, the messages are from another young Black boy just like me, and all you lot like to do is lock us up rather than get the real criminal.' He paused and briefly looked at the public gallery, and saw Tyrone with his phone in his hand, texting.

'We all act on the big white man's word. I don't even know who that white man is. All I know is that my boys have looked out for me in the past.' Emmett paused momentarily to catch his breath and avoided looking back up at the public gallery. 'When they told me to bring a knife to the park, I just thought we were going to try and scare someone. We aren't killers.'

An elderly white female juror gasped.

'What do you mean you thought you were going to try and scare someone?' Rosa asked, worried about the answer.

'We ain't all bad. Yeah, my friends might do some bad things but there's bigger fish organising the whole thing. Where do you think everyone gets their drugs from? Do you think we grow up in poverty but just manage to buy thousands of pounds of drugs to sell? You know it doesn't make sense.' The jurors were captivated and listened intensely. The judge was lost for words.

'Look, I know we ain't here for drugs, but you've got to think about why a random white man was killed. I can tell you one thing: my friends were working for someone.'

A lightbulb switched on in Rosa's head. Thomas settled his debts shortly before his death. Debts that made him so desperate that he'd tried to blackmail someone. Were these drug debts? The nurses had hinted that he'd been stealing drugs from hospital – when that was cut off, had he gone elsewhere, racking up debts along the way that he was then desperate to clear? Was that a missing piece of the puzzle?

Rosa wasn't quite sure whether this was where Emmett was going, or whether she was required to intervene to keep him focused. There wasn't really any focus, but she let him keep talking, and now he addressed the jury directly.

'You lot see white skin and presume innocence, Black and you assume guilt. It ain't like that.' Emmett was becoming more emotional. There was a fire behind his eyes. 'I'm not saying he, Thomas Dove, was into drugs, but it might be worth thinking a bit more about why and how he was killed, rather than locking up an innocent Black man!' Bingo.

'HOW DARE YOU!' a voice screeched from the other side of the courtroom, where Thomas Dove's family members were evidently sitting. They'd remained silent for most of the trial, Rosa had barely noticed they were there.

'We just come from a place where loyalty means a lot!' Emmett shouted back, no longer addressing the jury. 'I'm here for my brothers and I won't snitch on anyone. You lot just need to focus on catching the real killer because it ain't me. I can—'

'ENOUGH!' the judge shouted, causing everyone to swivel their heads.

'This is not a speech, Mr Hamilton! You answer questions. That's it! This is not your show!' The judge desperately tried to regain control of the courtroom. 'Ms Higgins, is there anything else because it's almost the end of the court day, and I don't want your client's evidence continuing on Monday morning. I think we all need a short break.'

'No, no further questions from me, My Lord,' Rosa said and sat down. She was still in shock.

CHAPTER 55

Rosa fled the courtroom desperate for some fresh air. She moved on autopilot, striding through the corridor, and bursting out of the grand doors, onto the street.

'Ms Higgins, do *you* have anything to say about your client's speech in there?' A woman with bright red lipstick and a blonde bob stepped into her path, forcing her to look up. Rosa was suddenly surrounded by members of the press. Cameras and microphones were shoved in her face as she tried to sidestep the commotion.

'Is Emmett Hamilton playing the race card?'

'Wasn't there supposed to be another witness. Where are they?'

She turned to follow the last voice, which sounded familiar. It was Matthew Weisberg from the *Daily Mail*. She pushed through the crowd.

'Are you *the witness*?' a voice called out to someone else in the opposite direction. Rosa turned abruptly.

Bouba was standing there, motionless.

'Unless you want to be charged with perverting the course

of justice, I suggest you all BACK OFF RIGHT NOW!'
Rosa screamed at the crowd. She paced towards Bouba and
grabbed her arm, hurrying her back inside.

'I 'eard what he said,' Bouba said softly to Rosa.

'Who?' she replied hurriedly. 'Emmett?'

'Yes.'

'He needs your evidence, Ms Ali. He really needs it.'

'Ms Higgins, are we proceeding with the evidence of Ms
Ali or not?' the judge asked upon Rosa's return. 'The court
cannot wait for the defence to get their act in order. I will
not be granting any additional time, and we now have no
interpreter!'

Rosa was startled and felt unprepared, but something told
her to follow her gut. She turned and looked at Emmett, who
nodded. Bouba was sitting and waiting for her in a small
room outside of the courtroom. She turned to the judge.

'Yes, My Lord, could I please call Ms Bouba Ali? Her
English is good enough.'

The judge huffed but didn't say anything further. The
court usher went to retrieve Bouba Ali. A few minutes later
she returned with Ms Ali, who looked at Rosa helplessly;
Rosa just smiled warmly and reassuringly.

Bouba looked again at Rosa and then at Emmett. She
made the sign of the cross and stepped into the witness box.
There was hustle and bustle in the press gallery as journalists
leaned forwards to take in her appearance. The courtroom
sketch artist began to scribble on his pad.

The court sat quietly, and Rosa let her settle into the

seat and watched her pour herself some water. The witness's hand shook as she took a sip. Rosa glanced up to the public gallery – Emmett's grandmother was sitting there alone, clasping her hands together as if in prayer. Just behind Joyce, Rosa noticed the young men she'd noticed the day before were clambering to their feet with panicked expressions on their faces. There were three of them and she watched as two darted out of the courtroom.

'Could you please state your full name for the court?' Rosa said slowly.

'Bouba Ali,' she replied with a shaky voice.

Rosa started with some easy questions to try and settle her. Bouba explained that she walked through that park every day, just to get some fresh air. She described that she tended to work during the night and so would sleep for a few hours at her flat, and her afternoon walk helped her to wake up and feel more refreshed. As she spoke, she began to relax slightly, and her hand stopped shaking.

'Could I now ask you, please, about what – if anything – you saw in the park that day?' Rosa asked, trying to ensure that she was not leading the witness in any way. Bouba paused and looked up at the public gallery and then around at the jury. She looked at the prosecutor. Her hand had begun to tremor.

'I can't remember everyzin'.' Rosa could see the panic on her face as she began to shut down – she didn't want to give evidence. The prosecutor's face remained neutral, but Rosa could feel his hope.

'Could you please tell the jury what you do remember?'

Rosa said carefully. She saw Bouba look around the court-room again. Rosa turned her attention purposefully at Emmett, and Bouba followed her gaze as Rosa hoped. Her eyes remained still and focused on him for a moment.

She looked up again at the public gallery and something or someone caught her attention. Her nervous expression melted away and a scowl formed on her face. Out of nowhere her demeanour appeared to change. She started to stand up and lifted her finger and pointed into the public gallery.

''Im!' she shouted loudly in English. ''Im!'

Rosa looked up to see where Bouba was pointing but the man had already stood up, turned his back to the court-room and was making his way to the exit. The boy who had remained to watch Emmett was gone. Rosa glanced at Emmett, who looked just as nervous as the man who'd left the room. She wasn't sure how to read that, but quickly diverted her gaze back to Bouba, hoping the jury weren't following her eyes.

Bouba's arm was still outstretched, pointing at the public gallery as she quickly and angrily spoke in accented English.

'Zat was 'im! Zat was who killed 'im! I just saw zem. Zey are 'ere!'

The doors of the public gallery swung open as the man, and a few other bodies, shuffled out.

Bouba continued to talk.

'I knew I'd know zem if I saw zem,' Bouba said in her thick accent. 'I knew it.'

'Ms Ali, please! Let's just take a moment,' the judge commanded.

'My Lord,' Mr Pankhurst called out, standing up to address the court, 'can the jury be invited to leave the courtroom?'

'Yes,' the judge replied. 'Members of the jury, please do go back while we get some order in this courtroom. Everyone just needs to get their bearings.'

The jurors stood up and followed the usher out of the courtroom. There was a buzz of chatter among them.

'Mr Pankhurst, I will leave you to speak to the Officer in the Case, who I can see just witnessed that show. I make no orders about what happens next, but it certainly seems sensible to try and find out who that witness was pointing to.' The judge closed his laptop and stood up to leave. 'Thank you all.'

At that moment, a male voice shrieked from outside the courtroom, cutting through the air. 'You were fucking *him*? *HIM?*'

An audible murmur ran through the courtroom, and people began to leave, curious. Rosa shoved her laptop into her handbag and rushed out behind them.

In the public waiting area outside, a large group had gathered around three people involved in a noisy confrontation. She craned to see what was happening.

'Are you fucking kidding me?' the same voice shouted.

A tall, dark-haired man was yelling at Claire Smith. He'd not attended the trial before now and Rosa was sure that he hadn't been in the courtroom. This was the first time she'd ever seen him. She figured it must be Claire's husband.

'Calm down, Steven. You're embarrassing yourself,' Claire muttered. She flushed pink. 'What are you doing here?'

Rosa hovered at a distance when suddenly she caught a hint a strong, sweet smell that she recognised. They were here – whoever had been following her, threatening her. She followed it and pushed gently through the crowd.

'Don't you fucking dare tell me to calm down. Calm down. You told me you only met him that day at the park! You were fucking someone else while carrying *my child*,' Steven screamed in Claire's face.

'Steven, *please*.'

'*Please*? After everything I've done for you. Risking everything for you. Risking my life, my freedom. I've given you fucking everything and you're fucking this ginger prick? Nah, I must be the world's biggest fucking idiot.'

Rosa stopped a few metres away from the courtroom door. The sweet smell of his cologne was overpowering. And she recognised the person she was face-to-face with: Tyrone.

'Please, baby, we can talk outside. Come on,' Claire begged nearby. Rosa's attention was pulled back to the fight.

'Who the fuck you calling a ginger prick?' shouted Mark McEvoy, who had mostly been standing aside until this moment. 'Yes, I have been fucking your wife. And just while she was pregnant? You're even more stupid than you look.'

Steven, without warning, charged at Mark, like a lion hunting his prey. But Mark wasn't scared. He raised his fists and punched Steven as he approached. Steven boiled with fury and tried to grab Mark's neck, but Mark resisted and grabbed his body. The men tussled and pulled each other to the floor. Claire started crying hysterically. Everyone else looked upon them in dismay.

'The last person who tried to fuck with my wife ended up six feet under,' Steven yelled, trying to overpower Mark.

'Oh, don't worry, mate, when I finish with you, you're gonna wish that's where you were,' Mark growled back.

The court security rushed towards the two men fighting like children in a playground. They separated them and tried to calm them both down. Both men were ordered to leave the court building and warned that if they continued, the police would be called.

Rosa took her chance to corner Tyrone. She took a deep breath.

'I'm Rosa, I represent Emmett,' she said.

'I know who you are,' he replied coldly.

'And you must be Tyrone?'

He stared at her, neither confirming nor denying.

'I, er . . . I just wanted to quickly talk to you.'

'I don't wanna talk to you,' he replied monotonously.

'I know this sounds slightly strange,' she continued. 'But I recognise your, er, your fragrance. It's quite distinctive.'

'OK.'

'Have you been following me?'

'Why would I do that?' he asked, his face still expressionless.

'Well, I'm not exactly sure. That's why I'm asking.'

'OK.'

'You followed me to my house?'

'I don't know what you're talking about, lady. Sounds like you might be a bit paro.'

'Did you send money to Joyce, to Emmett's grandmother?'

'I make sure she's looked after. You can tell Emmett he doesn't need to worry about that. I've got him.'

'Right. And Tanya?'

He stared at Rosa blankly, unwilling to fill the gaps in her sentence.

'Tanya Williams?' Rosa waited for him to speak but he remained silent. 'The teacher. Tanya. Did you tell her to stop speaking to me?'

'I ain't answering your questions, lady. I'm not on trial here. I'll be honest, I didn't think you could do it. Thought it would be better if . . . just one person got done. But now . . . I don't know how you've done it, but maybe you have. I'll leave you alone. You just need to focus on your job. You only have one – make sure Emmett is found not guilty.'

And without waiting for a response, he turned and walked away.

CHAPTER 56

'**M**embers of the jury, welcome back,' the judge said, following the short break. The chaos outside had calmed, but the courtroom remained flooded with frustration.

'Just before you were asked to go to your room, you heard Ms Ali give evidence attempting to identify the person she says killed Thomas Dove – within the public gallery.'

Some jurors nodded and others remained still.

'The only thing that you need to decide is whether or not you can be sure about whether Emmett Hamilton killed Thomas Dove. I will give further directions about that later on. For now, we will continue with the evidence,' the judge said.

Rosa asked only a few more questions. She clarified with Bouba that she saw someone else stab Thomas Dove. Bouba did not waiver in confirming that Emmett did not stab anyone.

Mr Pankhurst suddenly came alive during cross-examination. He questioned Bouba heavily, asking why she chose not to give a statement to the police, and why she initially said that she couldn't really remember anything.

Her evidence was clumsy and imperfect at times, but she maintained that she saw the entire incident and saw someone else stab Thomas Dove. She explained that the reason she hadn't given a description to the police before was because she was so scared about what would happen to her. Standing in the dock, in front of a room full of people, she looked deeply anxious.

'You didn't *really* see what happened, did you, Ms Ali?'

'I did.'

'No, you just wanted to help Mr Hamilton?'

'No, zat's not true.'

'So, you don't want to help Mr Hamilton?'

'Well, I do, yes. But—'

'So, when you said that wasn't true, that was incorrect, it was true.' Mr Pankhurst was tying Bouba in twists and knots, in what seemed to Rosa like a desperate attempt to confuse her.

'I don't know,' Bouba said reluctantly.

'Was it Emmett you knew, or his family?'

'I didn't know anyone.'

'Or perhaps he reminded you of someone close to you?'

Bouba stayed silent, which Mr Pankhurst recognised as an opportunity.

'Do you have children, Ms Ali?'

'Yes.'

'A son?'

'Yes.'

'How old?'

''E is seventeen, tomorrow.'

357

'A similar age to Emmett?'

'I guess so,' she mumbled.

'Did Emmett ever remind you of your son?'

'A little bit,' she said, truthfully.

'And that's why you decided to help him?'

'Yes.'

'You would be willing to lie about what you saw, to protect him? Like you would for your own son.'

'No.'

'You have made up this evidence because you feel sorry for Emmett?'

'No. Zat is not true.'

'You have actually risked committing a serious crime, misleading the court, to protect Emmett. Perhaps hoping someone would have done the same for your son?'

'No. I'm tellin' the truz!' Bouba protested. 'I don't understand. I swear on God. I might be deported just by bein' here.'

Rosa was surprised at her force and tried to smile at Emmett, but he didn't look her way, his eyes remaining fixed on Bouba.

'I see,' Mr Pankhurst said with a wry tone. 'I have no further questions, but if you could wait there because Ms Higgins may have some further questions in re-examination for you.' Mr Pankhurst sat down, evidently satisfied with his questioning.

Rosa stood up. This was her last chance to draw useful evidence out of Bouba. She looked her directly in the eye and placed her hands firmly on either side of her lectern.

'Ms Ali, is there anything else that you would like to tell

this court, based on what you've been asked today?' Rosa knew it was a risky question, but she needed to know that Bouba had told the court everything that she knew.

'Er, ze man wiz ze red 'air, I saw 'im 'olding a baby,' she said.

'When?'

'Well, 'e was in ze fight, and 'e 'urt 'is leg. Zen 'e kind of fell back; and zen I saw 'im pick up a baby and 'e was 'oldin' it.'

'Had the fight stopped?'

'No. It was still goin'.'

'Was there anyone else with him and the baby?'

'No.'

'Ms Higgins, can I just remind you that this is re-examination, not an opportunity for you to elicit more information. Is there anything else, relevant to the issues in this case?' the judge said, apparently not interested in Bouba's revelations.

'Not for this witness, thank you, My Lord,' Rosa said.

'This is the last witness?'

'My Lord, I have a few further questions for Ms Smith.'

'You are seeking permission to recall her?' The judge tipped his glasses down to stare at Rosa.

'I'm afraid so, My Lord.'

'What more could you possibly have to ask her?'

'My Lord, just a few follow-up questions. Ms Ali just said the man with the red hair – I assume that's Mr McEvoy – was holding a baby. I think we need to ask Ms Smith about this, since she was there . . . with her baby.'

The judge let out an exasperated sigh. This was clearly relevant. 'Right, is she here? Mr Pankhurst?'

'I don't think I can object, My Lord.'

'I'm not asking for you to object. I've made my decision. I'm asking if your witness is here.'

'Oh, sorry, right, well . . . ' Mr Pankhurst stuttered, and looked helplessly at the Officer in the Case. She pointed at the public gallery where Claire Smith sat, frozen and alone.

Claire avoided eye contact with Rosa as she made her way out of the public gallery and back into the witness box. She looked directly at the jury, awaiting the questions.

'I'd like to ask you about your baby,' Rosa began. 'When was your baby born?'

'Ten months ago.'

'Where?'

'My Lor—' Mr Pankhurst attempted to halt this line of questioning.

'In Whipps Cross Hospital,' Claire replied.

'Who was present at the birth?'

'My mum, and er, my husband.'

'What about the staff?'

'What do you mean, the staff?'

'My Lord, how is this possibly relevant?' Mr Pankhurst objected.

The judge looked to Rosa, who rephrased.

'Ms Smith, was anyone relevant to this trial present at your baby's birth?'

Claire hesitated and looked uncomfortable. She looked up to the judge.

'Your Lord, do I have to answer this question?'

'Well, I don't see why you wouldn't,' the judge replied. 'Is there an issue?'

'Erm, well, does the court have my medical records?' she asked apprehensively.

'That doesn't really answer Ms Higgins's question. Please just answer the question, Ms Smith.'

Claire searched the room as if looking for the answer on people's faces. She rested her eyes back on Rosa.

'Ms Smith—'

'Thomas Dove. Thomas Dove was there.'

Mr Pankhurst flushed red, and his jaw hung slightly ajar. The judge sat upright and scribbled a note. The jurors looked flabbergasted.

'And what was he doing there?'

'I think he delivered my child.'

'You think?'

'Well, yes, I remembered erm, the other day.'

'And did you know Mr Dove was in debt?' Rosa blurted out.

The prosecutor, who had remained sitting silently, rose to his feet.

'Mr Pankhurst, please sit down,' the judge commanded. 'Ms Higgins, I know what the objection will be. Is this a question this witness can answer?'

'I'd like to know that too,' Rosa replied.

Claire looked between Rosa and the judge, unsure of whether to answer. The judge nodded for her to speak.

'Why would I know that?' she asked.

'I'm asking *whether* you knew that.'

'I think he may have mentioned it, yes, maybe. I can't really remember.'

'Why would a nurse, helping to deliver your baby, mention that he was struggling financially?'

'I don't know, maybe he needed a friend,' Claire replied.

Rosa knew the judge would attempt to intervene again if she didn't think fast. Time to bring everything into the light.

'Did he ever try to blackmail you?'

'I don't understand. How?' she said in a higher-pitched voice than before.

'You said you and Mr McEvoy were in a romantic relationship?' Rosa asked. 'Can I ask you this Ms Smith, did Thomas Dove know about your affair?'

Claire began to cry. Tears rolled down her cheeks as she made groaning sounds and smeared her hands across her face.

'Do you need a short break?' the judge asked. 'Let's all take ten minutes.'

The short break destroyed Rosa's momentum. Claire appeared to have composed herself and returned adamant that Thomas Dove knew nothing about the paternity of her baby. The judge became irritated and asked her to move on. Mr Pankhurst re-examined her and she remained unshakeable. The rest of her evidence passed quickly, and the long Friday afternoon finally drew to a close.

'It seems we really are done with the evidence now,' the judge declared once the jurors had been escorted to the jury room. I do not intend to permit any other witnesses to be recalled. We'll start speeches tomorrow.'

CHAPTER 57

Rosa arrived at court out of breath and flustered, just before 10 a.m. on Friday, for what she hoped would be the final day of the trial. She'd somehow slept through her alarm, and in Nana's absence, looking after Toby had used up any remaining time she'd had.

The usher called them in, and they took their seats in the courtroom. While Mr Pankhurst started his speech, Rosa tried to catch her breath.

Mr Pankhurst told the jury that they could be sure of Emmett's guilt. He said that the prosecution, the Crown, had proved their case and that the jury could have no reasonable doubt as to Emmett Hamilton's guilt. He emphasised that two separate witnesses identified him as the murderer, and claimed it didn't matter what these witnesses did in their personal lives as it had no bearing on what they saw that day.

He invited the jury to ignore Emmett's alleged 'desperate' attempt to confuse them with a speech at the end of his evidence. He explained that the police had not identified any other suspects and described Bouba's public gallery identification as 'an inappropriate red herring'. He asked them to bear in mind that until now, Emmett had provided no explanation of his text messages and why he was in the park that day, and that could only be because he hadn't had the chance to invent the story he was now presenting.

'Members of the jury, you couldn't make it up,' Mr Pankhurst declared. 'He was quite literally found in the park, at the scene of the murder, with blood on his hands.'

It was Rosa's turn to address the jury. She stood up and held her hands behind her back to hide her nerves. She started by reminding the jury of the burden of proof – that it was the prosecution's job to prove the case. She reminded them of the standard of that proof, that in order to convict him, the jury must be *sure* of Emmett's guilt.

She paused and looked down, noticing that one of her blouse buttons was undone. Unfazed, she buttoned it up swiftly and returned her attention to the courtroom.

'Members of the jury, this is an unusual case. A lot of the evidence has only come out for the first time during this trial. That doesn't make it any less believable, it just means that you are faced with the additional task of trying to understand why a young Black boy who has been charged with a murder he didn't commit might not want to throw his friends under the bus.

'Or even why a woman who does not have secure immigration status in this country might be worried about speaking to the police about what she saw.'

She highlighted the key pieces of evidence and told the jury that they clearly could not be *sure* about Emmett's guilt.

He might have made bad decisions and got himself involved in something he knew little about, but he didn't kill anyone.

She finished her speech and sat confidently back onto the bench. She heard Nana's voice. *Well dun, Mercedes. Mi proud of yuh.*

Without stopping for a break, the judge began his directions to the jury.

'At the start of this case I explained to you all that you, the jury, and I, the judge, have different parts to play in this trial. I am responsible for all of the legal matters and will tell you about the law which applies to this case. You must accept and apply what I tell you about the law.' The judge paused, looking to the jury to ensure they were listening.

Rosa twisted her head to look at Emmett, who sat solemnly in the dock.

'Where you feel there is conflicting evidence, you must decide how reliable, honest and accurate each witness is. You may draw sensible conclusions from the evidence you have heard, but you must not guess or speculate about anything that was not covered by the evidence.' The judge paused to take a deep breath.

'Cases like this sometimes give rise to emotions. You must not let such feelings influence you when you are considering your verdict.' His voice was stern, and the smile had disappeared from his face. He began to recite the evidence they'd all just listened to. Rosa felt sick with anxiety.

The court usher handed out pieces of paper to the jury, which the judge explained were his written list of questions to follow when they considered their verdict. He added that if the jury answered these questions in order, they would reach verdicts which correctly considered both the law and their conclusions about the evidence.

The judge invited them to retire.

Rosa fled the courtroom and rushed to the bathroom. She made it to the cubicle just in time before lurching forwards and emptying her stomach. She wiped the splashes of green-coloured liquid from her hand and cheeks with squares of toilet roll, before cleaning the clumps from the toilet seat. Pulling herself up from her knees, she checked her suit for stains – fortunately there were none. She left the toilet cubicle and approached the sink. She cupped her hands and tipped a handful of water into her mouth, gargled it, and then spat it out. There was no soap in the dispenser, and having washed her hands vigorously with water, she then discovered there were also no hand towels to dry her hands on. She smeared her wet hands down the sides of her jacket and left the bathroom.

Craig was waiting for her in the hallway. 'Shall we head down and speak to him?'

'I can't, Craig. I just can't. Not right now,' she said in response. Craig looked at her perplexed.

'I just get a bit funny awaiting a jury verdict. A bit nervous, I guess.'

Craig smiled warmly and placed his hand on her shoulder. 'I'm OK!' she said forcefully, stepping back and hoping that Craig didn't detect the strong smell of vomit. 'I just, you know how it is. I just want to have done him justice.'

'Oh, you've done more than that!' Craig said kindly. 'You've done an absolutely brilliant job, Rosa. I really couldn't have asked for better and I mean that.'

'Don't speak too soon, we haven't got the verdict yet.'

'No, honestly, I mean that. I am so glad I gave you this case, no matter what the outcome is.' His lips turned upwards, and he revealed his crooked teeth again. 'Your granny would be so proud of you.'

'Thank you,' Rosa replied and attempted a smile back.

'I am so sorry to hear about her,' he said. 'I can only imagine how stressful it's been.'

Rosa could tell that this was genuine, but she felt uncomfortable allowing her personal and professional life to merge.

'Thank you, I've been managing,' she lied. She'd been dropping Toby off at the childminder's early every morning and picking him up in the evening after court finished. She had barely thought about how they'd cope long term – she knew that this was the new normal. She'd be a mother to Toby, and she still needed time to process it.

'That's great, real great. I'd really like to come to the funeral if you're happy with that,' he added.

'Of course.'

Again, she hadn't properly engaged with funeral arrangements. Orissa had helped her reach out to a funeral director, but funerals were so expensive that she'd have to apply for a bank loan before she could move forwards. She also needed to work out how to liaise with HMP Bronzefield to ensure her mother could attend. These were all things she was postponing until after the trial.

'Right, well, if you don't need me, I'm going to just pop into one of these rooms and get a bit of work done. I'll listen out for the verdict.'

'Can everyone in the case of Emmett Hamilton please return to Court 1?' the court speaker system announced.

It had been less than half an hour. Rosa's nerves started to bounce around in her stomach again and she clutched her belly tightly as she marched to the courtroom. Craig joined her at the door but said nothing.

She tried to distract herself.

'Craig, I've been meaning to ask. Is everything OK?'

'Er, yeah. Why?'

'Well, I don't mean to pry at all. I just know you've not been that well a few times during this trial. I've been so hyper-focused on the trial that I've not even asked whether you're OK.'

Craig smiled awkwardly and flushed red. 'Ah, yeah. Well, to be totally honest with you, Rosa, I've actually been fine but my wife . . . she requires a bit of extra care, you know?'

'Ah, I'm so sorry for asking,' Rosa said, embarrassed.

'No, don't be silly. It's life, isn't it? She hasn't been the same since the baby. I just try to help out as much as I can.'

Rosa nodded sympathetically; she didn't know what else to say. The verdict took over her thoughts.

As everyone gathered in the courtroom, she looked up at the public gallery, which was fuller than it had been at any point during the trial. Joyce was sitting there with her eyes closed and head lowered. The young Black boy she'd noticed sitting there most days, who she now knew was 'Ty', also sat there with nervous clenched fists, but his two friends were gone. Claire Smith tried to sit hidden at the back of the gallery, but her glossy hair and bright eyes stood out in the dull courtroom. Mark McEvoy was nowhere to be seen.

Once everyone had settled, the court clerk stood up and addressed the jury forewoman – tall, curly haired, fluffy-jumper woman.

'Have you reached a verdict upon which you are all agreed? Please answer "yes" or "no".'

The forewoman tucked her curls behind her ears.

'Yes,' she said.

'What is your verdict?' the court clerk asked.

Rosa bit her lip nervously.

'Not guilty.'

Rosa turned to Emmett. Large tears raced down his cheeks and his head fell into his hands.

A number of people wailed loudly from where Thomas Dove's family were seated, and one woman screamed out as if in physical pain. Rosa looked up to the public gallery and saw Claire Smith's head of glossy hair whirling about as she escaped out of the courtroom, passing Joyce, who sat sobbing softly.

The judge waited patiently for a minute, to allow the clamour to die down, then turned to address Emmett.

'Mr Hamilton, you have been found not guilty and you are free to go.'

*

Rosa explained to Emmett that he would be taken back downstairs to collect his things, that it might take a few hours for them to check him out of the cells but that he would be released that day. He barely listened and just grinned at Rosa.

'I knew you could do it,' he said. Rosa doubted that he'd always had such faith in her but thanked him all the same.

'Craig, you proved to be all right. My dad clearly knows how to pick a good friend!' Emmett joked.

'No problem son,' Craig said, ignoring Rosa. 'Let's be honest, it was all down to Rosa's hard work. Finding that witness and managing to get her to give evidence in front of the jury . . . I still don't know how she did it.'

Emmett smiled to himself, and then at Rosa.

'Thank you, honestly. Thanks for ending this nightmare. I owe you everything,' he added.

'No, you don't owe me anything. It was the right result.'

When he arrived at home, Emmett held his grandmother for more than ten minutes without letting go. They wept in each other's arms. She wiped the tears from his eyes with a floral handkerchief, but his eyes continued to pour.

At long last they released each other from their tight grip.

'I am so sorry, Granny.'

'My boy, you are home now, that's all that matters.' She closed her eyes and looked up. 'The Lord has brought my boy home.'

CHAPTER 58

'This interview is being recorded. I am Detective Sergeant Emily Boyles and I'm based at the Central London Police Station, and I am joined by my colleague Police Constable Malik Sayeed.'

The police interview room was a place where time appeared to stand still. The lighting was dim and yellow, and the walls were lined with a faded grey wallpaper. Even the officers wore tired expressions.

'Could you please tell us your full name for the recording?'

'Claire Jessica Smith.'

'Could you also please confirm your date of birth for us?'

'Thirteenth June, 1981.'

'The date is 27 November and the time is exactly 11 a.m. This interview is being conducted with the assistance of Ms Smith's lawyer, mister . . .'

'Mr Petrov.'

'Right. I'm just going caution you now, Ms Smith.'

She rocked nervously in her chair and rubbed tears from her eyes.

'You do not have to say anything, but it may harm your defence if you do not mention when questioned something you later rely on in court, and anything you do say may be given in evidence.

'Is there anything you'd like to tell us before we start our questions?'

Claire nodded.

'Please, go on.'

'I was blackmailed. I was blackmailed by Thomas Dove.' She struggled to speak as her tears began to flood down her face. 'Thomas befriended me. I needed a friend. He found out that Mark had got me pregnant and that I'd been having an affair. He knew my secrets. Thomas threatened—' She had to stop momentarily, to calm her erratic breathing. 'He threatened to tell my husband.'

The officers remained expressionless. Nodding and listening.

'But I knew his secrets too. Thomas was having money problems. He had an addiction. A drug addiction. It made him reckless. He gambled thousands – money he didn't have. That's what he wanted from us. He wanted money from me. From us. He wanted tens of thousands of pounds.

'We had to do something. We came up with a plan. Mark's friend told him about some boys who were willing to do anything for money, skint little thugs or whatever. Tyrone, I think the main one was called. He said he'd sort it out.'

She sniffed.

'Did you ever pay Thomas any money?'

'Yes. We gave him almost £10,000 to go away, but he just kept asking for more! He kept threatening me. We didn't even have the money to give him.' She stopped crying and her voice grew icy. 'We just needed him to disappear.

'Mark came up with the plan. We'd threaten him. Make him realise that he shouldn't mess with us. We wanted to frighten him a bit. We told him that Mark was a big drug dealer, and that he had young boys willing to do anything for him.'

She explained that didn't work. It only made Thomas greedier. He demanded more money.

'We planned to scare him in the park that day. We told him we'd meet him to give him cash. The boys would then rough him up a bit, you know, scare him.'

A clock on the wall ticked quietly.

'He was just so smug. He wasn't scared. The boys tried to scare him but he just didn't care. Mark tried to teach him a lesson.'

'What do you mean?' DS Boyles asked.

'He held the knife to him, it all happened very quickly.'

'Did Mark stab him?'

'No. Thomas actually grabbed the knife and stabbed Mark!'

'Who stabbed Thomas? I will remind you of the testimony of Ms Bouba Ali at the recent trial of Emmett Hamilton.'

Claire hesitated. She looked up at DS Boyles and stared coldly at her. Her eyes glistened.

'Me. I stabbed the prick.'

CHAPTER 59

Rosa clutched at Toby's hand as they walked into HMP Bronzefield. They'd decorated the reception desk in tinsel and placed a small artificial tree by the security scanner. She thought that a prison was the last place any child should have to be at Christmas. But Toby wanted to see their mum and Rosa knew it was probably about time that she visited too.

They put their personal belongings into a locker and walked through the security scanners with nothing but their locker key. Toby's excitement was only making Rosa's nerves grow. They sat in the holding room, waiting for their names to be called. Rosa tapped her foot impatiently and checked her watch every few minutes. She kept scanning the room, hoping not to see any relatives of a client. How would she explain this?

'Mercedes Rosa Higgins and Toby Arnold Higgins,' a slim, female officer sporting a Christmas hat called out. Rosa jumped out of her seat and tugged on Toby's arm. 'Please follow me.'

They followed the officer into another room and were asked to sit on two stools, a few metres apart from one another. A trained sniffer dog was brought into the room and guided around them both. This was so much more intrusive than when she visited as a lawyer.

Eventually they were called into the family and friends' visiting room and guided to two cushioned chairs. Seconds felt like minutes as they waited for their mum. Rosa's stomach flipped relentlessly.

'Mummy!' Toby called out and launched towards her from his chair as she was brought into the room. Rosa went to call him back but the officer smiled and indicated that it was OK. Toby grabbed his mum's leg and held on so tightly she couldn't walk any further. She chuckled and lifted him up.

'Ma'am, please put him down,' an officer said with a sense of urgency in his voice. Toby returned to the floor and scurried back to his chair next to Rosa, as though scared he too would get into trouble.

Rosa looked at her mum and felt a rush of warmth that she wasn't sure she'd felt since she was a child. She missed Nana so much and somehow her grandmother's memory felt more alive in her mum's presence.

She reached out her hand and the two women enjoined palms. They squeezed hard and Toby, not wanting to be left out, stood up and put his hand on top, making both Rosa and her mum giggle. They barely exchanged words but a sense of hope hung in the air like sweet perfume.

'How is work, Rosa? What's next for you?' her mum asked.

'Rest,' she joked. Her mum smiled. 'No, in all seriousness, I think I'm pretty well cut out for this defence work but I'm going to try prosecuting for a bit.' Her voice got quieter, realising where she was.

'Oh, really?' her mum asked, surprised.

'Yes. I think a good prosecutor has more power to make significant change. Half of these cases wouldn't make it to trial if they bloody did their jobs properly and exercised a bit of due diligence.'

Rosa's mum listened silently.

'But it's just easier to believe that there is no smoke without fire. To buy into the stereotypes. That needs to change. We're not all bad.'

'Some of us are bad, though, Mercedes.'

'No. You are not bad. You've made some bad decisions but you're not bad.'

'No, Sady, Mummy is bad. That's why she's in prison,' Toby declared loudly.

Both women laughed and hugged Toby between them.

'Mummy loves you,' their mum whispered in Toby's ear. 'And you, Mercedes.'

'I love you too, Mum,' Rosa said softly.

ACKNOWLEDGMENTS

There are so many people to thank for the birth of this book.

Thank you to my editor, Ed Wood, who has been my 'partner in crime' (metaphorically speaking, of course). He's never been more than a phone call, email or Zoom call away throughout the entire process. We've bonded over our love of Essex, but more importantly we have worked side by side in creating a book that I couldn't be prouder of. There have been illustrated timelines spread across my living-room floor; colour-coded Excel spreadsheets, and so much patience in weaving together this beautiful plot. Ed, words can't even begin to express my gratitude. Thank you for everything.

Thank you always to my agent, and friend, Hayley. Thank you for believing in me when this author journey first started. You've never placed a ceiling on me, and continue to push me to greater heights. I couldn't have asked for a better agent – someone who I can trust with personal bumps in the road, and who advocates for me no matter what. You're the best in the game, and I'm so grateful to have you in my corner.

My heartfelt thanks also go out to the whole team at Sphere/Little, Brown who have brought this book to life. Thank you, Hannah Wood, for designing this eye-catching cover, which draws you in but gives nothing away. I loved it the moment I saw it. Thank you to Niamh Anderson for your hard work in publicity, and to Lucie Sharpe for your incredible marketing. I am so grateful for the buzz around my very first fiction book.

I really can't thank Jon Appleton and Nithya Rae enough as project editors. They not only edited *The Witness* fantastically, but were patient with me as I juggled full-time work as an attorney in New York.

Thank you also to the brilliant eyes that helped to perfect this story – the copyeditor, Karyn Burnham, and the proofreader, Edward Wall.

Last, but certainly not least, a massive thank you to Tom Webster in production, and Hannah Methuen and the sales team. Thank you for being a big part of putting *The Witness* out into the world.

Thank you all so much. This is only possible with such an amazing team.